The Path
That Led Me Here
A Novel

Inspired by a true story ...

KIM NOTTINGHAM

Halo
Publishing International
www.halopublishing.com

Library of Congress Control Number: 2010927391
ISBN 978-1-935268-38-3

Halo ●●●●
Publishing International
www.halopublishing.com

Printed in the United States of America

For Blake and Kara, who make being a Mom wonderful . . .

For Brian, who never ceases to support my dreams . . .

I love you all.

A Note From The Author

I love to listen. To be able to completely focus on a person and allow the world around you to fade is a gift. Conversation can last but a moment or linger for hours. A quiet connection is made; eyes meet and lives touch. I have been blessed in my nursing career over and over by the patients for whom I've cared. At life's most vulnerable state, I have been entrusted with their care. Often afraid and alone, patients opened their hearts to me. Many may assume that nurses are too busy to care, jaded by the demands of the profession or detached to protect themselves from the suffering they see. It is quite the contrary. The act of giving of oneself and really listening to someone in need can unleash a multitude of blessings on the nurse. This book was inspired by those cherished moments of my career that have touched me deeply and given purpose to my work.

I have many to thank for this book coming to fruition. I thank God for gently nudging me to write this story that I've been carrying in my heart for years. To my wonderful editors, Emily Jones, Marsha McGregor, Mary Busha, and Kevin Hrebik from Halo, your unique and talented insight helped mold my work into the best it could be. To John Ettorre, thank you for your guidance and interest in this project. To the Greenwood Girls Book Club, your secret critique and review was priceless. Thank you "Father Flanagan" for your excellent advice on the book's ending. Thank you Jane and Bill for introducing me to my fabulous publisher, Lisa Umina at Halo Publishing. To all my family, co-workers, and friends, I have truly been blessed to have your love and support. Lastly, to my past and future patients, thank you for inspiring me to be the best nurse I can be.

− Chapter One −

A shock of cool air chilled Maddie as she stepped onto the front porch. Late night rain had left a blanket of leaves on the ground while exposing rheumatic tree limbs reaching toward the grey, overcast sky. Tentatively, she made her way down the slippery stairs and into the shelter of her old Bronco. The engine turned over with a loud growl as if in protest of being left out in the cold all night. The gravel crackled under the tires as she drove away from the house down the long driveway. The transition of coarseness to the smoothness of paved Route 33 began her systematic routine. With each white fence post she passed, her shoulders became less tense. When she made it the entire length of their front pasture, her chest muscles loosened and breathing became easier. Only when she could no longer see the farm would she allow herself to turn on the radio and, if feeling happy enough, might sing a few verses out loud as she drove the familiar ten miles into town.

Tuesdays were shopping days. It was the one day of the week that Ray didn't give her grief for leaving the house. Brewster's was the only grocery store in Westville. It was family owned and had a personal feel that the big box stores were unable to capture. Originally opened in the 1920s, the landmark had serviced the community well with its philosophy of highlighting the bounty of the land. The store's flyer faithfully showcased the item of the week, be it honey from Smith's Farm or apples from Shoemaker's Orchard. Clean-cut boys brought out your groceries, returned your cart to the store, and always politely declined a tip when offered. Brewster's was something the townsfolk could rely on as always being the same.

After parking her car, Maddie walked inside and selected a cart. As she began her usual route, the sight of crisp, red apples lined neatly beside the tart, green ones pleased her. The contrast of color was sharp, and the light reflecting from them gleamed as if saying, "Pick me! Pick me!" Maddie appreciated the sense of order amidst the disorder of her life.

Some women hated grocery shopping. For them, it was a dreaded weekly task that must be endured. Not so for Maddie. She admired the shine of the waxed floors, welcomed the hello from Carol who worked behind the bakery counter, and enjoyed the fresh glazed donut slyly appearing from her gloved hand. She had been shopping here for years and had memories of going to the store with her mother as a young girl. Her sister and her dad traveled the same aisles. There was comfort in knowing she was entrenched in family and tradition; it was the beauty of small town living.

As she shopped, Maddie was able to escape her world but for an hour, lulled into another state of mind by soft music streaming from speakers hanging on the store walls. She looked over the potatoes and green beans. They were locally grown and should easily pass for hers. The idea of canning this year's garden had been too daunting a task. The energy needed was not there, and she left the unused produce in the rows to spoil. It was symbolic to see the once healthy fruit wither away. Ray would notice at some point that their shelves were void of their usual bounty, for he didn't miss much. It would be something she'd have to worry about later; she was too tired to care right now.

When she reached the meat aisle, Maddie stopped to ponder which cellophane- wrapped items to purchase. Her choices were limited, chicken or pork, never beef. They had a side of that in the deep freeze at home. Bending down to pick up a roaster chicken, Maddie felt a sharp, stabbing

2

pain radiate through her abdomen. *"Oh, not here,"* she thought to herself. Maddie carefully placed the chicken in the cart. She hadn't had one of her spells in awhile, and this one caught her off guard. When at home, she could lie down or take a hot bath to try to deal with the pain. Maddie hoped the pain would pass and she could finish shopping.

After a few deep breaths, she steered the cart slowly, contemplating what she should do. The cramping intensified as she turned down the freezer aisle. Maddie paused and rested her arms on the cart. The pain became sharp and constant, different from her previous episodes. Beads of sweat formed on her brow, and breathing became a more concentrated and deliberate effort. She looked around to see if anyone was watching her. An elderly lady stood about ten feet ahead of her looking intently at the frozen vegetables, her lips moving as if in conversation with herself. Maddie noticed the woman's hands shake with a tremor as she attempted to open the freezer door. She would have helped the old woman if she weren't shaking herself. A young mother with a cranky toddler was coming up behind her. Maddie stood still as they passed.

"I want the Dora popsicles!" the curly-haired child whined.

"I know sweetie," said the young mother. "Mommy bought you popsicles last time we were at the store. We still have some at home. You can have one after lunch."

"No. I want Dora ones!" She whined more intently.

"Somebody's tired." Her mother commented.

"I'm not tired!!" The little one shouted.

"Okay, okay, we're almost done. Are you getting hungry?" The mother asked as she pulled out a small package of fruit snacks from her purse. The child nodded her head and greedily began putting the snacks in her mouth.

Maddie watched them round the corner and disappear from her sight. She took a few steps forward but had to stop again. If only she could sit down for a minute. Suddenly she felt very hot and decided to take off her jacket. Panic began to settle in, and Maddie became confused as to what to do next. Each step she took was worse than the last. There were two options. One was to leave the store and try to make it to the car. The other was to try to find the restroom. A feeling of heaviness developed with cramps that took her breath away. Maddie decided to abandon her cart and proceed to the restroom. The pain had disoriented her. When she tried to read the aisle signs hanging above her, the words blurred together, offering no direction. Using the freezer doors to steady herself, she walked towards the back of the store, gingerly turning corners, pausing frequently to recoup and gain strength. A young stock-boy stacking a cracker display was a welcome sight.

"Excuse me, I'm sorry to bother you, but I was wondering if you could direct me to the ladies room?" Maddie asked, trying to sound normal and not alert him of her current state of distress.

"Sure," the shaggy-haired teenager said and motioned for her to follow him. He walked slowly ahead of her. The way he walked with his hands in the pockets of his baggy, tan pants made her think of Matt. Her heart ached at the mere thought of him.

"It's over there next to the bakery," he said pointing to the far corner of the store.

"Thank you," she said and watched as he turned and walked back to the display he was stocking. The distance to the bakery was daunting but she slowly made it.

Once inside the ladies room, Maddie was thankful it was empty. She entered a stall, dropped her purse on the floor, and began fumbling with the button on her jeans. Her hands were sweaty and she felt dizzy. Out of

4

pure frustration, Maddie began to cry. Finally the button slipped through the hole and Maddie was able to lower her pants. With trembling hands she sat down on the toilet. She moaned as the pain became unbearable. In a matter of moments it felt as if all of her insides had escaped her. She panted as if in labor until the pain eased and she was able to compose herself. Maddie cleaned herself up as best as she could, horrified at the sight of her bright, red blood on the toilet paper. Slowly she rose and mustered up the courage to turn and look in the commode. She gasped at the site of large blood clots floating in the water. Bile rose in her throat and she vomited.

Once dressed, Maddie opened the stall door and carefully walked over to the sink. When she caught her reflection in the mirror she was startled. Her skin was ashen and her black hair was wet and matted against her face. She felt immediately cold and struggled to turn on the warm water in the sink. With her hands full, she splashed her face, hoping to wake from the fog she was in. As Maddie straightened, the dizziness returned and her vision narrowed. With ears ringing, she grasped onto the counter, tried to focus on the faucet to keep her head from spinning, then blackness.

* * *

The cold tile on her cheek was the first sensation Maddie felt. The second was a throbbing pain that came from the side of her head. Slowly she opened her eyes, squinting to adjust to the bright light of the restroom. Maddie scanned her surroundings and tried to orient herself. She recognized her purse sitting on the ground by a toilet. It occurred to her that she was still in the restroom of the grocery store. An attempt at lifting her head was excruciating so she lowered it back on the tile. A puddle of drool had formed from her lips and she struggled to reach her mouth with her hand. Maddie pondered how long she had been lying on the floor.

It surprised her that no one had entered the restroom. Surely someone would have to come in and find her soon. Maddie thought immediately of her cell phone. Her purse seemed a mile away, but if she could reach it then maybe this nightmare would be over. Pulling up one leg was a task; it felt numb and cold as if no longer belonging to her. With a grunt, she pushed against the tile with her shoe and inched herself a half a foot. With a second grunt, she gained a little further ground. Before she could make her third attempt, she heard voices and then the creaking of the restroom door. In walked the young mother she had noticed earlier.

"Okay, Emily, we're going to try to go potty before we go bye-bye," the woman said to the child she was leading with her hand. They walked toward the stall, then abruptly stopped when the mother noticed Maddie lying on the floor.

"Oh my goodness, are you okay?" the woman asked as she rushed over to her.

"I think I must have passed out," Maddie said weakly.

"Are you hurt?" the woman asked as she put her hand on Maddie's arm.

"I can't seem to get up," Maddie confessed. "I'm not sure I know what's happening."

"Oh my, you are bleeding from your head," the woman commented, then got up from the floor and grabbed some paper towels. She wet them with water from the sink and placed them on Maddie's forehead.

"What's wrong, Mommy?" the little girl asked as she clung to the back of her mother's leg.

"This nice lady fell down, honey, and she has a boo-boo on her head."

"Why is she crying, Mommy?" the little girl said, then buried her face into her mother's pants.

"She's hurt, sweetie," the woman said. "I think I need to go get some help. Will you be okay if I leave you here for a minute?" the young woman asked with concern.

"I'm fine. Thank you so much for helping me," Maddie said, not recognizing the weak, hoarse voice that was emanating from her mouth. She watched as the woman led the child through the door. Maddie tried to calm her nerves but her body was shaking uncontrollably.

The first to appear were the frosting-covered workers from the bakery. Carol, her donut-wielding friend, knelt down and held Maddie's head in her lap. Another woman put fresh cool towels on her head. Two more people entered the small bathroom inquiring about the status of the woman who had collapsed. Words of concern and questioning surrounded her. Maddie felt overwhelmed and embarrassed. The door suddenly opened again and a tall gentleman dressed in a shirt and tie began ushering people out of the bathroom. Ambulance workers filed in and immediately began assessing her. One man was standing towards the side with a clipboard, calmly writing down what the other men were calling out: "Respirs of thirty, pulse one-forty and regular, Bp 70/45." Their words were foreign to Maddie. A needle pricked her hand, the sensation of coolness followed. She tried as best as she could to answer their questions but found it hard to remember the simplest facts about herself. She remembered her purse and mentioned it to the man with the clipboard.

"I have a purse here somewhere," Maddie said, forgetting where she'd seen it earlier.

"Hey, Jack, check in the stalls to see if you see a purse."

"Okay," a raspy-voiced man said.

Maddie listened as the doors to the stalls swung open.

"This it?" A stocky, blond-haired man said as he swung Maddie's black purse over her head.

"Yes, thank you," Maddie murmured.

After asking Maddie's permission, the man with the clipboard opened her purse and found her wallet. From her license, he began recording her personal information. With a quick warning and a one, two, three, the men hoisted her onto a stretcher. Once the safety straps were secure around her, the cart started moving as they wheeled her out of the bathroom. "Maddie, everything is going to be just fine. We'll get you to the hospital in no time," the man with the clipboard said. Suddenly from behind them the tall man from before appeared. His face looked familiar but in her confused state she couldn't place it. She assumed he knew her by the look on his face; the instant change from shock to concern. He reached his hand out and softly touched hers as she passed by him. He had but a moment to look into her eyes and speak her name, "Maddie..."

CHAPTER TWO

The ride to the hospital was a blur. Maddie kept her eyes closed the entire time and tried not to listen to the conversation around her. Once inside the emergency room, she was immediately taken to the treatment area. Bright lights surrounded her. Another heave-ho and she was jostled to another cart. New faces peered down at her, each with their own set of questions. Maddie answered as well as she could. She felt more pokes on her arms, then her clothes were removed and replaced with a gown. Her head was throbbing, and when she mustered up the nerve to say something about it, the doctor promised that as soon as the testing was completed she could have pain medicine.

After a few moments, she was taken down for x-rays, then returned to the emergency room. Less than fifteen minutes later, she was wheeled down for a CAT scan of her head. Someone mentioned an MRI but that would be awhile because they had a fresh trauma that took priority over Maddie. Once back in the treatment room again, a doctor she had not seen before wheeled in an ultrasound machine. After a quick introduction, the soft-spoken man sat down on a stool beside her bed. "I need to take a peek at your abdomen," was all he said, then lifted Maddie's gown, exposing her stomach and everything else. He squirted cold, ultrasound jelly on her abdomen and began pushing on it with a wand of some sort. She looked over at a screen and saw a mesh of colors that made no sense to her. There was a method to his movements and Maddie tried to study his face for clues as to what he was seeing.

The doctor looked unkempt with his scrubs wrinkled, stubbly chin, and his hair sticking up as if he had just woke from a nap. The furrow of his brow revealed that he was not happy with what he was seeing. After briefly visiting each quadrant of her abdomen, he concentrated on the area where her uterus lay. He would move the wand to a certain area and then pause. With his other hand he would type something into a computer. This went on for quite a while. It was a dancing of clicks and pauses and writing. When he was finished, he abruptly stood, told Maddie he was through, and left the room. She was left alone staring at the ceiling, wondering what they would put her through next.

After the ultrasound test was finished, a nurse came in to check on her. She took Maddie's blood pressure and pulse again.

"How are you doing with your pain?" the nurse asked.

"I'm alright. It's much better than it was before."

"Do you need more pain medicine?" she said as she wrote something down in Maddie's chart.

"No, I'm fine," Maddie said.

"Anything else you need? A drink? A blanket?"

"A blanket would be nice," Maddie admitted. She didn't want to be a bother to the nurse, but she was freezing wearing just a thin gown with only a sheet covering her.

"I'll be right back," the nurse said and left the room. Moments later, she returned and carefully tucked a warm blanket around Maddie's body.

"Can I ask you a question?" Maddie asked softly.

"Sure," the nurse said kindly.

"Do you know the results of my tests?"

The nurse was quiet, then placed her hand on Maddie's. "The doctor will be in to talk with you soon. Why don't you try to rest a little bit until he comes in? Use the call light if you need me."

"Thank you," Maddie said. She then stared again at the ceiling. Thoughts of Ray, her husband, entered her mind. She wondered if he had checked the messages yet. He had never taken to the whole cell phone idea and preferred to use walkie-talkies, radios, or a landline phone. The paramedics had called Maddie's home, and she had given them instructions to leave a message on the machine. When Ray came in for supper, the first thing he would notice was that his meal wasn't ready. He would then wonder why she wasn't there.

Maddie looked at her watch. It was five-thirty. She had gone to the store after lunch and was surprised that so much time had passed. Ray usually came in to eat supper around seven. Life on their dairy farm was scheduled like clockwork. Mealtimes were seldom changed. If they were, it was as if the equilibrium of the place was off kilter. She still had a good two hours before he could possibly get to the hospital. Maddie had purposefully not asked them to call her sister or her dad. She had to think through what she would say to them. Maddie rubbed her temples and rested her arms over her eyes to shield them from the light.

Things weren't going as she had planned. It wasn't supposed to happen like this. Her health had been declining for quite some time but it had been manageable. Almost too easy, she thought to herself. The weight-loss was disguised with baggy clothes; her decreased appetite went unnoticed by Ray. She managed to keep up with the housework enough to make appearances and snuck in a nap whenever possible. She rarely left their property so when her episodes hit she was almost always at home. The decision to succumb to her illness had been made in the course of the two years since her son Matt's passing. With the suspicion that she had cancer like her mother, Maddie formulated a plan to let herself go. It was the easiest way to stop the pain. Ray continually cemented her plan with his repeated acts of unkindness.

– Chapter Three –

The hospital admitted Maddie at six-thirty. At home, as Maddie had suspected, Ray had come in for dinner. When he entered the kitchen and saw that she was not there and, more importantly, that there was no dinner for him, he became immediately annoyed. Ray called out for her and when she failed to answer he stomped around the house. When he came back through the kitchen, he noticed the answering machine light was flashing. After listening to the message, he grabbed his coat and keys and headed to the hospital.

After reviewing her tests, the doctor decided to admit Maddie to the intensive care unit for observation. Alone and scared, they wheeled her to a private room. The nurse placed leads on her chest and a blood pressure cuff on her arm, explaining it was needed to measure her pressure every half hour. A nurse performed a quick assessment, followed by another from the resident doctor of the ICU. Once left alone, Maddie closed her eyes and in a moment was fast asleep. She awoke to see Ray standing by the window of her room. He turned when she stirred, looked her in the eyes, then returned his gaze to the window. He said nothing to her. A few minutes passed, and Maddie was the one who spoke.

"Have you been here long?"

"Few minutes," Ray replied.

"You should have woken me."

"You look tired," he said flatly.

"I'm beat. They put me through so much today."

"What's wrong with you?"

"They don't know yet. My doctor is supposed to come in later." She paused, allowing herself to calm her nerves.

"Did you hear about what happened at the store?" Maddie continued.

"Yeah, some of it. They said you passed out in the bathroom. Have you been sick lately?" He turned to look at her.

"I've been tired but that's not unusual. I just really didn't feel well when I got up today." Ray walked over towards her, then stopped and leaned against the wall. She could sense that he wanted to reach out to her but stopped himself. It saddened her that they had reached the place in their relationship where they could no longer comfort each other. She would have hugged him if he were the one lying in the bed instead of her. Although he wasn't kind to her, she still cared about him. It would have been nice for him to show some emotion.

"You realize how much all this is going to cost me?" Ray said with a tone of disgust.

"I know, I thought about that, too," Maddie said, trying not to cry. "Can you do me a favor and call Dad and Lisa? I was going to but I fell asleep. I don't have the energy to explain everything to them now." He looked annoyed by her request. "Please, Ray. I won't bother you for anything else. I don't want them to worry. They might have already found out by now anyway."

"Alright," he said. "I'm going out for a smoke and then I'll call them on the payphone." He left the room. Maddie felt tears begin to form and belittled herself for letting him upset her again. She knew better than to expect anything more from him than what she got. At least he had shown up. Taking a few deep breaths to ward off the sobs, she looked out the window and thought about what to say to her family when they got there. She guessed that someone had already called her sister Lisa. Westville was a small town and she was sure one of Lisa's friends would have jumped at the chance to spread the news. Maddie felt guilty that she had not had someone call her sooner.

She then remembered the familiar voice and soft touch of a man's hand on hers at the store as she was being wheeled to the ambulance. Even in all the confusion, Maddie knew when she heard him speak that it was Kevin, her old friend from high school. She had not seen Kevin in years but immediately she had known it was him. Maddie found it strange that the brief touch and sight of him stirred something in her.

Ray returned to her room and left her no time to ponder this further.

"Did I miss the doctor?" Ray asked.

"No. No one's come in since you left." Maddie paused to see if he'd respond. Instead he searched for the TV remote and turned on the TV.

"Did you get hold of Lisa?"

"It was busy," he said as he stared at the television, flipping the channels quickly.

"How about Dad? Did you try him?"

"No. He's your dad. Why don't you call him?"

"If you turn the TV down, I will," Maddie said and cringed. Ray shot her a look.

"It don't matter how sick you are, Maddie. You don't sass me. Got it?'

Maddie didn't have the chance to respond. The nurse had tapped lightly on the door and entered her room.

"Maddie, you have a couple more visitors. Unfortunately, we can only have two at a time in the room with you. Your husband would have to step out for a moment in order for them both to come in."

"I'll be back," Ray said and abruptly left the room. He passed Maddie's Dad and sister, said a quick hello, then kept walking in the direction of the hospital's cafeteria.

Lisa poked her head in Maddie's room. "Okay if we come in?"

"Of course. Hey sis. Hi Dad," Maddie said as her family embraced her. "Ray tried to call you but couldn't get through."

"He didn't try very hard. Carol from the store called just a little while ago. She wanted to check to see how you were doing. You can imagine how shocked I was to hear about what happened," Lisa said.

"I'm sorry I didn't tell you myself. I meant to call but fell asleep."

"You doing okay, honey?" Jack said and held onto his youngest daughter's frail hand.

"I'm alright, Dad."

"What's the matter with you, sweetie? What are they saying is the cause of all this?" Jack wore a look of deep concern.

"So far, they've said I lost a lot of blood. It could be due to some female problems I've been having. They ran a lot of tests but I don't know all the results yet."

"You never told me you were having problems, Maddie," Lisa said.

"I thought it was normal, maybe early menopause. Plus that stuff is not something I like to talk about. Try not to worry, you guys. I'll be fine."

"So, what are they going to do now?" Lisa asked.

"I'm not sure. Tonight, I think they'll just watch me. My doctor will be around in the morning to explain it all to me. My nurse said everything is stable now."

"I hate to see you like this, Maddie," Jack said, trying not to get emotional.

"Do you hurt anywhere?" Lisa asked. "You look so tired and pale."

"I'm just very tired. Today was exhausting." Maddie noticed the nurse coming through her doorway. She gave the family a five-minute warning before they needed to leave.

"Do you want me to stay the night with you? I can, Maddie. I don't mind," Lisa said.

"No, no. You go home. I'll be fine. I hope to get some sleep. We'll know more in the morning. I promise I'll call you as soon as I know anything."

"Promise?" Lisa said in her motherly tone.

"I promise," Maddie said and weakly smiled. She gave them both a hug goodbye and watched as they left. A minute later, Ray returned.

"Nice that they took up all the visiting time. The nurse says she'll give me ten more minutes," Ray said with disgust.

"They were worried, Ray. I'm glad they came to see me."

"Has the doctor been in yet? I'll be ticked if your family caused me to miss him."

"Only the resident from earlier. He said my doctor won't be in until the morning. She'll discuss the results then."

"I have to milk in the morning, you know." Ray let out an irritated sigh. "It's ridiculous to make us wait until tomorrow to find out what is going on. I ought to call that doctor at home and tell her to get over here and do her job."

"Ray, whatever she has to say can obviously wait until tomorrow. They wouldn't wait until then if it was something serious."

"Still, it ain't right. We have to pay for a night in this intensive place, and maybe you don't even need it. I swear it's a way they can make more money. It's a crying shame how they run these places. That's my sweat they're spending."

"There's no use getting all worked up over it. We can't change the way they operate. Did you get something to eat? You must me hungry."

"I went to the cafeteria and ate a burger."

"Good. It's late. Why don't you go home so you can get your evening work done and get some rest. I'm just going to try to go to sleep. I'll call you in the morning."

Ray contemplated her suggestion. "I think I'll swing by Smitty's for a drink, then head home." He zipped up his coat and fished in his pockets for his keys. "You call me as soon as you wake up, you hear?"

"I will," Maddie said, waiting to see if he'd dare to touch her.

"Alright, then. See you tomorrow." Ray turned and walked out the door.

"See you tomorrow," Maddie said with a sigh. She wished it wasn't so.

CHAPTER FOUR

At five a.m., a phlebotomist awakened Maddie, request-ing to take some blood samples from her. After filling three vials, the woman placed a bandaid on her arm and left the room. Now awake, she attempted to get up to use the restroom. Dizziness enveloped her and she had to quickly sit down. The nurse came in and gently scolded Maddie for not calling for assistance. It was hard to humble herself and admit she needed help. Once back in bed, she turned on the TV to distract herself. A soft knock presented Dr. Brown, her gynecologist, into the room. She hadn't changed a bit in the three years since Maddie last saw her. She had auburn hair cut short that framed her light green eyes. Tall and lean, she made an impressive entrance, carrying herself with a grace that few women possess. Wearing taupe pants, a light blue sweater, and a crisp, white lab coat, she definitely looked the part.

Dr. Brown closed the door behind her and asked if she could sit on the end of Maddie's bed. She held a blue chart with Maddie's name on the front written in black marker on a white sticker. She folded her hands and rested them on the chart. "Well, it's been a long time since I've seen you, Maddie, too long." She gave Maddie a motherly, concerned look.

"I'm sorry I couldn't come to see you last night. I had to give a presentation and couldn't be in two places at once. I have been in contact with my residents though and have been updated frequently on your status. Did you have a chance to get any rest last night?"

"I slept a little. It's hard to sleep with so many people coming in your room all night."

"I know. Hopefully by tonight we'll have you on a regular floor with fewer interruptions." Dr. Brown glanced around the room, then back at Maddie. "Are any more of your family around by any chance? I was hoping they would be here when I talked to you."

"My husband was in last night but won't be able to make it in until later this morning. I don't know if you remember we are dairy farmers. He has a lot of work to do early in the morning."

"I see," Dr. Brown said, opening Maddie's chart on her lap.

"I'll call him when we are through talking."

"That would be good. Now let's talk about yesterday. I'd like to get a good picture of what happened from your point of view." Maddie imagined Dr. Brown readying her mental notebook for a big entry. She then began to describe her sudden attack in the store, at least what she could remember before she passed out.

"Has this ever happened before?" Maddie silently nodded yes and let her doctor continue. "How long have you been feeling badly?" Dr. Brown inquired. "Do you remember your first symptoms?"

"To be honest, I can't remember when it all began, maybe a year or so ago. It was a slow process. I was losing a little bit of weight, which I didn't mind, and I began spotting. It started pretty slowly so I thought maybe I was going through early menopause. After awhile, I was getting tired easily so I cut back on working in the barn, and that helped some. I had my good days and my bad days. I guess you could call yesterday a bad day," she said with a nervous laugh. This was hard.

Dr. Brown wore a look of concern. "It puzzles me that you didn't come to see me when you first started having problems."

"I thought about it, I did, but I think I thought it would just take care of itself."

"Maddie, it has taken care of itself but not in a good way." She looked at Maddie with a grave face. "I suspect you may have cancer." Dr Brown paused to let her statement sink in. "There is a large tumor growing in your uterus. From the scan you had yesterday, it looks as if the tumor has also grown through your uterine wall to the area outside your uterus."

Maddie listened, trying to understand what her doctor was trying to tell her. The doctor continued, "From your history of endometriosis, I would gauge that you developed endometrial cancer, which is an abnormal tissue growth on the lining of your uterus. This cancer usually affects women over fifty so, at forty, you are quite young for this. Now I can't diagnose the cancer for sure until I get a biopsy of the abnormal tissue, but from what I see, Maddie, it doesn't look good."

"I had a feeling from the way the doctors were acting yesterday things didn't look normal." Maddie found it hard to look into her doctor's face. She felt terribly guilty for hiding the truth from her. There is no way she could admit that she was letting herself get sick on purpose. She just hadn't planned on getting caught.

Dr. Brown looked briefly at something in Maddie's chart. "What I'd like to do is put you on the surgery schedule for this afternoon, if that's okay with you. We need to remove your uterus and possibly your ovaries. I'll have to see how involved the tumor is when I get in there. The surgery should last anywhere from one to three hours. We will take samples from the tumor and surrounding tissue to be biopsied. I'll also biopsy lymph nodes in the immediate area. Once I get the results back I can stage the cancer—Stage I is the best scenario, and Stage IV is the worst. Am I talking too fast, Maddie?"

"No, please continue. It's easier to just hear it all at once."

"When I find out what stage it is we can formulate a plan of care."

"You are pretty sure I have cancer, aren't you Dr. Brown?"

"Let's just say I'd be extremely shocked if you didn't. I don't mean to scare you, but I think it's best to prepare you now for the worst, then backtrack from there if we should be so fortunate. I'm so sorry, Maddie, I just wish you'd come to me sooner."

Maddie stifled a cry and tried to compose herself. Dr. Brown reached for her hand. "What time are we thinking for surgery?" Maddie asked, fearful she would become too emotional and let out her secret.

"I think I can squeeze you in around three. You haven't had anything to drink or eat today?"

"No, not since last night."

"Good. I just need the okay from you to go ahead with the surgery. I'll call the operating room to get you on the schedule. Do you have any questions for me before we proceed?"

"I don't think so," Maddie said, and then mustered up the courage to proceed.

"Dr. Brown, I'd like you to promise me something."

"Okay," she said in an apprehensive tone.

"I don't want anyone to know I have cancer." Maddie had a serious, steady tone when she spoke.

"I don't understand. Not even your family?" Dr. Brown was shocked.

"No. I want to do this myself."

"That's your right, Maddie. I just don't understand why you would want to go through all of this alone. You are going to need a lot of support . . . much more than you realize."

"I'll be fine. I can't put my Dad and sister thought this right now. It was awful to watch my Mom die of cancer. I don't want to burden them with the thought of me having cancer unless I have to. And my husband . . . he is still grieving the loss of our son two years ago. I need time to process all this myself before I tell anyone else. It's just something I need to do. I know it must be hard for you to understand. I can always change my mind and tell them later if I need to." Maddie knew this would not be the case but thought that Dr. Brown wouldn't pry too much if she offered a little hope of her giving in later.

"I just feel bad that you are going to go through this alone."

"I won't be. I'll have you and that will be enough. Can you give me that?"

"Of course, Maddie. I'll do all I can for you," Dr. Brown said.

"I appreciate it. I'll talk to my family and give them enough information for them to understand why I need surgery. I'll handle their questions."

"Alright. I respect your wishes and will leave this in your hands. If you change your mind, I'll gladly talk to them."

"Thank you, Dr. Brown. You have been very kind."

"I just want what's best for you. I'll do everything I can to help you survive this."

"I appreciate your concern for me."

"I'll see you this afternoon," Dr Brown said, then left the room.

Maddie pulled the covers up to shield her face while she allowed the doctor's words to sink in. It was official. Her suspicions had been right all along. The ball was in motion. She had let herself go and now there was no turning back. She had prayed for this—prayed that she would get sick in order to escape the pain of her everyday existence. She remembered thinking that dying would be a welcome relief from her suffering. The loss of her son had been just too much to bear. Not only had it left her empty but had turned her husband into a man of whom she was afraid. Maddie knew she couldn't face years of Ray's coldness. She was too tired and just wanted this all to be over soon. Her body now was cooperating with that plan.

– CHAPTER FIVE –

Maddie called her Dad and Lisa to let them know about the surgery. They promised to come and sit with her before the operation. Reluctantly, she called Ray at home to tell him the plan for the day. Profanity was his first response, but then he settled down and told her he'd try to get to the hospital as soon as he could.

The hours passed awkwardly as Jack, Lisa, and Ray sat with Maddie in her hospital room. She was still tired from the previous day but felt she couldn't rest with the tension in the room. Maddie noticed her Dad was unusually quiet.

"You okay, Dad?" Maddie asked. "You are very quiet over there in your corner."

"I'm alright, honey. It's just hard to see you in this condition. You look so much like your mother. It brings back a lot of memories of when she was sick."

"I'm sorry, Dad," Maddie said. "I don't want you to be upset by all this."

"It's nothing that can be helped. It's not your fault. She was brave like you; always looking out for everyone else," Jack said and glanced at Lisa. "I wish you girls would have gotten the chance to know your mother better. You'd see so much of her in yourselves."

"I remember coming to see her in the hospital," Lisa reflected. "Maddie was always scared to go in her room, but Mom always had a treat for us and would pull us both into her bed to watch cartoons together. Do you remember that, Maddie?"

"I do," Maddie said, touched by the memory. "She'd tell us that the mean old nurse didn't let her have sleepovers or else she'd let us stay with her. We nick-named the nurse, Meanie-neanie."

"She shouldn't have told you girls that," Jack laughed. "Do you realize how hard it was to take you to your check-ups at the doctor after that? If the nurse was the slightest bit old looking, Maddie would start to cry, instantly thinking it was the dreaded 'Meanie-neanie.'"

Lisa laughed. "I haven't thought of that in years."

Jack got up from his chair to stretch. The clock on the wall read two p.m. "This wait is eternal. I wish this would be over already. I just want you to be well again."

"Me, too," said Lisa. Ray, who had ignored the conversation, continued to stare at the TV. Lisa looked his way in annoyance. Lisa and Ray had exchanged words on many occasions. There was a mutual dislike of each other but, for Maddie's sake, they kept it civil. Maddie had no idea how much Lisa knew of Ray's comings and goings around town. For the sake of her sister's happiness, she had kept what she learned to herself.

The nurse came in around 2:15 and began to get things ready to take Maddie to the operating room. She asked the family to say their goodbyes, then left the room.

"We'll be waiting for you when you get out, Maddie," Jack said and kissed her forehead.

"You'll do just fine, sis," Lisa said. They turned to see what Ray would say.

"Do you mind?" Ray said with irritation and pointed to the door.

"Of course not," Jack said and led Lisa from the room.

"Well that was three hours of sheer torture."

"They're not that bad, Ray."

"Speak for yourself."

"Are you going to wait around until I get out of surgery? Or do you need to get back home?"

"I really should get back to the farm, but I guess I'll stay."

"Well, I guess I'll see you when I'm all done."

"You scared?"

"Terrified."

Ray leaned down and kissed her cheek. "You'll be alright."

"If you say so."

Once Ray left the room, the nurse immediately entered. Maddie watched as she checked the IV site in her arm, pushed a few buttons on the machine to which it was attached, then wrote some numbers on a piece of paper. Next she unwrapped some plastic leg wraps and put them on Maddie's lower legs. She explained that they were used during surgery to help with blood circulation to her legs and to help prevent blood clots from forming. Maddie pretended she understood. Another nurse entered the room holding Maddie's chart in one hand and some paper surgery caps in her other hand. Laying the chart on the end of Maddie's bed, she gave caps to the other nurses and Maddie. The nurses tucked their hair into the cap and Maddie figured she should do the same. The thought crossed her mind that the caps made the nurses look very unattractive. They then unplugged the bed and tossed the cords over the headboard. As they pulled the bed towards the door, one of the nurses told Maddie to keep her hands by her sides.

Once outside the room, the nurses wheeled her past the nurse's station. Everyone at the station stopped what they were doing for a moment and watched as she rolled by. Maddie felt like she was an animal on display at the zoo. It was horrible to be led out in the open in just a thin gown, no make-up, and wearing a silly cap. To make matters worse, the operating room was on the first floor. She had to go down the elevator in the bed and then be wheeled down the hall again, close to the main lobby. She hoped she would not see anyone she knew.

When they finally entered the surgery department, Maddie felt the cool air envelop her immediately. "I'll get you some warm blankets once we get you on the table," the ICU nurse said to Maddie as she wheeled her towards operating room three.

"That sounds nice," Maddie said, wondering why it had to be so cold. Common sense would dictate that a body should be kept warm. The smell of the room to which they took her was hard to place, like a mixture of alcohol and plastic. Maddie briefly thought of burnt flesh but didn't want to entertain that idea. Slowly, she looked around the room. There was a narrow, stainless steel bed in the center of the room. It had a thin mattress covered with a white sheet. Above the bed were very large lights with blue rubber handles. At the head of the bed stood an array of machines with flashing lights and colored buttons. There were poles with IV bags dangling and a table with various bags of supplies nearby. A man stood off to the side, pulling little vials of medicine out of a red metal cart. She watched him use a needle to draw up a milky-white mixture.

"That's for me," Maddie thought to herself. The man had on dark green scrubs and a black cap decorated with red peppers. She noticed that he was a very hairy man and made an assumption that he was bald under the ridiculous cap he was wearing. Although he wasn't directly looking at her, he was carrying on a conversation with one of the nurses. She then noticed there were several other people in the room, each of them busy doing one task or another. The nurse from the intensive care unit had left, replaced by a new nurse; a somewhat gruff, portly woman named Patty. She wore light blue scrubs that were a size too small. A few random brown curls defied her paper cap, dangling down her neck.

"Okay Maddie, I'm Patty. I will be the nurse taking care of you while you are in the operating room. This is

Paul. He is the surgeon's assistant." Maddie turned her head to the left to acknowledge him. She guessed him to be in his forties. He had red hair and light brown freckles covered his body.

"Hi there," Paul said, his smile revealing silver braces. Maddie hadn't expected that.

"Maddie, I'm going to have Paul help me get you onto this table." The two grabbed the sheet underneath her and pulled it taught. "You ready Paul? One, two, three." With that, Maddie was thrust onto the surgical table. Patty and Paul each took one of her arms, holding them out away from her body, then resting them onto arm boards.

"We have to strap you down now," Patty stated flatly. "Paul, can you believe Jane called off again?" It was apparent Maddie was no longer included on the conversation.

"I heard. I don't see how she still has a job here," Paul said as he buckled the strap on Maddie's left wrist. He then moved toward her middle and waited for Patty to follow suit so they could fasten the lap belt.

"I know. It's ridiculous! If she expects me to fill in for her tomorrow, she's in for a big surprise because I'm not doing it. I've worked five days straight and I've had it with this place," Patty complained, making Maddie feel uneasy that the nurse in charge of her was frustrated with her work. They moved down to her legs and applied straps there as well. Maddie wondered why she needed so many restraints. Wasn't she supposed to be completely asleep? It made her nervous. Paul came back to the top of the bed.

"You doing okay, honey?" he asked.

"Uh-huh," Maddie managed to say.

She was beginning to feel anxious and tried to calm herself. The man with the pepper cap started talking to her and it was strange not to be able to see his face. He was talking fast and she could only understand bits and pieces of what he was saying. She couldn't see what he was doing but she was pretty sure he was turning back and forth as he was talking. She thought that was rude. Maddie suddenly noticed a cold sensation traveling up her arm. A moment later, the cuffs on her legs started to squeeze and release. It felt like there were bugs crawling on her.

The commotion subsided somewhat once everyone had accomplished their duties. Someone told Maddie the doctor had called and was running late but would be there in about 15 minutes. Maddie was fortunate Dr. Brown was also a surgeon. She felt comfortable with her and trusted her. Maddie didn't like the fact that she was given time to think about what was happening. Patty surprised her and brought new warm blankets. Maybe she wasn't that gruff after all. The blankets distracted her for a minute but then she noticed again how uncomfortable she was. She couldn't move and felt trapped. She wished they would just put her to sleep.

She noticed for the first time that classical music was playing. She guessed it was supposed to relax everyone but it did nothing to ease her nerves. She again looked around and wondered who might have had surgery before her. Who had lain on the same table as she was now on? What had brought them to the same place? What was their outcome? Maddie wondered how many people had died here. How many people had not realized this room was the last thing they would see before they died. Maddie wondered if she would die during surgery. She thought it would be an easy way to go, but it also scared her to think about it. Her heart must have started racing because Dr. Pepper, Maddie's new name for the anesthesiologist, asked her if she was okay. She said she was fine, although her heart rate on the machine told him otherwise.

Finally, her doctor entered the room. It was strange to see her so casually dressed. She was wearing light green scrubs and, unlike Dr. Pepper, her cap was a light gray paisley print. Upon entering, she went directly to Maddie and greeted her.

"Hello, Maddie. I'm sorry to keep you waiting," Dr. Brown said with sincerity.

"It's okay," Maddie said, meaning it.

"No, it's not. I pride myself on being on time. Today there was something that came up that took more time than I had scheduled." Dr. Brown scrubbed her hands while talking and then went over to a nurse who was holding a towel. She dried her hands and next put on a paper gown and sterile gloves. Maddie had wondered why the doctor had kept her wet hands in the air while she was talking to her. Now it made sense. She had to keep her hands from touching anything after she washed them. The doctor walked back over to Maddie's side.

"Alright Maddie, I think we're ready to get started. I'll talk to you again after the surgery. You're going to be fine." The doctor gave Dr. Pepper a nod, her signal to him to start. As the medicine began to dull her senses, she heard her doctor talk to Paul. Dr. Pepper mumbled something to Maddie but it sounded far away. She heard a few beeping sounds, then nothing.

– Chapter Six –

The first thing she remembered after surgery was hearing the rhythmic beeping of the EKG machine at her bedside. Maddie opened her eyes and squinted at the lights shining down from the ceiling. She tried to move her legs but they were heavy from the anesthesia. A sweet, young nurse was sitting at her bedside. Maddie turned her head to face her.

"Hi, Mrs. Stevens, my name is Kelly. I am your recovery room nurse. I'll take care of you until you're ready to go back to your room."

"Nice to meet you," Maddie said. "I guess I made it through surgery okay."

"Yes, you did. Your vital signs are stable, and there was no excessive bleeding."

"Good," Maddie mumbled, her throat feeling scratchy and dry.

"Are you comfortable?"

"It's really starting to hurt now. Is that supposed to happen?" Maddie asked.

"Let me give you some more medicine. Once the anesthesia starts wearing off, the pain sets in pretty fast."

After about an hour in the recovery room, a male nurse's aide wheeled her back to her room. Oddly, her family sat in the same chairs as before surgery. After she got settled, it was only a few minutes and Dr. Brown came in. She introduced herself and began to discuss the surgery. Maddie was nervous that her doctor might say too much and not respect her wishes.

"Well, the surgery went smoothly and, as expected, I did a total hysterectomy and removed your ovaries. That should take care of the bleeding you were having. I'm going to leave you on the pain pump overnight to help with the pain. You'll have to get up to go to the bathroom, which will be painful, but I want you up and moving as soon as possible. I'd like you to get some rest," she admonished Maddie, then said to the family, "So if we can keep the visit short that would be best for Maddie."

"We will, doctor. Thank you for all you've done," Jack said and reached out to shake Dr. Brown's hand.

"When can she go home?" Ray asked.

"In a couple of days, if she's feeling up to it. We'll see. It was a big surgery." Dr. Brown then turned to address Maddie again. "I'm going to dictate on your case, then do some rounds. I'll be back to check on you before I leave for the night."

"Thank you, Dr. Brown," Maddie said, grateful that the doctor had kept her promise to keep her situation private.

After the doctor left the room, Lisa and Jack gave Maddie a hug goodbye and said they'd call in to check on her. Ray stayed for an hour after they left, then needed to get back to the farm. He said goodbye quickly, void of emotion. Maddie was too groggy to care.

The nurses taking care of her seemed nice, but the way they looked at her made her feel uncomfortable. They looked at her with such pity in their eyes. It dawned on Maddie that they had access to her chart and knew exactly what was going on. They knew what she was hiding.

As promised, her doctor returned to check on her. She found Maddie to be alone and was able to talk freely. Maddie was told she had Stage III Endometrial Cancer. The tumor had spread outside the uterus but not outside the pelvis. It had not affected either her bladder or rectum. Dr. Brown was still waiting on the biopsy of the lymph nodes and would tell her the results as soon as they were available. Maddie listened quietly to her diagnosis. It seemed surreal. Dr. Brown said she'd talk with her more tomorrow when Maddie was more coherent. She didn't want to burden Maddie with any more details tonight.

By morning, she was feeling more level-headed. The nurse taking care of her that day removed the pain pump and gave her pain pills instead. Maddie didn't like the way the morphine made her feel. She only took one of the pills and that was enough to make her pain tolerable. The nurse removed the catheter from her bladder and Maddie felt liberated. By lunchtime, she had taken a small walk in the hall and had been able to eat lunch while sitting in a chair. When she had finished eating, she slowly made her way back to her bed. She positioned herself with the pillows and turned on the television. She was switching the channels trying to find something to watch when Dr. Brown walked into her room.

"I heard you were a busy lady today," Dr. Brown said and smiled at Maddie.

"I couldn't stand to be in the bed one more minute. I'm not used to being so still."

"I'm glad you did so well getting up. The pain is worse when you lie in bed. Your body gets stiff and the immobility can also lead to other complications." She positioned herself in the chair beside Maddie's bed. "So how is your pain today? I hope we didn't take you off the pain pump too soon."

"I actually prefer the pills. That other medicine was too strong for me."

"Good. Listen, I came to talk to you about your treatment plan." She looked for a reaction from Maddie. "I decided I'd like you to get started on radiation treatments while you are here. The radiation oncologist will be in tomorrow and will be able to get your markings done and possibly give you your first treatment. His name is Dr. Dillon. You'll really like him. He will explain your treatment regimen for outpatients. He'll also take over your care for the cancer. I do the surgery, but that is the end of my scope of practice. Sometimes they will put you on hormone therapy as a treatment, so don't be surprised if he brings that up. I think you'll do fine. You've done really well with surgery and I have every hope for the best chance of recovery."

"When do you think I'll be able to go home?"

"I'd like to keep you here tomorrow, then if everything goes well you could go home the next morning."

"That sounds good. I'd love to sleep in my own bed."

"Soon," she said, smiling at Maddie. "So we're on for tomorrow?"

"Okay." Maddie faked a smile. She didn't know anything about radiation and had not thought this part through. She was caught off guard and now had committed to it. She felt a wave of anxiety wash over her.

"Alright then," her doctor said and stood up. "I'll go write some orders. See you tomorrow."

"Thanks for all you've done," Maddie said and she meant it. Her doctor had been wonderful.

"No problem." She turned and started walking to the door.

"Um, Dr. Brown?" Maddie said inquisitively.

She turned again towards Maddie. "Yes?"

"I was just wondering . . . does the radiation make your hair fall out?"

"No. You may have a loss of appetite, diarrhea and, sometimes, difficulty with urination."

"Oh." She paused. "That doesn't sound pleasant."

Dr. Brown looked at her with concern. "Maddie, I think you should really consider talking to your family about all of this. You need their support."

"I'll think about it," she said to appease her.

"I hope you do. It's the best thing you can do for yourself."

She waved goodbye and left the room. Maddie again was torn and confused. She wished she could go somewhere and hide out until this was all over. There were too many people involved, too many people to explain things to. It would be easier, she told herself, once she got home. She would just have to pretend she was fine. Dr. Brown did say that the radiation would help with any residual pain. That would be nice. To no longer be in pain would make things a lot easier. Plus, who said she had to make it to every treatment?

– CHAPTER SEVEN –

Later that afternoon, Maddie again was alone in her room. The quiet was both calming and unnerving. She had turned over her doctor's words over and over in her head. If she could just keep it together until she got back home, she knew she could hide everything better there.

Maddie's thoughts drifted towards Kevin and how suddenly he had reentered her life when she had passed out in the store. She remembered her high school days and how she and Kevin had become friends. It was their last semester before graduation and they were paired up in art class. She had known who he was but had never really become friends with him. They ran in separate circles. He was one of those kids who was neither popular nor a loner. He fell somewhere in between. As a requirement for graduation, he had to take an art class and had done his best to avoid it until then. Maddie, on the other hand, lived for her art classes. Maddie's artistic talent amazed her teacher and she secretly lived for the praise and encouragement he bestowed on her.

It was routine for the teacher to pair a "struggling artist" with a more seasoned one. That was where Maddie fit in. She was both excited and sad about her last art class. Kevin, on the other hand, couldn't wait to get through it. His attitude, however, changed on the first day of class when the teacher placed him next to Maddie. He couldn't believe his good fortune. She was one of the most popular kids in school and he thought she was absolutely gorgeous. They formed a friendship that may never have developed had he not been required to take that class. He was in all honors classes and on the fast track for both college and graduate school. Always expected to excel, he was happy to be out of the spotlight for once in his life. It felt good to let someone else shine. Maddie enjoyed his company, and secretly it felt good to be able to teach something to someone so much smarter than herself.

Outside of class, when Ray wasn't around, Maddie would say hello to Kevin in the hall. Ray was the jealous type and made fun of Kevin anytime Maddie talked about him. Ray was really good-looking and popular. He was the typical, smart-mouth kid who thought he was "too cool for school." He didn't participate in sports or clubs. He managed to squeak by with average grades. His future was on the family farm so he felt it was pointless to work hard at school. He worked hard enough when he got home. He walked the halls like he was "it," with Maddie right there beside him. She was just as enamored as the rest of the girls and was more desirable because she was his girl.

Maddie was well liked by teachers and her classmates. She was a good girl from a good family. Her sister Lisa had paved the way for her. She didn't even have to try to be popular; she just was. It didn't hurt that they had their mother's dark hair and dark eyes.

Kevin was tall and lanky but had a handsome face and a perfect, white smile. What was most attractive about him was his sense of self. He was nice to everyone. He didn't get caught up in all the social antics that typically plagued the high school scene. He didn't gossip like everyone else. Once, Maddie had tried to turn one of their conversations that way and felt embarrassed she had. He didn't care about what other people were doing or about who was dating whom. He was looking ahead to college and a better future. It was as if he knew this was a step he had to take; something to endure until he was really where he should be. Kevin knew there was life after high school. This amazed Maddie, who herself was all wrapped up in the social scene. She knew college was not in her future so she lived for the football games, parties, and dances. She was also completely awestruck over Ray. Sometimes he was all she talked about. Kevin didn't like Ray, and his demeanor would change when Maddie brought him up. It took a little while, but Maddie finally figured out that Kevin was enamored with her. When he looked into her eyes it felt as if he was looking deep within her soul. To this day, she had never felt that way again. No man had ever looked at her and saw who she really was or really listened to her like he did. Kevin tried several times to convince her to go to art school, but she would always brush the idea aside and say that her life was moving in a different direction.

Graduation was the last time she had seen him. Their eyes had met across the crowd and they had smiled to each other. He hadn't attended any of the graduation parties and Maddie always had regretted not being able to say goodbye to him. She heard he had left for college, had met and married a girl from there, and had become a successful businessman somewhere in the northeast.

The summer after graduation, Maddie married Ray and settled into the life of a farmer's wife. She had tucked away her art supplies and, along with them, her dreams of school. It was the right choice for her at the time. With everything that had happened since then, she questioned how her life would have been different had she never met Ray.

A soft knock on the door broke her train of thought. She was surprised to see that it was Kevin in the doorway! He had an uneasy smile on his face. The sight of him instantly warmed Maddie.

"Is it okay if I come in?" he asked softly.

"Sure, come on in, Kevin." She pulled the covers up to her chest and tucked her hair behind her ears. "It's good to see you. It's been a long time."

"It has. How are you? You gave me quite a scare at the store."

"I'm really sorry I caused such a scene. I'm embarrassed about what happened. I cringe when I think about it."

"Don't worry. Everyone is just hoping you are okay," Kevin said and took the seat next to her bed.

"It's been a crazy few days, but I'm doing much better. I had surgery yesterday. I should be able to go home the day after tomorrow. I'm sure I look a fright. A lot has changed since high school, huh?"

"I think you look great. Since I've been back, I've wondered when I would run into you. I didn't think it would be this dramatic, but I'm glad I got to see you just the same," Kevin admitted.

It struck Maddie that Kevin had been thinking of her. What did that mean? She brushed off the thought. "I wish it had been a more dignified reunion."

"When someone told me a lady had collapsed in the bathroom, my heart sank. Then when I found out it was you," Kevin let out a sigh, "I just wanted to drive over to the hospital right away, but I knew it wasn't my place. I waited as long as I could, then thought, 'heck with it,' and came over today."

"I'm glad you did," Maddie said. She was touched by his concern.

"What are they saying caused all this? Are you okay now that you've had surgery?" he said with genuine concern. It struck Maddie that Kevin showed more empathy than her husband.

"I'm going to be fine. Just some female problems. It's really sweet of you to care."

"I've always cared about you, Maddie. Time doesn't change that." He looked deeply into her eyes. Maddie noticed that time had given Kevin a boldness he did not have in his youth.

"What the hell are *you* doing here?" An annoyed voice spoke from the doorway.

Kevin and Maddie turned their gazes towards the door and saw Ray standing with his hands on his hips. A wave of anxiety overcame her. She felt a strange and urgent need to protect Kevin. "He came in to see how I was . . . being the store manager and all."

"I wasn't talking to you," Ray said as he glared at Kevin. "He has no business being here and he knows it." Ray let his jealous nature overtake him and stepped closer to Kevin. Time had not softened Ray's dislike of Kevin.

"Ray, he was just being nice. There is nothing to get upset over," Maddie pleaded.

"If he knows what is best for him he'd better get out of here," Ray said, not taking his eyes off Kevin.

"Are you threatening me, Ray?" Kevin said and stood from the chair. A lot had changed from their younger days. Kevin was a good foot taller than Ray and was much more intimidating.

"Call it what you want but I'm giving you two seconds to get out before it gets ugly," Ray said intently.

Kevin turned to face Maddie. "I'm sorry you have to deal with this loser . . . unbelievable."

At that Ray lunged at Kevin, swung his arm and missed Kevin's face. Kevin ducked and returned a reactionary swing, nailing him in the jaw. Ray hit the floor and Maddie screamed. Before she realized it, the room was full of people. As the brawlers were being removed from the room, Kevin turned, eyes connecting with Maddie's, and he mouthed, "I'm sorry." She could hear Ray yelling as he was led down the hall. The nurse came in to console Maddie and reassured her that the men would not be allowed to return to the hospital again. Maddie was grateful for the solitude. She needed to process what she had just witnessed.

– Chapter Eight –

Ray's rude display of chivalry worked to her advantage when Dr. Dillon came to see her in the early evening. Warm brown eyes and an easy smile accompanied the tall frame that came into her room.

"Mrs. Stevens, I'm Dr. Dillon. Dr. Brown told you I was coming?" He reached out and shook Maddie's hand.

"Yes, it's nice to meet you."

"I wish I could have made it to see you earlier, but I've been running like mad today."

"It's okay, I've had a big day as well."

"I talked at length with Dr. Brown about your situation. Fortunately, there is no sign of the cancer after the surgery, so you are in better shape than we thought. I'd still recommend radiation treatments just in case. You are young and I'd advise outpatient radiation for you. There is something called internal radiation, but I don't think we need to do anything invasive at this point. Your tumor also tested to be responsive to hormone therapy. I'd like you to get started on that right away."

"How long will I have to take the radiation treatments?"

"We're looking at five days a week for several weeks. What I'm thinking is having you come to my office Monday morning. That will give you a chance to rest over the weekend and we can then formulate a schedule starting next week. I'd like to have you set up at my office so we'll have your records there. Sound like a good plan?" Maddie thought he was awfully chipper, but she immediately liked him.

"Okay," Maddie replied.

"Here's my card. Give my office a call to set up an appointment. Ask for Cathy, my office manager. I'll let her know you'll be calling. Any other questions for me?"

"I don't think so."

"Alright, then. I'll look forward to seeing you on Monday."

After he left, Maddie felt more confused. Everyone was so helpful and nice; eager to help. She didn't know what to do and again had agreed to do something that was against her plan. She began to doubt if she was doing the right thing. She thought of Ray and how on earth she could explain going to the doctor every day for weeks. It was impossible. The phone rang and it was Ray on the line.

It was a cold, brief conversation, the majority of which was filled with questions about Kevin. Maddie, being well versed in appeasing her husband, explained again why Kevin was in her room. She was glad for the physical distance between them but could still imagine Ray's brow furrowing and the tenseness of his body as he held the phone. She could read his tone like a book. He called again the morning of her discharge. A half hour before he was to come pick her up, he made up an excuse as to why he couldn't do it. Her sister, Lisa, came instead and drove Maddie home.

Lisa took on a maternal role and stayed at Maddie's to lend a hand for a couple of days. She drove to town and shopped for groceries, then went to work preparing several meals. She froze most of them but put a few in the fridge that could be heated up when she left. Maddie was grateful for her help and tried to rest as much as she could.

Ray only came in for meals while Lisa was there. As they were eating, Lisa would think up random topics to discuss, but neither Ray nor Maddie contributed enough to make it an actual conversation. There was an unspoken tension growing between Maddie and Ray. Had Lisa not been present, Maddie knew Ray would not be able to keep quiet about what had happened at the hospital. He was biding his time until her sister left. Maddie felt the tension in every glance, sigh, or abrupt movement he made. Even though it wasn't her fault, he would wear her down until she believed it was. Maddie tried to tell herself that she wasn't afraid of him. If she could just find the nerve to stand up to him, then maybe things would be better. She only wanted peace, just to be left alone.

When Lisa gave her one last hug and then drove away, the full brunt of dread enveloped her. Lisa lived only five miles up the road but she already felt a million miles away. Lisa was her safety net. Ray shrewdly kept his cool around her family. He had them all fooled, or so he thought. Maddie turned and gingerly walked back up the steps to the porch. The old, grey boards creaked under each step she took. Before going inside, she straightened the braided rug lying in front of the door with her foot. Maddie was still very sore from her surgery and hadn't taken any pain pills since the night before. When she made it into the kitchen, she decided she'd better take one. As she shook a few pills in her hand she picked one up. Her doctor had said she could take two. She felt like sleeping the day away so she popped two into her mouth. Ray would be out in the barn for several hours so she had plenty of time for a nap.

Knowing she would feel the effects soon, she climbed the narrow, dark stairway of the old farmhouse. Once on the landing, she stopped and held onto the railing to steady herself. Her doctor had told her she could only climb the stairs once a day and now she understood why. Her incision was stinging and Maddie held her swollen belly with her hand to ease the pain. She was unable to stand up straight so she kept herself in a hunched over position. Her intention was to lie down in her bed, but when she glanced in the opposite direction she caught sight of Matt's room and felt the familiar pull to go inside.

She opened the door and let the light spill in from the hallway. She scanned the room with her eyes. Everything was in its place. His bed was adorned with a quilt made by her grandmother. A hat rack above it still displayed his collection of ball caps. The worn-out Cincinnati Reds cap was his favorite. She walked toward his dresser and ran her fingertips over the picture frames and trophies that decorated the top. Each photo pulled at her heartstrings. "Oh, how I miss you Mattie," she whispered aloud. She walked over to his bed and sat on the side of it. She smoothed the quilt with her hand and reached for his pillow. Cradling it in her arms, she tried to breathe in his scent, even though it was long gone.

Thoughts of their last day together slowly formed in her mind. She tried to fight them but it never worked. She had been down the same path so many times. Once they crept in, it was almost impossible to stop them. It was two years ago on a hot summer's evening. Matt had been working in the barn all day with his Dad. His childhood buddy, Jesse, had been working alongside them as his summer job. They did their fair share of goofing off but managed to get enough work done to please Ray. Maddie loved to hear the sound of the boys belly-laughing about whatever eighteen year-olds found amusing. They had come in to dinner and had asked Ray if they could go for a swim at Johnson's pond. It was a local hangout for the high school kids. They would swim and camp out there during the summer months. Matt was very responsible and she and Ray had let him go since the previous summer.

"You can go but you better be prepared to work in the morning," Ray said.

"We will be," Matt chimed in. The boys couldn't get their stuff packed fast enough. Usually they had more work to do after dinner so they were grateful for an early start to their evening. Maddie had suspicions that girls were involved but she didn't say anything. She didn't want to embarrass Matt. She walked out on the porch to watch them leave.

"That was a great supper as usual, Mom!" he had said, smiling at her.

"You guys behave and don't break any hearts," she teased.

He rolled his eyes at her playfully. She remembered how the fading sun had silhouetted his hair and cast a glow on his youthful face. It was hard to believe he was eighteen and no longer her little boy. "Don't stay up too late, or you'll have to answer to your dad tomorrow," Maddie had called out to them.

"Thanks for dinner, Mrs. Stevens," Jesse had yelled out the window of Matt's truck.

"You're welcome. Have fun." She had watched as they pulled out of the driveway. The next time she saw the white truck was when Jesse drove it recklessly up their driveway, two hours after they had gone to the pond. He had returned alone.

Every time she remembered the events, it seemed as if they were happening in the present moment. Maddie heard the tires screech to a halt on the slab-stone driveway and she dropped the dishtowel in the sink. She opened the screen door quickly to see what the noise was all about. Maddie hadn't expected the boys back so soon. She walked out onto the front porch and saw a very distraught Jesse coming towards her. His face was red and blotchy and it was obvious that he had been crying. He was nervously rubbing the palms of his hands up and down his thighs.

"Mrs. Stevens, I . . . I . . . I don't know how to tell you this . . . it's bad, it's *real* bad."

"What happened, Jesse? Where's Matt?" Her voice was beginning to shake as a feeling of dread crept into her body.

"Matt, he . . . oh, man . . . he . . . he's been hurt real bad." Tears were flowing down his face and Jesse began to sob. "He's dead, Mrs. Stevens. Matt's dead!"

In one steady stream, all of Maddie's breath left her chest. Her mind went numb. Her mouth was open but no words came out. She felt Jesse's hands on her arms. He was talking to her but she couldn't hear him. The roar of reality had deafened her and suddenly she realized she was screaming.

Ray came running from the barn to see what the commotion was about. Jesse backed away as he came near. Maddie looked at her husband and felt herself go limp. Ray caught her and lowered her to the ground. He looked up at Jesse. "What the hell is going on, Jess?"

"Mr. Stevens, there was an accident at the pond. I came over here as fast as I could to tell you," Jesse said.

Ray stood up and faced Jesse. "What happened?" he demanded intently.

"A bunch of us guys were swimming—" his voice cracked, "and you know the rope we use to swing with?"

"Yeah?" Ray knew it well. He used to swing out on it himself when he was Matt's age.

"Well, Matt was up on the bank and, just as he was taking off, the rope snapped and he fell backwards and landed on his head. We all rushed over to him and pulled him out—" Jesse was crying so hard he could barely finish, but the look on Ray's face made him continue. "When we laid him down he didn't move or breathe or nothing. Somebody called 911 and we tried to do CPR but he wouldn't respond. The ambulance came about fifteen minutes later, and they worked on him for awhile, then said he was dead . . . said he probably broke his neck."

"Are they still there? Why in the hell didn't anybody call us?" Ray demanded.

"I'm sorry, sir. It was all happening so fast and I

couldn't think straight. I went into a panic. It was awful. Just plain awful!" Jesse said as he suppressed a sob.

Ray had the look of a man half-crazed. "Help me get her into the house," he barked. They both lifted Maddie and carried her inside. Ray pointed to a list of numbers taped on the wall by the phone. "You call this number and tell Maddie's sister to get over here right away!" He grabbed the keys and ran out the door. The slam of the door awoke Maddie from her dazed state and she jolted up from the couch. She flung the door open and ran out to the truck where Ray had just gotten in and started the engine.

"Wait!" she yelled, "I'm going with you!"

"No, you stay here," Ray said pointing his finger at her.

"Ray, I'm going. I need to go!" Her voice was frantic.

"No, Maddie. You go in the house. I'll be back and tell you what I find out."

"I'm going with you. Please, Ray, I have to go to my boy. I need to see my son," she pleaded with him.

"You don't need to see whatever it is I might see. You go on inside." Ray put the truck in reverse and Maddie tried to hold on to the door. "Go!" Ray yelled at her as he backed up.

"Ray!" she cried out, "*Ray!*" He pulled out of their driveway and screeched down the road. Jesse cautiously walked towards where she was standing. She turned to him and started to shake. "Why? Jesse? Why? He was my only boy. He was my only baby. Why?" She pleaded with him. He looked at her but helplessly said nothing. "This can't be happening. It can't. Please tell me you're wrong, Jess! Please tell me it was someone else. Not my Matt. Not him!"

"I'm so sorry, Mrs. Stevens," he cried, "I'm so sorry I couldn't help him." She looked at the broken boy in front of her and wished she could comfort him, but she couldn't.

She was incapable of empathy for anyone else in the world at that moment. She turned towards the barn and took off running down the footpath that cut through the woods. Jesse stood with a confused look on his face, tears streaming down his cheeks. He started to walk toward the path onto which Maddie had run. After a few steps, he stopped and turned toward the house. Once inside, he found the phone. With a shaking finger, he pushed each number, listened to the rings, and with a broken voice spoke into the phone.

Lisa and her husband, Doug, arrived a short while later and began searching the farm for Maddie. They looked for over an hour, and finally found her slumped over a rock near the creek at the far side of the farm. Doug lifted her and carried her back to the house. They laid her down on her bed and Lisa lay beside her, gently stroking her hair. Ray returned home well after midnight and they all knew by the look on his face that indeed Matt was gone. Life as they had known it forever changed at that moment.

*   *   *

Sarah, their golden retriever, entered Matt's room and laid her head on Maddie's lap. This gesture of love brought her thoughts back to the present, and she stroked the dog's coat. "You miss him too, don't you, girl?" Maddie motioned for her to get on the bed. Sarah lay close as Maddie petted her softly until they were both fast asleep.

– Chapter Nine –

The slam of the kitchen screen door awoke Maddie from her deep sleep. She jolted up in Matt's bed, biting her lip to stave off the urge to yelp from the sudden surge of pain from her abdomen. With her heart booming in her chest, she eased up from the bed as quickly as she could. If Ray caught her in Matt's room again, he would be furious. She made it to the landing before he called her name. His shadow preceded him, and then he was in full view at the bottom of the stairs.

"Where's dinner?" he asked gruffly.

"I'll be down in a minute."

"Hurry up. I'm starving!"

Maddie slowly crept down the stairs. When she turned toward the kitchen, she saw Ray seated at the kitchen table nursing a beer. Ever grateful that Lisa had prepared meals, Maddie went to the refrigerator and took out two plates wrapped in plastic wrap. One by one, she heated them in the microwave. The minutes seemed like an eternity as she waited for them to be ready. Ray sat silently except for the sound the beer bottle made when he set it on the yellow, speckled, Formica table after each drink he took.

Quickly and deliberately, Ray ate his meal in silence. He stared at Maddie as he chewed, only looking down when he needed to refill his fork. It was impossible to avert his glaring eyes, for her peripheral vision was acutely aware of his position. She had learned it was best to endure the game. She knew he was in no mood for the rules to be changed. Ray had calculated the moment of his attack. He pushed his empty plate to the center of the table.

"So how long have you been seeing him behind my back?"

Here we go again, Maddie thought. "I don't know what you are talking about, Ray."

"The hell you don't. I ain't no fool, Maddie. I knew it wouldn't take long for that pompous jerk to come sniffing around you again."

"Come on Ray, you know me better than that. You won't believe me but that day at the store was the first I've seen him since we were in school. That's the honest truth."

"You're a liar and a slut. Why would he think he had the right to come and see you at the hospital if you two weren't friendly—and I don't mean in a buddy sort of way."

"You're going to believe what you want, so I don't know why I even try to talk to you," Maddie said.

"You ain't got nothing to say because you know I'm tellin' the truth. If you hadn't just got out of the hospital, I would send you packin' and off my farm, you little tramp."

"Ray, that's enough," Maddie said.

"Number one, you don't tell me when I'm done. Number two, if I ever catch Kevin anywhere near you again, I swear it won't be pretty. They'll have to take me away in cuffs once I'm through with him."

Maddie stayed silent. She was horrified at his ranting.

"I don't expect him to have much interest in you now though. You're a sorry specimen of a woman if I ever saw one. My sows would fetch a better price than you would." With that biting comment, Ray pushed himself back from the table. As he rose, the table moved forward and jammed into Maddie's abdomen. She couldn't control the moan that escaped as she bent over in pain. Ray stood still as if shocked for a moment at what he had done.

"You okay?" he coldly asked.

"Mm-hmm," she muttered, holding back the tears.

Ray pushed his chair towards the table and then

grabbed the rest of the case of beer out of the refrigerator. He adjusted his hat, then stomped out of the kitchen, slamming the door without another word.

— Chapter Ten —

It had been three weeks since her surgery. Maddie never made it to Dr. Dillon's office. She had called to make the appointment but ended up canceling. She told them she didn't feel well, which was the truth. She said she'd call to reschedule but up to this point had not done so.

Maddie stood at the kitchen window and gazed outside. It was two in the afternoon and the sun illuminated the red and yellow leaves of the trees. She and Ray owned over four hundred acres and there was a clear view of the countryside from any window in the house. She could see the barn set on the left side of the house, maybe fifty or so feet away. The whitewashed wood had the words *Stevens Dairy* painted in black letters above the door. She opened the window and allowed the cool air to drift inside. It was unusually quiet. Ray and the hired hands had finished up early and had headed to town. They were going to look at some new equipment, catch an early dinner at Smitty's, then go to a farmer's meeting. Maddie hated Smitty's. It was the town's greasy spoon. Ray was a regular there and fit right in with the locals who had kept the restaurant in business for over fifty years. Located in the center of town, its windows glowed from before dawn until well after sunset. They were known for their breakfasts, hamburgers, and they were always packed for Friday night fish fries. On the rare occasion Ray took her out, he always insisted they go there. He swore you couldn't get any better food in the county than at Smitty's. Westville was the county seat and a city of around twenty thousand people, situated in western Ohio not far from the Indiana border. It was a small, farming community with burgs situated twenty miles apart. All the action was in Westville. They had the annual May-Fest, the county fair, and then the Pumpkin Festival in the fall. Maddie had lived there all her life.

Maddie filled her stockpot with water and put it on the stove. She was going to make lasagna. She made a pan for her and Ray to eat tomorrow and made another to take to her dad. He had invited her over for the evening. In the three weeks since she'd been home from the hospital, this would be the first time she'd been off the farm. Lisa had a meeting in town and told Maddie she'd pick her up and take her on her way. Her Dad, Jack, lived in an apartment near the center of town. After her mom died and the girls were out of the house, he had sold their childhood home. He had told Maddie it was just too lonely there with all of them gone. Jack worked in town and now could walk to work if he wanted to, which he did whenever the weather permitted. He had retired two years before but found that he missed working, so he decided to work as a consultant for the glove factory. It afforded him a bit of fun money and also kept him busy enough. Most evenings, you could find him at Smitty's for dinner. He told Maddie that he was too lazy to cook for himself, but she knew better. Jack was sweet on Gina. She was a little mouse of a lady ten years his junior. She had never married and still lived with her aging mother. She had been too shy to date much, so she spent most her time working as a waitress or reading. She was well liked at the restaurant and was able to come out of her shell a bit while she was there. Jack had appreciated the way Gina always remembered how he liked his coffee, and she always seemed to save him the best piece of pie. It made Maddie smile to think of him going there almost every night to see her. He missed having someone take care of him. Gina was just what he needed.

Maddie was excited at the prospect of having a free night without worrying about Ray. She knew he wouldn't be home until the wee hours of the morning. As part of his routine, he would end up at a bar with others like him. He would make it home somehow and pass out on the couch. He used to come up to bed and expect her to respond to his advances, but he hadn't done that in a very long time. She was thankful for that. The love in their lovemaking was long gone, and to have to be physical with him was sometimes too much for her to bear. Rumors circulated around town about how he was being satisfied. Maddie found it easier not to think about it.

When the lasagna pan was cool enough for her to handle, she placed a piece of aluminum foil on it and set it on the counter near the door. She jotted down a quick note to Ray just in case he decided to change his plans and come home early. Lisa chatted as they drove to town. She dropped Maddie off at the sidewalk because she was already ten minutes late. Lisa would call when she was ready to pick Maddie up. She walked up to her Dad's private entrance and rang the doorbell. He had a small patio to the right of his door that was big enough for a grill and a small table. She had enjoyed many dinners out there with him and more recently with the company of Gina. Her Dad greeted her with a hug and went on about how good the lasagna smelled. Gina said hello from the kitchen table. They had been playing cards. It was almost seven and they had already had their supper, so Jack put the food in the refrigerator and said they would enjoy it tomorrow. He poured Maddie a cup of coffee and asked her to join them at the table. They played gin rummy for over an hour. Maddie watched the two playfully flirt with each other. She noticed the way Gina would touch his hand when he said something funny or how he would tap her back when she won a round. His hand would linger a bit and Maddie witnessed Gina blush several times. It was evident they were fond of each other. Maddie could see the years melting away from her Dad as she watched him. It was good to see him so happy.

"Who wants ice cream?" Jack said, interrupting Maddie's train of thought.

"Whatcha got?" Maddie asked.

"Nothing," he grinned. "I thought we might walk up to the Dairy Twist and get a cone. My treat. Are you up for the walk, Maddie?"

"I think I could give it a good try," Maddie said. The exercise would do her good.

"I'm in," chirped Gina. She weighed all of ninety-eight pounds and Maddie was continuously amazed at the amount of food she could consume. She was only five-foot-two and had Irish-red hair. You could see her from across town with those locks.

"Let's go then," Jack said as he held the door open and let the ladies pass through before closing and locking it. Maddie took a deep cleansing breath and let her tensions escape her. It was almost magical how relaxed Maddie became when she was around her Dad. She could fall back into the role of being his little girl and feel completely protected by him. When her Mom passed, he made sure that the girls would be taken care of. Even though he worked a lot, he made sure they still got to do fun things together like swimming and camping. He never remarried but always made it a point to have females included in their lives. He wanted them to have good role models and to be able to learn what their mother never got the chance to teach them.

Jack was a loving father and still involved in his daughters' lives. It hurt him to see Maddie unhappy. He wasn't fond of Ray at first but gave him a chance nonetheless. They formed a workable relationship and he didn't want to meddle in his daughter's marriage. It was only when Ray took to drinking heavily that Jack felt he had to say something. He had pleaded with her several times to leave Ray but to no avail. He told her he would be there for her no matter what she decided, but it wasn't easy. Jack felt guilty sometimes that he was so happy and she wasn't. Maddie knew everyone was right. She should leave Ray. Unfortunately, it wasn't that cut-and-dried. There were too many factors involved. It exhausted her to think about it.

Maddie trailed behind her Dad and Gina a bit. They held hands as they walked and, from time to time, Gina would rest her head on his shoulder. Even though she was younger than Gina, Maddie felt so much older. Her life was a mess and Gina, although it had taken her fifty years, seemed at the moment to have the world at her fingertips. How wonderful it must be to feel adored.

Maddie glanced at the storefronts as they walked along Main Street. The Pumpkin Festival kicked off the following day and ran from Friday to Sunday. The downtown was already peppered with food stands and display tables. Bales of hay and mums decorated the storefronts. Rafters were being erected for the live entertainment. They passed the bank with its smoky windows trimmed in gold. "Come in for Pumpkinfest Coupons" read a bright, yellow sign from the bank's window. Dan's Shoe Repair was sandwiched between the bank and the post office. Maddie remembered that she had forgotten to mail the bills that day. Oh well, there was always tomorrow. Smitty's was located across the street next to Brewster's and was hopping as usual. The Dairy Twist with its bright lights was situated on the corner of Main and Sycamore. It stayed open until the Pumpkin Festival and then would close up shop until the May-Fest in the spring. The owners were an elderly couple who always jumped on a plane for Florida the day after closing. They would return the week before the Fest to clean The Twist and would be there every night it was open. They were a Westville mainstay and knew everyone in town.

Maddie, Gina, and her Dad crossed the street and took their place in the back of the small line that had formed. It wasn't as if The Twist was the only ice cream place in town. The *Dairy Queen* was just up the road but they didn't get nearly the business that The Twist got. Gina decided on a chocolate malt. Maddie's dad talked her into a big hot fudge sundae. He was getting one and didn't want to be the only glutton in the group. Maddie struggled to make a dent in it as they talked with a few of the people who had gathered there for an evening treat. Maddie found an easy out of the conversation and rested over on a nearby bench. She was going to have to throw most of the ice cream away. It was starting to make her feel sick. Then she heard a familiar voice and saw Kevin walking her way.

"Hey there, Maddie. How are you?" Kevin said as he neared where she was sitting. "Mind if I join you?"

"Not at all." She moved from the middle of the bench to one side. He sat down beside her, cradling a large vanilla cone with crunch coat topping on it.

"You didn't get very far with that," he said as he motioned toward her sundae.

"I know. Don't tell my Dad or he won't bring me again," she joked. "I'm absolutely stuffed. He talked me into it so I guess he's to blame." They both looked over to where Jack and Gina were standing and they waved.

"You're not the only kid who had their parents take them for ice cream tonight," Kevin said, motioning to where his parents where seated, enjoying their treats as well. "I'll finish mine, though. I haven't had this ice cream in ages. I forgot how great it is," he continued. "So, how are you feeling? You look great, by the way."

"Thanks, I'm doing much better."

"I'm glad to hear it."

"How's your dad doing?" Maddie inquired.

"Oh, he's hanging in there. His doctor thinks he should get a pacemaker but Dad's freaked out by the shock part of the deal. I'm working on him though. He's just beside himself that I decided to move back. Mom said he's sleeping better at night. Before I came, he was worrying so much about the store."

"You're a good son. He's lucky to have you," Maddie added.

"It's been a lot of fun, to tell you the truth. I've enjoyed reconnecting with the community." He looked into Maddie's eyes as if to say more, then looked in front of him at his parents. "They're just too cute together." Kevin's face turned serious and he looked at Maddie. "I've wanted to talk to you about the incident at the hospital. I'm so sorry it happened. I feel like such a jerk."

"Please don't," Maddie replied. "It wasn't your fault. Ray . . . he's just so difficult sometimes. He hasn't changed since you knew him. He's just as jealous as ever."

"I figured as much. I just feel bad that you had to witness that behavior. I'm embarrassed by it. It's not in my character to get into fist fights. There is something about Ray that brings out the worst in me. I'm disappointed my visit with you ended the way it did." They sat in silence for a few moments and watched the people walking by.

"Have you found a place to stay yet or are you still living with your parents?" she asked, trying to change the subject.

"Oh, that sounds awful. Being my age and living with my parents, that is," he laughed. "Seriously though, I've had my eye on that little house by the library. It's not far from here. They just listed it a few weeks ago. I think the owner died and the family has it up for sale. At least that's what my realtor told me," Kevin said.

"Your realtor's right. Mr. Watts used to live there and he passed away from Alzheimer's. He was staying in a nursing home for a year or so before he died. His daughter stayed there when she came into town to check on him every couple of weeks."

"I went through it a few times and I think it has a lot of potential. It's pretty dated inside but would be a lot of fun to restore. I would be able to walk to work, which would be great. I put an offer in but there is another potential buyer so we're going to have to duke it out." He grinned, and then popped the remainder of his cone in his mouth. Maddie smiled at him.

"Do you think you are going to miss the city life?"

"There are parts of it I will definitely miss, I'm sure, but I feel like my life is moving in another direction, and it feels good. It's a slower life, I've found, but I like it. The city has so much activity and so much to experience. I loved the restaurants and being able to go to the bookstore and have coffee at midnight if I wanted to. It's those things that will be hard to adjust to not having at my fingertips. I guess I'll have to develop a taste for Smitty's," he said as he looked at her and winked.

"Let's hope not. I can't stand that place."

"So what can you stand?"

"Anything but Smitty's," she laughed. "My sister and I go out once a month. It's usually *Red Lobster* and a movie. Exciting, huh?"

"It could be." Kevin was looking at her but Maddie decided to look ahead. There was more to what he was saying and she didn't want to acknowledge it. "So, are you still painting?" he said as he leaned back on the bench and stretched his legs in front of him. Maddie caught a hint of his cologne and liked it. She tried not to look at his legs but found it hard not to. He was wearing shorts and running shoes. His legs were tan and toned. The evening air was crisp and he wore a gray sweatshirt. Maddie thought he looked handsome.

"No, I haven't touched my paints in years. It just wasn't a priority. I had my hands full being a wife, a mother . . ." Her voice trailed off and she looked away from Kevin. She didn't want to stir up her emotions.

"Maddie, I was so sorry to hear about your son. I have kids of my own and I couldn't imagine."

"I don't think any of us can until we're wrapped in the middle of it." Maddie looked down to her feet and tried not to become tearful. "So how many kids do you have?"

"I have a son, Ryan, who is going to architect school at Kent State. My daughter, Molly, is a senior at a private high school in a suburb of Chicago. She lives with her Mom."

"I'm sure you miss seeing your family. Are they planning on moving here with you?"

"No, they're not. My wife and I got divorced a little over a year ago. Ryan is closer now that I'm in Ohio, so I can drive over to see him whenever he feels cool enough to see his dad." Kevin laughed. "Molly and I have a strained relationship since my wife and I broke up. She's very angry with me. I write to her often and hopefully time will heal things."

"I hope so, too," Maddie said. Before she could continue, her cellphone rang. Lisa called to tell Maddie she'd swing around and pick her up in ten minutes. Maddie decided to remain seated on the bench with Kevin until she came. "That was Lisa. She should be here soon to pick me up."

"I guess I'd better make the most of those ten minutes. Do you mind if I sit here with you until she comes?"

"That would be nice," Maddie said, then had a realization that made her nervous. She looked over to Smitty's, then at her watch. There was no way Ray could still be there. No way he could be watching her. It was nine and he was probably still at the farm meeting. The carefree mood of the evening suddenly dissipated and Maddie felt uneasy.

"So, where's Ray tonight?" Kevin asked, his tone changing as soon as he said Ray's name.

"He had a meeting, so that's why I came over to see Dad. It gets lonely out on the farm sometimes."

"You two have been married a long time," Kevin commented.

"Yes, we have. It's been over twenty years." Maddie tried not to sound despondent when she said it even though that is exactly how she was feeling.

"Are you happy?" Kevin said looking intently in her eyes, no hint of humor in his voice.

"Happy enough," Maddie replied, then felt someone embrace her from behind. She looked up to see her sister, Lisa.

"Are you two getting reacquainted?" Lisa said and immediately went to hug Kevin. "How are you, Kevin? It's been a long time."

"Nice to see you, Lisa. I was just enjoying the company of your sister."

"That's not hard to do," Lisa said and squeezed Maddie's shoulder.

Jack and Gina soon joined them and they talked about the upcoming festival. Maddie motioned to Lisa that she needed to get home. They hugged their dad and said goodbye to Gina and Kevin. As they were walking to the car, Kevin called out to Maddie. She motioned Lisa on.

"Are you coming back for the festival this weekend?" he asked.

"I don't think so. I'm still not feeling like myself yet, so I'll have to pass on it this year. I'm exhausted with this little outing tonight."

"If you need anything, please let me know."

"I will. Thanks, Kevin."

"See you around?" he said and smiled warmly.

"Okay. Goodnight."

When Maddie got into the car, Lisa started. "What was that all about?"

"He wanted to know if I'd be back for the festival."

"I think he still has feelings for you, Maddie."

"I think you're crazy, Lisa. I'm an old, married woman."

"I saw the way he looked at you."

"We're just old friends, that's all."

"I don't know," Lisa said as she turned the car toward home. "I don't think he'd come to see you at the hospital like he did if he wasn't thinking of you as more than a friend."

"Enough, Lisa," Maddie said. "What difference does it make? I'm not in any position to even entertain the idea. So lets just stop talking about it."

"Okay," Lisa said. "I'm just saying that I think there's a new man in town that still holds a flame for my little sister." Maddie rolled her eyes and they both broke into refreshing laughter.

$-$CHAPTER ELEVEN$-$

Winter came in with a fierceness that Maddie had not known before. By mid-January, they had broken record snowfalls twice. Sheets of ice lay on the roads; days void of sun and warmth to melt them. The alarm went off at five a.m., and Maddie swatted it with her hand until silence again filled the room. With a groan, she pulled her body to a sitting position and glanced toward the window. It was dark and frost covered everything. She felt the cool draft encircle her feet and was tempted to return to her warm covers. Duty called, so she stood and reached for her robe. She needed to get breakfast started and then join Ray in the barn. The bad roads had kept most of their workers home. Some might make it in later, but by then the majority of the morning work would be completed. After finishing breakfast, she changed into her work clothes, making sure to put on extra layers. She was having trouble staying warm this winter.

As Maddie began measuring the feed into the morning rations, Ray led the first of the herd to the milk machines. She kept her thoughts to herself as she watched the kernels flow like water and the fine dust rise from them. It used to be a sweet smell to her but these days it nauseated her. The whole farm life was becoming more of a burden. The romance of the farm was but a memory. The early days had brought such promise, and she had loved being a farmer's wife. She'd delighted in the praise she used to receive for her home-cooked meals and special treats she would bring into the barn in the afternoons. Ray was so happy to see her then. She used to miss him when he was out in the barn and would think of excuses to go out to see him. Back then, he didn't want her working in the barn. He wanted her to stay clean and pretty. He said that made his hard work worth it.

69

He didn't realize that she, too, was working hard to make their home spotless and to have meals warm when he came in. She made it a point to always look her best for him. They were young and carefree then; completely wrapped up in each other. After they added Matt to the family, she felt complete.

Maddie glanced out one of the barn's windows and caught a glimpse of Ray's tractor. He had coveted it for years until it finally was his own. One of her sweetest memories would always be connected with what to her now was nothing but a green beast. They planned carefully and endured sacrifices until finally they'd saved for half the tractor's price. Meeting this goal assured they would be able to afford the monthly payment on the balance.

Matt was a lanky, quick-witted six-year-old who sat between his Mom and Dad as they drove Ray's truck to the *John Deere* store. Wide–eyed and amazed, Matt looked at the giant machines that were every farmer's dream. The Kelly green paint shone against the yellow trim. Thick black tires with treads in which Matt could fit his fists bore the weight of the massive workhorses. With each model they passed, Matt would eagerly ask if he could sit in the cab and touch the steering wheel.

Ray took his time looking at all the models and didn't let on to the salesman that he was there to buy. Maddie patiently played along with this game, mostly for the benefit of Matt, who was having much more fun than Ray. When they finally made their intentions known, they were led to a desk near the back of the store. The salesman sat on one side of the desk and Ray and family on the other. It took a few minutes for Matt to catch on to what was happening.

"We getting the 4850, Daddy?" Matt asked excitedly.

"Yes, son, we are," Ray said proudly and patted Matt's head.

"We want the 190 horsepower one," Matt said to the salesman.

"I think we can make that happen, little guy," the salesman said and smiled.

"And Daddy wants five front head lamps—not four, mind you, he needs five," Matt said and raised his hand up extending all five fingers.

"You got it, buddy," the salesman chuckled.

"That rear lift needs to lift over 900,000 pounds," Matt said.

"I think around 9,000 pounds should do us fine, son," Ray said and shook his head, laughing.

"Oh, yeah, right. I mean 9,000 pounds. Yep, 9,000 pounds," Matt said as if satisfied with the new number. "And one more thing, mister . . . make sure we get the green and yellow one, 'cuz the red one we got at home ain't worth a darn!"

It took a moment for the adults to compose themselves. It was a story they retold for years. Ray had beamed with pride at his son. Matt had listened to his daddy talk about someday getting a *John Deere*. He wanted to make sure his daddy got exactly the one he wanted.

The sound of Ray's impatient voice startled her out of her reverie and she turned in his direction. "What's wrong with you, woman! I've been calling you for five minutes." Ray stood with his hands on his hips.

"Sorry," was all Maddie could say.

"Come over here and help me. The machine's acting up again." Maddie stopped what she was doing and walked over to him. She was careful not to look him in the eyes. He was easily agitated; one wrong look and she would be sorry. "Now hold this lever and don't let go until I say so. I have to crawl underneath and check something out." Maddie held on as long as she could, until she felt her muscles tighten. Her fingers could no longer match the tension and she had to let go. She heard Ray yell several obscenities and braced herself for more. He came out from under the machine and looked at her with evil in his eyes.

"Can't you do one thing right? I swear you must be stupid or something."

"I tried to hold it as long as I could, Ray."

"I don't know why I even bother to ask you to do anything around here. You're useless! You know that? Useless!" Ray barked.

Maddie turned and started walking towards the barn door. She knew better than to stick around when Ray got agitated.

"Where do you think you're going?" He barked.

"I'm going back into the house." She turned to face him.

"No, you're not. You're going to stay here and help me," he demanded.

"I can't, Ray. I'm going in." Maddie turned to start walking again and felt Ray's hand on her shoulder. He roughly spun her around.

"You'll do as I say, you hear?" He had a stern look on his face as he spoke to her.

She suddenly felt brave and talked back. "I'm not one of your hired hands, Ray. Leave me alone!"

"You're my wife and you WILL obey me." He had her cornered against a wall at this point. She could feel his breathing getting harder and felt his grip tighten on her shoulders. How could this be the same man she had been daydreaming about moments before? Maddie just looked at him and said nothing. Her insides were churning. She was truly frightened of him and regretted talking back to him.

"You make me sick, Maddie. Look at you. The clothes hang on you and you're as white as a ghost. I don't know why I even bother having you around anymore. I'm embarrassed of you."

"I'm embarrassed of you, too, so I guess we're even." She couldn't believe her boldness. She was bracing herself to be hit. Maybe he would put her out of her misery.

"You've got a lot of nerve talking to me like that. You're in very dangerous territory Maddie. Who do you think you are?" Ray's face was close to hers and she could smell his foul breath.

"I'm a woman who has wasted a lifetime on you." Maddie flinched as she watched his hand rise up. She closed her eyes waiting for the blow to come. He had come close to hitting her before but never followed through with it. Now she knew there was no turning back.

"Stop it, Ray! Stop!" Maddie opened her eyes to see Johnny in the doorway. Johnny had worked on the farm for two years. He had blond hair and stood six feet tall. He was twenty-one. He looked up to Ray and was glad for the work he provided for him and his younger brother, Randall.

"This is none of your business, Johnny. You get out of here, boy," Ray said with authority.

"Come on, Ray. Let her go." He was trying to sound tough but couldn't pull it off. Johnny didn't want to get Ray mad at him. Johnny walked over to where they were standing. Maddie could see Ray's temples pulsating. She held her breath to see what he would do next.

"Ray, you don't want to do this," Johnny held his ground.

Ray looked at Johnny then back to Maddie. He then did something that shocked everyone. He spit in her face. The only sound after that was the gasp that came from Johnny. Ray backed away and said, "Come on, John, we got work to do."

Maddie took the opportunity and quickly slid by them. She wiped her face with her hands and choked back the tears that were welling in her eyes. She didn't want them to see her cry. She had been humiliated enough. Once through the barn doors, the frigid air slapped her in the face. She struggled back to the house through the heavy snow. It was hard to breathe and cry at the same time. Once inside, she kicked off her boots, laid down her coat, and lowered herself to the floor. She cradled her legs in her arms to comfort herself. She didn't know how much more she could take. How much more of this life did she have to suffer through? Over three months had passed since her diagnosis and things seemed worse than ever.

"Why, God? I know You are listening. Why do I need to be here to endure this? I am so tired. If You really love me, You'll take me. Please take me. I don't want to do this anymore. Please, God," Maddie pleaded. When she was finished crying, Maddie pulled herself up to a standing position. She straightened her hair and her clothes. It was time to start making lunch.

—Chapter Twelve —

When lunch was finished, she cleared the table. Ray hadn't acknowledged his behavior in the barn and ignored her during the meal. Upon leaving the kitchen, he told her not to bother coming back out to the barn. The workers had arrived and Randall, Johnny's younger brother, had come since school was canceled. He was a quiet boy and a hard worker. Maddie enjoyed it when Randall came in to eat with them. He was polite and always complimented her on her cooking. It was nice having a young person at the table again.

The house now was quiet again and Maddie tried to collect her thoughts. She was startled when the phone rang. It was her sister, Lisa.

"Hey Maddie, how are you feeling?" she asked.

"Oh, I'm alright," Maddie said with a sigh.

"You sound tired."

"I am. I had to help Ray in the barn this morning and I'm already feeling it in my bones."

"That was some storm, huh?"

"Yeah, I was shocked to see so much snow on the ground when I woke up. Are the boys enjoying their day off?"

"Oh, yes. Doug took a snow day as well. He and the boys went sledding."

"And who's taking care of the barn?" Maddie teased, knowing firsthand that a farmer can't just take an afternoon off.

"John and Bill are here to hold down the fort," Lisa said. Unlike Ray, Doug had brothers who worked the farm with him. They had equal shares of the six-hundred acres passed down from their grandfather.

"There's plenty of snow for sledding, that's for sure."

"You're not kidding. I can't remember the last time we had this much. Ty and Trevor were as giddy as eight-year-olds and couldn't get their snow-pants on fast enough," Lisa said, laughing. Lisa and Doug had twin boys who were seventeen. Their oldest child, Rachel, was away at Ohio State studying to be a teacher.

"Ah, to be young and carefree again . . . I'm sure they are having a ball," Maddie said.

"I'm sure it is now, but I can hear Doug complaining already about his back. He gets all caught up in the moment and then forgets he's forty-five! If he thinks he'll get the boys out in the barn tonight, he's in for a big surprise. They'll be grumpier than all get out," Lisa laughed.

"You'd better hide because he'll come looking for you to help him," Maddie teased.

"Oh, he knows better than that. My feet will be propped up by then and I'll be watchin' my shows," Lisa said, sounding like she wore the pants in the family.

"Well, have a good time with your grumpy men. I'm going to try to be productive for a little while."

"Alright, I'll talk to you later," Lisa said.

"Thanks for calling. Bye." Maddie hung up the phone. She was grateful for Lisa. She talked to her at least once a day as part of her routine. Maddie went down to the basement and began the laundry and ironing. When she finally made her way up the stairs again, two hours had passed. She was exhausted and all she wanted to do was to go back to bed. After the morning's incident, she could have crawled into a cave and never returned. She had an hour before she needed to start dinner, so she decided to lie down for a little while. Maddie walked upstairs and into her room. Ray's crumpled socks and dirty pants lay on the floor from the night before. She didn't want to be near any part of him, so she grabbed the throw draped on her desk chair. She put it over her shoulders and made her way to Matt's room. She pulled down the blinds to darken the room. After lowering herself on the bed, she rested her head on the pillow. She was in view of the nightstand beside his bed and studied the framed picture resting on it. It was Matt's prom picture from high school. He looked so handsome that night. Matt reminded her of how Ray looked when he was young.

She began to daydream and her thoughts settled on the night of her Spring Formal. She had been so excited that night. Two weeks before the dance, her dad had driven herself and Lisa to the mall to pick out her dress. Lisa had been out of high school for a few years and was excited to help Maddie prepare. They went to all the major department stores and she tried on over twenty dresses. She still couldn't decide on one so her Dad treated them to lunch. Once refreshed, they went on the hunt again. She finally found the perfect dress. It was light yellow with pink roses embroidered into the bodice. Layers of sheer fabric swayed when she walked. The capped sleeves and scooped neck showed off her delicate shoulders. She was allowed to pick out shoes and a purse to match. Lisa reminded Maddie of their mother's jewelry, and Dad nodded his approval. To top off the day, they stopped for ice cream on the way home. She couldn't have loved her Dad anymore than she did that magical day. He was so patient and never rushed her. He was like a Mom and a Dad to her at the same time. He had touched her heart with his thoughtfulness.

The day of the dance was warm for the end of April. Lisa came over early to help Maddie with her hair. She had used hot rollers to tame her wild mane. The way Lisa pinned it up made Maddie look like a princess. A pale, yellow rose tucked behind her ear finished the look. Tears welled in Maddie's eyes as Lisa fastened her mother's pearl necklace around her neck and placed the teardrop earrings in place. Maddie felt so grown up. She couldn't wait to see Ray and hear what he would say about her.

He was fifteen minutes late picking her up, but she didn't mind. It gave her extra time to make sure everything was perfect. When she walked down the stairs, she blushed when she saw him. He was so handsome in his tie and jacket. He even had on dress shoes. She had only ever seen him in his cowboy boots. It meant a lot that he had made an effort to look nice for her. He pinned a corsage of pink roses to her dress. She felt her stomach flutter at his touch.

"Man, you look sexy," he whispered to her as he was walking her down the steps of her house. They turned to wave at her Dad.

"Be back by eleven-thirty, please," Maddie's Dad stated.

"Yes sir," Ray acknowledged.

"Bye, Dad," Maddie called out. She felt giddy.

"Have fun, sweetie." He looked at Ray, with his voice turning stern, "Eleven-thirty."

"Yes, sir," Ray said, then mumbled to himself, "I heard you the first time." Ray walked Maddie to the car and got her settled in the passenger seat. He rounded the front of the car and winked at Maddie. Once he had driven the car far enough away from her house not to be seen, he pulled over.

"What are you doing?" Maddie asked.

Ray leaned over and kissed her on the neck. His hand rested on her thigh and toyed with the fabric. "I don't know if I can wait until after the dance to make out. You look downright irresistible."

"Ray . . ." It was hard to concentrate when he did this to her. "Ray, please. I spent hours getting ready—not to be all fussed up before I got to the dance. Be patient, honey."

"Alright, alright, I'll be good. But you've got to be good to me later." He grinned at her. His smile could melt her in a minute. It was becoming harder and harder to hold him off. Ray was more experienced than her and wanted more than she felt comfortable giving. Going all the way seemed to be the only thing on his mind, and it scared her to death. He had given her a promise ring at Christmas and said he intended to marry her as soon as he could afford it. They only had one month left of high school and then they would graduate. She wondered what the summer had in store for them.

They arrived at the dance and turned heads as they made their way through the crowd. Maddie felt on top of the world. She smiled at all the faces admiring her. They found the table with all their friends. After dancing for over an hour, Maddie decided to go to the bathroom with some of her girlfriends. On her way back to her table, Maddie spotted Kevin coming towards her.

His eyes gazed at her from head to toe as if he were trying to take her all in. Once he reached her, he smiled widely. "Maddie—" he started shaking his head.

"What?" she said playfully with her hands on her hips.

"You look so beautiful."

"Aw . . . you're so sweet, Kevin."

"I'm serious. You take my breath away."

She blushed at his compliments. She motioned to her friends. "You guys go ahead. I'll be there in a minute." She turned back to him. "So, are you having fun?"

"It's okay, I guess."

"I'm having a ball." Maddie was giddy and she was having a hard time containing it. "So who did you come with?"

"Erin Jones. We're just good friends, nothing more," he said as he looked directly in her eyes. "I couldn't take who I really wanted to go with. She already had a date."

"Oh Kevin," she said and rolled her eyes jokingly. She gave him a playful smile, then looked over to where her friends were sitting. "Listen, I'd better get back. It was good to see you! Try to have some fun tonight," Maddie said as she pointed her finger at him.

"If you say so," Kevin replied.

"I'll see you Monday," she said and smiled.

"Bye," he said as he watched his crush walk away.

She was almost to her table when she turned to look back at Kevin. He was still watching her and waved. She felt pulled suddenly and was swept into the air and spun around by Ray.

"I thought you'd fallen in," he said as he embraced her.

"Would you have come in to rescue me?" Maddie teased back and returned his embrace. She looked beyond his shoulder to see that Kevin was gone.

"Of course I would, baby." He pulled back and gave her a kiss. She smelled alcohol on his breath.

"Ray, have you been drinking?" Maddie asked with alarm.

"Oh . . . well, when you girls went to powder your noses, we guys decided to go outside for some air," he said with a laugh.

"Ray, you're crazy! You could get busted. You can't afford to do that. We're almost graduated. You can't go screwing things up now. I won't let you," Maddie insisted.

"Who are you, my mother? You sure know how to kill a buzz." He pulled away from her and sat down next to his buddies. Maddie wished she hadn't said anything. Now he was mad at her and she hated that. She was just so worried he would get into trouble and they wouldn't be able to get married. He was already treading dangerous water with her dad.

A fast song started playing and Maddie's friends pulled her to the dance floor. They danced through several songs, and her mood had elevated when Ray joined her. He twirled her around and held her close. Moments later, they announced it was time for the court to come to the stage. Maddie's heart raced. Once on stage, she positioned herself with the other girls. She looked over to see Ray standing with the other guys who had been nominated for king. Maddie beamed as the crown was placed on her head. She looked at Ray. He winked at her and then turned to face the crowd. He was grinning and adjusted his jacket and tie in anticipation of being crowned. When the announcer said Todd Bishop, the basketball star, was the king, Maddie felt her heart sink. She didn't know what to do. She saw the happiness drain from Ray's face and become replaced with a look of anger. He glared at Todd and wouldn't look at Maddie. She had to stand locking arms with Todd while the other nominees were escorted off the stage. Then came the dance. It was the longest slow dance she had ever danced. As they swayed back and forth, Maddie strained to see past the bright lights into the crowd. She could only see shadows of heads and people dancing. Finally, the dance was over. She thanked Todd, then hurried down the stairs back to their table. She noticed that Ray was not with her friends.

"You guys, where's Ray?" Maddie felt herself beginning to panic.

"He left," her friend Katie said uneasily.

"What do you mean, he left?" Maddie searched the crowd but couldn't see him anywhere.

"He came off the stage, grabbed his keys and took off," Katie answered.

"Did he say where he was going?" Maddie felt the tears start to well up in her eyes.

"Bill and Jamie ran after him and they haven't come back yet," Katie said apologetically.

Maddie grabbed her purse and headed out to the parking lot. She found Ray's friends, Bill and Jamie, standing next to their cars smoking a cigarette. Maddie walked quickly towards them. "Have you seen Ray?" she asked frantically.

"He was really ticked off, Maddie. He got into his car and peeled out of here. We tried to get him to stay but he wouldn't," Jamie said.

"I can't believe he left me!" Maddie tried to keep it together but started to cry despite her efforts. Jamie put his arm around her. A few minutes later, the rest of their friends joined them.

"Why don't you come with us, Maddie?" Katie said.

Maddie knew they were all going as couples back to Jamie's house. His parents were out of town for the weekend. She was supposed to go with Ray.

"Thanks guys, but I think I'm going to stay until the dance is over in case Ray comes back for me."

"What if he doesn't?" Jamie said. He knew how stubborn Ray could be.

"I'll call my sister or my dad to get me. You guys go have fun. I'll be fine."

She watched them go, then walked back to the dance. She felt silly wearing the crown and promptly took it off. She smoothed her hair and walked back to the cafeteria to use the phone. She decided to call Lisa instead of her dad. It would be easier to explain to her. She was digging in her purse for some loose change when she heard someone call her name. She turned to see Kevin standing there. She tried not to look disappointed. She had hoped it was Ray.

"Oh, hi, Kevin. I thought you had left already."

"Nope, I'm still here. Hey, congratulations on the crown."

"Thanks," Maddie said flatly.

"Um . . . I saw Ray leave without you outside. I was leaving myself, and then I thought about you, so I came back in. I've been looking everywhere for you and I'm glad I found you."

"Where's your date?" Maddie said as she looked around.

"She caught up with her friends and wanted to hang with them tonight. It's cool."

"Oh." Maddie began searching her purse again for money.

"Do you need a ride home?" he asked hopefully.

"Thanks, but I'm just going to call my sister. She'll come and get me when the dance is over. I want to wait and see if Ray comes back."

"How about I'll wait with you and if he comes back, that's good for you and, if he doesn't, it's good for me. I'd have the pleasure of driving you home," Kevin offered with hope evident in his voice.

"It's really not necessary. I'll be fine." Everything was becoming so complicated. How could such a perfect night come to this?

"Maddie, I wouldn't feel right leaving you here. As your friend, could I please take you home?" She looked at him and knew he was being sincere. She had no right to be rude to him. He was just looking after her. Kevin always was nice to her. Guilty at her behavior, she agreed to go with him. They waited by the front of the school until eleven, but there was still no sign of Ray. Maddie needed to get home by her curfew, so she reluctantly agreed to leave with Kevin. She was crushed that Ray had not returned for her.

Maddie followed Kevin out to his car and allowed him to open the door for her. As Kevin drove the car out of the parking lot, she looked blankly out the window. If only she could find a way to see Ray tonight. She had to make sure things were okay with them. He would freak out if he knew she had allowed Kevin to drive her home. She had a small hope that somehow he wouldn't find out about it.

"Are you doing okay?" Kevin asked.

"I'm worried about Ray." She turned to him. Tears were forming in her eyes. "I wish I knew where he went."

"I can't believe he would just leave you like that. You deserve better than that Maddie," Kevin said in a disgusted tone.

"He was upset, Kevin. He must have been humiliated up on the stage. Everyone had talked for weeks about how we would be king and queen. I don't know what happened." Her voice was defensive. "You wouldn't understand, Kevin. Everything comes so easy to you. Ray has had to fight to make it through school. He doesn't have a good family to support him. He's not as smart and respected as you. He acts all tough but he really does care what people think. He really wanted to be king."

Kevin turned to look at Maddie. "Do you think my life is so easy?" Now he was being defensive. "I may be smart but that doesn't mean my life is perfect. I want to have fun like everyone else . . . to fit in. I've always been labeled as the smart kid. Not many people take the time to get to know me; to see that there is much more to me than my stupid grade point average. Everyone has this preconceived notion of who I am. They have no idea." He pulled the car over to the side of the road and turned to face Maddie. "When I was seated next to you in art class . . . and we started to talk and laugh together . . . I felt so good about myself. I could relax and be myself. You have no idea how much I look forward to that class. What luck I have had that the prettiest girl in school sits beside me each week," Kevin boldly confessed.

Maddie didn't know what to say. She sat in silence.

She didn't want to look him in the eyes, so she stared down at her hands now resting on her lap.

"Can I be honest with you Maddie?" Kevin asked.

"Yeah, I guess," Maddie muttered.

"I think you are the most interesting, beautiful person I have ever met. You have so much talent it amazes me." Maddie felt herself blush. "I think you could go so far in this life. You have so much potential. I guess I have a really hard time seeing what draws you to Ray except for his looks."

Maddie was taken aback by his comments. Her first instinct was to yell at him, but she stopped herself. She looked at her watch. "I really need to get home. I'm going to be late." Kevin sighed and shifted the car into drive. There was silence between them for a few minutes, and then she spoke again. "I can't explain it, but I'm drawn to Ray. It's like he's my destiny or something."

"But he doesn't have to be. Have you ever thought of being with someone else? With someone who would treat you right? How do you know he's the one if you've never been with anyone else?"

"What are you saying, Kevin? I should go out with you?" Maddie said sarcastically.

"Would that be such a horrible idea?" Kevin asked, exasperated.

"Give me a break, Kevin." She let out a big sigh. He didn't say anything. "You're serious, aren't you?" She looked at him but he didn't look at her. She hoped she hadn't just hurt his feelings. She didn't mean to sound so cruel.

"I just think you could do better," he said defensively.

"And you would be better?"

"I could be."

"Kevin, I'm flattered by your offer, but I'm with Ray and I love him."

"And I love you." There, he'd said it. There was no turning back now.

Maddie was stunned by what he had just revealed. What had she gotten herself into? Things were turning from bad to worse. Kevin loved her?

"I'm sure that's not what you want to hear right now," he continued, "but it's true. I think about you all the time. It's been driving me crazy. I've wanted to talk to you about it but never had the chance. You are *always* with Ray."

"He's my boyfriend, Kevin. What do you expect?" Maddie said emphatically.

"I just wanted you to know how I felt."

"Do you feel better now?' She knew she was being insensitive, but she was anxious to get home and out of this conversation. "What to you expect me to do? I have a boyfriend."

"I know." Kevin pulled the car into the driveway of her house. Maddie grabbed her purse and opened the door. She paused before getting out. "Kevin . . . I am touched that you have feelings for me, I am. If I wasn't with Ray, who knows? But the fact is that I am. I hope I haven't hurt your feelings. You are a really great guy and have been a good friend to me. Thanks for the ride home." She got out of the car but before closing the door she said, "See you in class." He gave her a weak smile and she closed the door. As Maddie rushed up the walkway to her front door, he backed out of the driveway and drove away.

Once inside, she said a quick hello to her dad, gave him a few details about the dance, and modeled her crown. She learned that no one had called for her and she went up to her room. Once inside, she sat on her bed and dialed Ray's number. No answer. She redialed it and, again, got no answer. Maddie decided to change and wash her face. She was becoming increasingly anxious. She crawled into bed and cradled the phone, deciding to call one last time.

On the fifth ring, someone answered. It was Ray's dad and he was drunk.

"Um . . . Hi. Is Ray there please?" Maddie said tentatively.

"He ain't here," the man grumbled.

"Oh . . . um . . . well, could you tell me where he went?"

"He's out with his friends."

Maddie's heart sank yet again. "Do you know where they could be?"

"No," he said as if she had annoyed him by the question.

"Could you please tell him that Maddie called?"

"I'll try to remember." Click. He hung up the phone. She began to cry. Why didn't Ray call her? Where was he? She was so worried. She began to sob and had to muffle her cries in her pillow. She tried to stay awake for as long as she could but finally succumbed to sleep.

*   *   *

Maddie was half awake when she heard the sound of footsteps on the stairs. She shot up in bed and listened intently. She was a bit disoriented and tried to wake herself to the present. Her heart started racing. She listened as the doorknob creaked and the heavy wood door opened. The light from the hallway spilled in and illuminated a dark silhouette. Maddie squinted her eyes to make out the figure standing in the doorway.

"What the hell are you doing in Matt's bed?" he barked. It was Ray and she wasn't dreaming anymore.

– Chapter Thirteen –

Ray ordered Maddie to come downstairs. She was disoriented and unsure of what time it was. He stomped down the stairs and she slowly made her way out of bed. She smoothed her hair and her clothes. She could hear Ray downstairs banging the kitchen cupboards. Slowly, she made it to the kitchen, fearing the consequences of being caught in Matt's room. He glared at her as she entered the room. She looked over at the clock above the stove. It read seven-thirty. She was surprised she had slept that late. Maddie took two plates out of the cupboard and spooned the chicken and dumplings that had been simmering in the crock-pot all day. She took homemade applesauce out of the fridge and ladled it into two bowls. She poured two glasses of milk for them and placed them on the table. Ray sat down and pushed the milk aside. "I want some beer. We're out of beer."

"I'll get you some tomorrow. If you give me a minute, I can make you some tea."

"I don't want any tea. I want some beer and something good to snack on. Get yourself together. I want you to go to the store."

"Ray, it's late and I don't have the energy to go tonight."

"You just got out of bed!" he said, throwing his arms in the air.

"I know but I'm still tired." Maddie hated that she was whining in front of him but couldn't help it.

"You can go to the store for me, then go to bed when you get home."

"Can't you run out? Then you can get what you want. Besides, the roads are terrible," she pleaded with him. Maddie dreaded going back to Brewster's. She was embarrassed to face people there.

"You can take the truck," he said with authority.

"Alright, I'll go," she said with resignation. Ray had won.

"I'll be waiting," he grumbled.

Maddie changed her clothes and put on a little make-up. If she was going to be humiliated, she might as well look good doing it.

One good thing about shopping at night was that there was hardly anyone in the store. She said a few quick hellos and, surprisingly, no one pressured her for any details about her recent episode at the store. Most people just wanted to know if she was feeling better. Since she now felt more comfortable in the store, she decided to get all the things she needed. It would mean she wouldn't have to come back for a while. When her cart was full, she made her way to the checkout. She was grateful when the bag boy offered to follow her out to her car to help load the groceries. She gave him a couple of bucks for being so helpful. She drove home and, as she pulled into the driveway, she noticed Ray had a bonfire going in the clearing behind the barn. She thought it was a bit strange but brushed it off. She didn't understand much of what Ray did these days.

It took her several trips to carry in all the groceries. It was past eleven when she finally got everything put away. Ray hadn't come in since she got home. She guessed the beer wasn't that important after all. She made herself a cup of tea and decided to turn in for the night. Holding her tea in one hand and a *People* magazine she had just purchased in the other, she climbed the stairs. She slowly walked down the hall and, as she passed Matt's room, a sickening realization came over her. She backed up and looked in. Except for the furniture, the room was completely empty. The linens were stripped from the bed. The curtains were gone from the windows. The walls were bare of the posters that reflected Matt's personality and interests. She walked slowly to the closet and saw that all of his clothes were gone. Only empty hangers remained. Nothing was left. She felt the teacup slip from her hands. It shattered on the floor and the hot liquid splashed on her legs. She didn't feel a thing. By instinct she grabbed a towel from the linen closet and began mopping up the mess. A sliver of glass cut her finger and Maddie watched the blood trickle down her hand. She sat with her back against the door. She was confused.

"Why did he do this?" Maddie said aloud. "I want it all back. All of it." She was angry and tried to think of where he would put everything. She stood and held the towel to her hand. She went to the window to look to see if Ray was there. He was still standing by the fire and was looking up at the house. It was like he was waiting for her to come to the window. She looked at the fire and a horrific thought entered her mind.

"Oh, no . . . Oh, *no!*" Maddie moaned. She ran as fast as she could down the stairs, flinging the kitchen door open as she burst through the doorway. She tried to run but found it too painful. When Maddie made it to the bonfire, she was out of breath. She must have looked like a crazed woman with her mascara running in streaks down her cheeks. Looking into the fire, she was able to recognize a few charred items that once had belonged to their son.

"What have you done?" she yelled at him. "How could you, Ray? How could you?" she moaned.

"It's for the best, Maddie. It's time to move on," Ray said, devoid of any emotion.

"How dare you!" she sobbed. "How dare you tell me when to stop mourning my son?"

"He was my son, too, and I'm tired of looking at his things everyday. It's not right," Ray said.

"I needed those things Ray. They were the only things I had left of him." She fell to her knees and placed her head in her hands. She rocked herself back and forth.

"He's never coming back. You need to realize that. I thought it best to get rid of that shrine of yours," Ray barked.

"I can't believe you. You're nothing but pure evil!" she screamed. "I can't do this anymore. I can't. You broke my heart tonight, Ray. You broke my heart." She pushed herself off the ground and turned to walk back to the house.

"You'll thank me for this one day," he called out to her. "Now maybe you can get on with your life."

She stopped and turned around to face him. "What life, Ray? I would welcome death right now, anything to get away from the torture that is my life. Anything to get away from you!"

"You don't mean that," Ray yelled to her.

"Test me on it," Maddie said and walked back to the house. As she lay in bed that night, she prayed the cancer would take hold if there was any left. There had been no treatment since her hospitalization. No radiation or hormones to stop any cells that were left behind. She welcomed its growth and hoped she could will it to return. The sooner she was gone the better. She prayed to God for strength to face the end, whatever it entailed.

– Chapter Fourteen –

In the morning, she closed the door to Matt's room and vowed never to open it again. There was no quiet place to retreat to anymore. His room had been a place where she could be surrounded by him. Still angry from the events of the night before, Maddie didn't want to risk being around Ray. She couldn't trust what would come out of her mouth.

He would have to fend for himself as far as his meals. She needed to get away. Bundling up in her coat, she grabbed her purse and keys and left the farm. Unsure of where to go, she started to drive. An hour passed, and she ended up in the quaint college town of Miami University. It was the school Matt was to start the year he died. He planned to commute the first year and, if he did well, they had promised he could live on campus the next year. Matt had been so excited to go. He had worked hard and had been beside himself when he got the acceptance letter. Good at numbers, he planned to get a business degree.

Maddie parked the car and decided to walk around. She imagined what it would have been like to come and visit her son at college. Maybe she could have lived vicariously through him, not having gone to college herself. Matt would have been the first in Ray's family to have a college degree. It was not mentioned much, but Maddie knew Ray had great pride in that.

She watched the kids, loaded with backpacks and laptops, walking briskly on sidewalks, across lawns, and some in the street. Others sat on benches talking on cellphones, laughing with animated body movements. Couples strolled and stole kisses. Surrounded by such promise and bright futures, she felt sadness for Matt's missed opportunity. His good looks and charm would not have been lost here. His small-town upbringing would make him stand out, but he had a wisdom and confidence that carried him in any situation. She wondered if he would have met his wife here or lifelong friends from all over the country. He would have loved this.

Maddie walked into the University bookstore and leafed through books, read some greeting cards, and left after she'd purchased a bottle of water. Next, Maddie went to the library. Once inside, she looked around aimlessly, then decided to ask for help finding medical books. She settled into a comfortable chair and read from the books she found on oncology. Drinking in the information on endometrial cancer, she made mental notes on the possibility of reoccurrence and symptoms to look for. A couple of hours passed without Maddie realizing it. She was engrossed in what she read, looking for clues as to whether her cancer may return.

When she had exhausted herself with the flood of information, Maddie headed for home. As she drove away from the college, she was surprised that she had gone there. It was not a planned trip but had proven very beneficial.

Pulling into Westville, she decided she wasn't ready to return home, so she stopped and purchased some flowers. She made her way to the cemetery and found the rose-colored stone that bore her mother's name. She placed the bouquet in the vase attached to the stone. Her fingers traced the name inscribed and paused at the date of her mother's death. She was only thirty-eight. Maddie began to pull some of the weeds from around the stone.

"Mom, I've had a pretty rough day. I wish you were here so I could talk to you." She toyed with the weeds in her hands. "Today, I went to where Mattie would have gone to college. I imagined him there. You would have been so proud of him. He was such a great kid," Maddie said and sighed. "I have to tell you about the terrible thing Ray did last night. He burnt up all of Matt's things. Cleaned out every little piece of him and threw it in the fire. I can't believe he could be so cruel. Mom, I just don't understand. Why does God let awful things keep happening to me? Why did you have to die so young? It's not fair. I wish you were here for me. I need you so much. I can't tell anyone else this, but I can tell you. I prayed again that I would die soon. I have blown off my treatments and still nothing is happening. I wish you could tell me how you felt when you were diagnosed with cancer. I wonder if you ever regretted going through everything you did. When you faced this, you were at a different place in life than I am. You had a loving husband and two girls to fight for. I have nothing. I am actually being driven in the opposite direction. I have no motivation to fight."

Maddie heard voices in the distance. She looked up and saw a young couple, hand in hand, walking along the center path of the cemetery. They reached a plot a few rows from where she was sitting. They nodded to her in acknowledgement, and Maddie did the same in return. She watched the man place his arm around the woman's shoulders and saw her dab her eyes with a tissue. Everyone had a story. Everyone suffers in this world at one time or another. Maddie wondered whom they had lost. Maybe it was a sister or brother, a parent, an aunt. "Oh Mom, am I doing the right thing?" She thought of her dad, her sister. She imagined them standing by her grave. They would be very sad. She knew she was being selfish. She knew it was not fair to keep this from them, but when was life fair?

She watched the couple walk back to their car, back to their real world. The moment of sadness would pass. It quickly would be replaced by the busyness of life, until the slightest expression, word, or sight would bring it back again. Her family, too, would adjust to her not being around. They would cope and, on occasion, take a few moments to linger at her grave and remember her.

– CHAPTER FIFTEEN –

Things slowly returned to normal around the farm. It had been six months since her surgery. Maddie had regained her strength and welcomed the respite from the pain and weariness she had experienced. It surprised her that she was doing so well. Each morning, she wasn't sure if the bottom was going to drop out from beneath her. Today, she was eager to go outside and enjoy the cool spring day. She no longer helped out in the barn, so the morning was hers. After the night of the bonfire, Ray had stopped insisting that she come out and work. She was unsure if it was because of guilt or if he just didn't want to be around her now. Lately, he walked around with a look of worry instead of the usual scowl on his face. She was curious about what was bothering him, but she dared not ask. She was afraid to break whatever spell had been cast on the farm. Everyone worked quietly and left each other alone. It gave Maddie plenty of time to think.

After breakfast, she decided to take a long walk. As she made her way down the steps of the porch, she noticed Johnny and his younger brother, Randall, getting into their truck. He was not as tall as Johnny, and his hair was brown as opposed to his brother's blond. If she hadn't known they were brothers, she would have never suspected that they were related. She had heard stories of their mother and the many men with whom she had company. She worked at the bar where Ray liked to frequent. That is where he first met the boys and offered Johnny a job. Maddie waved to the boys as she walked towards the path that led to the northern end of their property. It was her favorite place to walk.

How long the path had been there, Maddie didn't know. Ray had grown up on the farm, and she envisioned him running limitlessly, jumping over fallen tree limbs in effort to make it to the creek bed. Each curve and bend had a pace that, if you ran just right, you were in rhythm with the land; not having to stop a beat to make it through.

Matt had loved to spend hours collecting minnows and crawdads for fishing. He could hardly contain his excitement whenever he found a mess of tadpoles, a few of which would find a new home in a pail on the front porch. Matt always hoped he'd see them transform into frogs before his eyes. But, time after time, they would die off. Matt would scratch his head, dump them on the ground, and return to the creek for more.

Once Maddie crossed the bridge that spanned the narrow creek, it was only a few yards until the woods met the back field. It was a quiet corner of the farm; easily accessible from the woods and hidden from the main road.

She made it to the old wood fence that marked the end of their property. It was beside a country road that was a vessel off the main road to town. Used mostly by the locals, it was perfect for the tractors to travel on. She looked across the road to the old farmhouse that belonged to the Shultz family. They no longer lived there and had rented it out. The younger generation had decided farm life was not for them. Maddie wondered why they didn't just sell the place and be done with it. That would make Ray happy. He'd had his eye on it for years.

Maddie studied the house. It was in a state of disrepair. The white paint was peeling and the shutters were faded. The front porch was not level anymore and the stairs looked dangerous. The flowerbeds were neglected. Only a few tulips were scattered here and there, the lone survivors of a once glorious garden. She moved her gaze along to the side of the house. A rusted swing set and a trampoline graced the space that used to occupy Mrs. Schultz's prized vegetable garden. She was sad to see it gone. The heart of the farm stopped beating when Mrs. Schultz was put in a nursing home several years ago. She suffered a massive stroke and barely survived. The family was not prepared and that left her bedridden with a feeding tube for two years before she finally passed. It was hard to see such a wonderful woman in that state. It was no representation of the beautiful lady she had been.

Maddie remembered herself as a young bride when she used to walk this path with hopes of finding Mrs. Schultz outside. When Mrs. Shultz caught sight of Maddie, she would always wave her over. What began as an occasional visit became more of a routine. Maddie would sit by Mrs. Shultz as she tended her garden. They would talk and laugh, sharing the stories of their lives. Maddie began to learn from her the art of gardening. She also learned the art of being a farmer's wife. These new skills did not go unnoticed by Ray. He praised her cooking and the way she kept up the house. Maddie had even planted a garden of her own. When Matt was a baby, she would take him along with her and, as he grew, he loved to run around while they visited. Mrs. Shultz was like the grandmother he would never have and the mother Maddie so dearly missed. Maddie cherished those times. They were magical in a sense. It was sad to see the way things had turned out. There had been such love in that old place.

The warmth of nostalgia faded and Maddie felt the chill of the air cool her. She crossed her arms to hold in the warmth and turned to make her way back. As she neared the house, she saw Sarah, their golden retriever, pacing in front of the barn. When she saw Maddie, she started barking loudly. Maddie recognized the nature of the bark and wondered what was bothering her. She reached the dog and tried to calm her down, to no effect. Sarah continued to bark frantically. Maddie decided to put her in the house and then look around to see if she could see what the matter was.

With Sarah secured, she went back outside and looked around the perimeter of the house. Nothing seemed out of order. Maddie noticed that the boys were still gone and Ray's truck was parked in the driveway. She walked into the barn. The lights were on but it was very quiet. The animals were outside and she could hear only the dull hum of the milking machines. She walked towards the back where they kept their small office. She called out Ray's name before she got to the door. He did not answer. Slowly, she opened the door and found Ray seated at his desk. His head rested on his arms. Maddie slowly tiptoed back and closed the door. She was afraid to wake him.

Maddie went back to the house to see how Sarah was doing. The dog had calmed down while Maddie was gone. Maddie crouched down to where Sarah was lying. "It's okay, girl. What spooked you?" She stroked her and watched as she drifted off to sleep. Maddie sat at the kitchen table, still puzzled by Sarah's behavior. After a few moments, she thought of Ray. It was unlike him to sleep in the middle of the morning. Actually, he had never taken a nap since they had been married. She looked over again at Sarah. How could he sleep through the racket of her barking? Maddie felt sick all of a sudden. She felt a sudden sense of dread; a pit formed in her stomach. It dawned on her that something was really wrong. She was terrified. She knew she needed to go back to the barn. She had to go check on Ray. With tentative steps, she walked from the house toward her fears. Maddie called out to Ray as soon as she was inside the barn, but there was no answer. She felt tightness in her chest as she reached the office. She placed her hand on the doorknob and gingerly turned it until it clicked open. The sound of the door creaking open unnerved her. Ray was in the same position as she last saw him. She softly called out his name, "Ray." She paused. "Ray, are you awake? Are you okay?" There was no answer. She studied his back to see if there was any movement and did not see the gentle rise and fall of his chest that would indicate breathing. His face was turned in the opposite direction, facing away from where she was standing. For what felt like an eternity, Maddie stood and stared at him. When she had worked up the nerve, she reached out to touch him. He didn't move. Maddie recoiled at the stiffness of his body. She was shivering as she walked to the other side of the desk. She gasped at the site of Ray's pale blue face. His eyes were open and his mouth was twisted in anguish. Ray was dead.

—Chapter Sixteen —

Once the realization that Ray was gone had set in, Maddie slowly backed away from the desk. When her body touched the wall, she slid down to the floor, her eyes never leaving Ray. She felt a ringing in her ears, and each breath she took was uneasy and shallow. Maddie didn't have the strength or ability to move. She studied the slump of his shoulders, the curl of his boot around the chair. She concentrated on his back and strained to see if his chest would move. It did not. Her gaze traveled down his arm and she could see a glimpse of his hand. It was purplish in color, like a bad bruise. The thought of his cold, dead skin and the wretched look of his face made her stomach churn. She felt a rise in her throat and could not stop the heaving that ensued. Luckily, she had not eaten much that morning. She wiped her mouth with the sleeve of her coat. Normally she would have taken her coat off right away to rid herself of the foul smell. Instead, she sat covered in her own vomit. She looked down at the mess. She did not smell an odor, nor did she feel the cold, cement floor under her. She knew it must be cold but it was as if all senses had failed her, except for her sight.

Maddie had been crouched in the office for over an hour when she heard voices. The hairs on her body stood at attention. Her breathing quickened to a hyperventilating state. She looked at the door anxiously. They were getting closer. She felt the vibrations of their footsteps. The door pushed opened further and the conversation ceased. Neither Johnny nor Randall noticed Maddie in the room. Johnny went to the desk, took one look at Ray, and began to swear. Randall approached to see for himself and then turned to walk out. At that moment, he spotted Maddie on the floor. Randall knelt down and reached out to her. His touch made her shudder. Before she could object, the boys lifted her and carried her to the house. They took her inside and laid her down on the couch in the living room. Randall made sure her head was on a pillow and gently put a blanket over her. Johnny used the phone in the kitchen to call 911.

The boys waited outside for the ambulance to arrive. The sheriff's car followed behind it. Bill Parker was a round man in his late fifties. He had held his post for over twenty years. When he reached the boys, he questioned them and Johnny was talking a mile a minute. "Slow down and take a breath, son," the sheriff told him, finding it hard to follow Johnny in his frantic state. When Johnny stopped talking, he immediately started to cry. Randall motioned to the sheriff and led the way to the barn.

"We left him just the way we found him, Sheriff. We didn't know if you'd need to take a picture or something."

"That was real good of you, Randall. I sure do appreciate it." The sheriff winked at the EMT workers, making sure that the boy didn't see him. He didn't have the heart to ask the boys to leave so he motioned them to stand against the wall. The ambulance workers examined Ray's body and found no signs of life. The police took a few pictures, and then the body was taken back to the ambulance. No flashing lights were needed for the trip to the hospital. The sheriff waved them on. "I'd like you boys to come back to the house and help me out with some details," Sheriff Barker said, motioning Randall and Johnny to follow as he walked toward the farmhouse. He needed to talk with Maddie. This was the part of the job he disliked the most.

They found Maddie sitting up on the couch. She had changed into fresh clothes and sat with a blanket draped over her lap. Bill Parker took a chair from the dining room table and placed it close to the couch. He took a seat and gave her an apologetic look. The room was silent but for the ticking of the clock on the wall, which seemed unusually loud to Maddie now. The boys stood against the wall with their hands in their pockets and their heads down. Bill cleared his throat. They could all hear him swallow. "I'm sure sorry about all this, Maddie." He had known her since she was little and he counted her as a friend. He hated to push her but he had to get the details of what had happened. "I know it will be hard to do now, but I really need you to tell me about what happened today."

Maddie hadn't spoken in hours and just then noticed how dry her mouth was. "Could someone get me a glass of water from the kitchen?" she croaked softly.

"Yes, ma'am," said Randall, grateful to have something to do to get out of the room, even for a minute. He returned and handed the glass to her. "Thanks, Randall. Please sit here next to me," Maddie said. He did as she requested and Maddie gave him a weak smile. After she took a drink, she set the water on the end table and began to tell the Sheriff what he needed to know. "Well, Bill, it was an ordinary day," she began. "I made Ray breakfast as usual. The boys were here early so they ate with us. Ray was quiet but that was not unlike him." Maddie toyed with the tissue in her hands. It would be in shreds in a matter of minutes. "They left for the barn when they were finished eating. I cleaned up the kitchen and decided to take a walk. I didn't see Ray when I went outside. He must have still been in the barn. Then I headed out for my walk."

"Where do you usually walk? Was it far?" the Sheriff inquired.

"Oh, I usually take the path beside the barn. It goes clear out to where our property ends. I stayed out there awhile, rested a bit by the fence, and then came back home. I guess I was gone maybe an hour and a half. Two hours, tops."

Bill pondered what she had said. "So, whatever happened to Ray must have happened after the boys left and before you got back. The boys said he was fine when they left for town." He scratched his head and took a few moments to gather his thoughts. Johnny nervously coughed but no one looked his way. The Sheriff continued with his line of questioning. "Tell me what happened then, on your way back from your walk."

"As I was drawing near to the barn, I heard Sarah barking. At first I ignored it, but as I was heading toward the house, I stopped to watch her. She was pacing and, once she saw me, she started barking like crazy. I went over to calm her. With a lot of effort, I practically dragged her into the house. I thought maybe she was hurt or something." Maddie paused to take another drink of water. Her throat felt like cotton. "I left Sarah inside and went out to the barn, and that is when I found Ray—I thought he was asleep. I went back to the house and, when I saw Sarah, I remembered the loud commotion she had made just outside the barn," Maddie said, her voice beginning to shake.

"It's alright, Maddie. Take your time, honey," Bill said in a fatherly tone.

"I . . . I realized that there was no way Ray could sleep through all that barking. He was a very light sleeper. It also made no sense that he would be sleeping in the middle of the morning. That's when I realized that something was terribly wrong. I went back out and that is when I found him . . . and when I realized he was dead. I just took one look and I knew he was dead." She began to cry.

He gave her a few minutes to collect herself before continuing. "So you realized he was gone . . . then what did you do?" the Sheriff said, prompting her to continue.

"I remember sitting down but I couldn't move after that. I don't know how long I was there before Johnny and Randall came in. The next thing I know, they had carried me into the house." She lowered her head and was quiet.

The Sheriff turned his attention to the boys. He asked

a few questions to verify what they had done during the morning with Ray, their errand into town, and what they witnessed when they returned. "Well, that should do. Sounds pretty straightforward to me. Is there someone I can call for you, Maddie?"

"I'll be okay, Bill. I'll phone my sister after you guys go. She just lives up the road a bit."

"Good enough." He stood and put his hat back on his head. "I'll be getting word to you when we have more details as to what may have caused his death. You'll need to start thinking of funeral arrangements for him." They heard a soft whimper and turned to see Randall, red-faced and fighting back tears. Maddie's heart went out to him. On instinct, she reached over and wrapped him in her arms. She felt his body relax and he cried like a wounded child. As she stroked his hair, she looked over at Johnny and found he was biting his lip to fight off his own tears.

"I'll walk you out, Sheriff," Johnny said. He knew his brother would be embarrassed about this later and didn't want him to feel worse than he already did.

"That would be good of you, son." Bill nodded to Maddie and turned to leave.

Once Bill and Johnny left the room, she turned her attention to the sad boy in her arms. It felt good to hold him. It made her feel like a mother again. She patted his back and whispered encouraging words to him. Randall was still, and Maddie felt his crying taper off until it was just the rise and fall of each other's chests that they heard. He slowly straightened himself and she released him from her embrace. They looked each other in the eye and a quiet understanding passed between them. She could tell he felt uncomfortable so she spoke. "I'm here if you need me, Randall. You can stop by anytime you want to."

"Yes ma'am."

"You're a fine young man. I'm proud of you and all you've done to help around here. Ray was real proud of you, too."

"Yes, ma'am." His head was lowered as he spoke. "Thank you for your kindness."

They heard Johnny come back into the house. "You ready, Randy? We best be getting home." Randall nodded to Maddie and started towards the front door.

"I'll stop by tomorrow to see what needs to be done," Johnny said.

"Thank you, Johnny. I appreciate that," Maddie said.

"You sure you'll be okay tonight?" Johnny asked.

"I'm sure. You go look after your brother. He's going to need you."

"Yes, ma'am."

He turned and left the house. Maddie walked to the kitchen and looked through the window in the door. She watched Johnny get into the truck. Randall was already in the passenger side. She could tell by the movement of his body that he was crying again.

"Oh, Ray, look what you've done," Maddie said in almost a whisper. As she watched them leave, she realized that, while her love for him had been dwindling away these last few years, it had been replaced by the love of two boys. They truly loved Ray and for that she felt very sad.

– CHAPTER SEVENTEEN –

When the truck disappeared from her sight, Maddie turned and took a seat at the kitchen table. The house was still and quiet. She looked at the clock and it no longer governed her day. There was no longer anyone for whom to cook dinner. It didn't matter if she got the laundry done. She was now accountable to no one. She felt her chest tighten and tears brimmed in her eyes. She hadn't planned for this. She looked around the kitchen and suddenly felt very afraid, and very alone. Even when Ray didn't come home until the early morning hours, she had always felt safe at the farm. He always ended up coming home, and she felt comfort knowing he was downstairs on the couch. He was most likely passed out, but he was there. Every sound in the house now was magnified. Even Sarah was asleep and therefore was no comfort to her. For the first time in her life, Maddie was totally alone.

"What am I going to do?" She said aloud as she started to cry. "I don't know what to do." She rested her head on the table. She sat silently there for a long time. She then got up and aimlessly wandered the house. Maddie felt like she was in a daze. When she passed the mirror in the dining room, she paused to look at her reflection. Who was this stranger in the mirror? She had no identity anymore. It had been a long time since she had been a mother and now could not call herself a wife. She was just Maddie, and she had forgotten how to be that person.

After a few moments, a sudden, terrifying thought came to her mind. "Ohhhhh," she moaned. "*Oh no . . .*" she said breathlessly. "What have I done to myself? Oh, what have I done?" The tears returned and she began crying heavily again. She suddenly realized that, in the process of ignoring her cancer, she had severely limited her chance

109

at survival now that Ray was gone. She had been so busy trying to die that she hadn't thought about her options if Ray died before her. Never in a million years did she think she would outlive Ray. He was as strong and stubborn as a mule. She couldn't believe this was happening to her. What a cruel twist of fate! It would have been better if she had just died. If she hadn't gone to the store that day, she would have collapsed at home. It would have been hours before Ray would have found her. The scenario raced through her head. She let her shoulders slump and she sobbed freely. "What am I going to do now? What am I supposed to do? Oh . . . you stupid woman. You stupid, stupid woman."

When she had finished berating herself, Maddie felt exhausted. Her body was tired and her heart heavy. She knew she had to call Lisa but dreaded what that would bring. She toyed with the thought of drinking enough wine to pass out but didn't think she could go through with it. It would have been much easier if she could.

Lisa arrived fifteen minutes after Maddie called her. She bolted through the door and found Maddie seated at the table. Her emotional embrace was almost too much for Maddie to handle. Her body felt like it was all pins and needles, and the touch of her sister was uncomfortable when it should have been comforting. She struggled to tell her the details of what had happened. It was only the second time she had told it but that was draining enough. By the end of their conversation, Maddie felt nothing but cold and numbness. By instinct, Lisa led her upstairs. She drew a hot bath and helped her sister undress. She left Maddie alone but kept the door propped open. She made her way downstairs again and into the kitchen, where she began to make Maddie some hot tea and chicken noodle soup, something easy on the stomach yet nourishing.

When the bath water had turned cold, Maddie mustered up enough strength to get out of the tub. Lisa had set out a nightgown and robe on the counter along with clean underwear.

With heavy hands, Maddie managed to dress herself. She wanted to crawl into bed to try to forget the day had ever happened, but she could smell the aroma of the soup coming from the kitchen. She wasn't hungry but knew that Lisa would insist she eat a little bit. Flashes of Ray stiff at his desk haunted her. She tried to think of how he looked this morning. It didn't make sense. Nothing made sense anymore.

When Maddie had eaten enough to satisfy her sister, she made her way into the living room and sat on the couch. Lisa got some blankets and pillows and sat beside her. She turned on the TV, knowing that Maddie had no energy left for talking. Maddie had decided over dinner that she didn't want to sleep upstairs. Even though Ray had not slept with her in their bed for quite sometime, she had no desire to sleep there any longer. She felt it would spook her to be lying up there in the dark, knowing her husband was dead. Maddie was grateful that Lisa was spending the night with her. It wasn't long before she was fast asleep.

Maddie woke up around five a.m. Squinting in the darkness, she could see her sister asleep in the recliner. The TV was still on but the rest of the house was dark. She was surprised she had slept that long. She massaged the kink in her neck that had developed overnight. After quietly using the bathroom, she grabbed the blankets from the couch and went out on the front porch. Maddie positioned herself on the porch-swing and wrapped the blankets snugly around her. The first rays of the sun were just beginning to tint the sky. She let her eyes scan the land before her. So much had happened on this farm. She had experienced the thrill of love, the joy of family life, and the agony of losing a child. Maddie had lived with the despair of a failing marriage, the fear of being abused, and the deception of her cancer. Now the land was witness to another turning point in her life. The farm's caretaker was gone. The one person who had given his life for this place had perished. Slowly, over the last few years, Maddie had removed herself from feeling any love for the farm. She couldn't remember the last time she had felt joy here.

The creaking of the screen door startled her. Maddie was comforted by the sight of her sister coming outside carrying two mugs of steaming coffee. "You freaked me out there for a minute when I woke up and found you gone," Lisa chided as she handed Maddie a mug and then sat down beside her.

"I'm sorry. I woke up and couldn't lie there anymore. I needed to get some fresh air."

"I'm surprised we slept as long as we did. My plan was to wake up before you and get breakfast ready. I guess the coffee is a good start," Lisa said.

"I'm fine really. I'm not even hungry," Maddie replied, thankful to have such a genuinely caring sister.

"Just let me know when you're hungry and I'll make you something."

"Okay." She placed her hand over Lisa's. "Thanks for staying with me."

"Anytime," Lisa said, squeezing Maddie's hand affectionately.

They sipped their coffee and watched the sun rise to brighten the day. Sarah lay close by, at Maddie's feet. She could feel the warm rise and fall of the dog's chest. Sarah had not left Maddie's side since yesterday's incident. She sensed that Sarah knew that Ray was gone. The dog's routine of going out to the barn early each morning with Ray had ended. She was quiet and had a look of sadness in her eyes. Maddie bent down and stroked her fur. Only the girls were left now.

The phone rang, and Maddie and Lisa both jumped at the sound. They scrambled to get inside, and Maddie picked it up on the fifth ring.

"Hello, Stevens' residence."

"Mrs. Stevens, please," said the deep voice emanating from the receiver.

"Speaking," Maddie said.

"Oh, I apologize, ma'am. My name is Dan Embers. I am the county coroner. We have the results of your husband's exam."

"Uh-huh," Maddie said as she sat down on a kitchen chair. Lisa sat as well, perched on the edge of her seat. She was hanging onto Maddie's every word.

"We did a thorough examination and have come to the conclusion that your husband died of an abdominal aneurysm." He paused and was met with silence. He continued, "What happened was that one of his major arteries that travels from his heart down to his legs had an area that swelled out and weakened the vessel. Eventually, too much pressure is put on this weakened area and it ruptures. That's what happened with your husband. It could have happened while he was working or simply sitting at his desk. I believe that is where he was found?" Mr. Embers asked.

"Yes," Maddie stated.

"Well, I want you to know, Mrs. Stevens, that there was absolutely nothing you could have done to save him, even if you had been there when it happened. He would have bled to death in a matter of a minute or two. He didn't suffer, I can tell you that much. It all would have happened very quickly."

"I understand."

"I'm very sorry for your loss. He was very young."

"Yes he was," Maddie replied.

"The next step for us is to take him to the funeral home of your choice. Have you thought about where you would like him to go?"

"I'd like him to go to Billing's in town."

"Very good. I'll take care of transporting Ray over to the funeral home. You'll need to call them and set up a time to meet with them to discuss the details of the funeral and viewing."

"Thank you. I'll call them today."

"Good. If you have any questions or concerns, please feel free to call me. Goodbye, Mrs. Stevens."

"Goodbye." Maddie placed the phone back on the receiver. She rubbed her hands back and forth over her face. She couldn't believe all this was happening. She looked at Lisa, who was waiting with baited breath to hear what the coroner had said. She explained to her as best she could what he had said. Neither one of them knew much about aneurysms but it all seemed to make sense.

Lisa offered to call the funeral home but Maddie felt she should do it herself. They would need to be at there at one o'clock to meet with the funeral director. It was past nine by now and, again, Maddie felt exhausted. It was as if the mere thought of what lay ahead drained every ounce of energy from her. Lisa suggested Maddie go take a nap while she ran home to check on things and get freshened up. "I'll be back around eleven, in time to wake you up so you can hop in the shower before we head to town," Lisa offered. It sounded like a reasonable plan, so Maddie agreed. "I'll call Dad and fill him in on the details," Lisa said, knowing Maddie would not have the energy to make the call. Maddie couldn't have been more grateful for that gesture.

Surprisingly, Maddie was able to fall back into a deep sleep. She didn't even hear Lisa return to the house. She gently tapped Maddie on the shoulder and encouraged her to sit up and have a little lunch. Lisa had whipped up chicken salad sandwiches before she woke Maddie up. Maddie was hungry and finished the carefully made sandwich set before her. She appreciated the added details of lettuce and chopped celery Lisa had been sure to include, just like their mother had done when she used to make them. She then showered and got dressed. Maddie paused, considering what to put on, not knowing if she should be wearing black to the meeting. Did that start right away? She was a stranger to the role of being a widow, especially under these circumstances. Her marriage to Ray had been at a very bad place when he died. There was so much distance between them; so much left unsaid. She was still unsure as to what she was feeling at the moment. She had no idea how to act or how people would expect her to act. She chose to wear grey slacks and a matching turtleneck sweater. Smoothing her black hair back, she secured it into a loose bun.

Maddie and Lisa arrived at the funeral home fifteen minutes early. Maddie had been there numerous times over the years. Only two times before had she been invited in on the planning session of the service. Frank Billing, the silver-haired funeral director, escorted them into a tastefully decorated office. He motioned them to sit in the rose-colored, Queen Anne chairs and he took a seat behind a highly polished, cherry desk. A black binder, tissue box, and a vase full of fresh cut flowers were the only items on the desk. They watched as Mr. Billing reached into his sports-coat and removed a shiny, silver pen. He then opened the binder, arranged the papers neatly before him, and turned his attention to Lisa and Maddie. It was as if time had turned back several years and Maddie was the young girl with her sisters and father planning her mother's funeral. She remembered clearly studying the older man before her. He had a smooth, calm voice and caring eyes. He used to keep a clear, glass jar of old-fashioned peppermint sticks on his desk. Even under the sad circumstance of losing her mother, she remembered how she had wanted to try one but had been too afraid to ask. She had seen them again when she and Ray sat in the very same chairs to plan Matt's funeral. They were gone now, and this puzzled Maddie.

The meeting went well and Maddie was grateful for Mr. Billing's guidance. He took her step-by-step through the whole process. She picked a simple, black casket with white, satin interior. She would need to bring in his suit by tomorrow morning so they could get him ready. After Matt's death, Ray had told Maddie his wishes for his funeral should he pass before her. She decided to have a simple service under a tent at the gravesite. He didn't want a service in a church. He hadn't been to church in years. She remembered him saying that he had no business going there once he was dead. The plan was to have the viewing tomorrow evening, with the funeral the following morning.

After all was said and done, they had been there for over an hour. Mr. Billing gave her the opportunity to see his body but she declined the offer. Maddie thanked the director for his help and, as they were leaving, she paused to ask a question.

"Mr. Billing?" she said, "can I ask you one last question?"

"Sure."

"What happened to your jar of peppermint sticks?"

He gave her a fatherly smile and answered, "It's my diabetes that took them away. Peppermints are my downfall."

– CHAPTER EIGHTEEN –

Ray was dressed in his ten-year-old black suit with a simple, white dress shirt. Maddie opted not to bring a tie for him. He was not the tie-wearing type. She thought his hair was combed in an unflattering way, but aside from that he looked okay. It was strange to see him so still and expressionless. She half expected him to bolt up and berate her for staring at him. Instead, he was cold and motionless, pasty from the freshly applied make-up and powder. She was glad for the opportunity to see him alone before everyone arrived. She had tried to think of something sentimental she could put in the casket with him but had a hard time finding anything. She would have put one of Matt's things in the casket had Ray not burned it all. She did manage to find a picture of Sarah as a puppy being held by Matt. This would have to suffice. Then Maddie considered what piece of her she wanted to leave with him. She slowly turned to see if anyone was watching her. There was no one else in the room. Her dad and Gina were in the gathering room with the director. It was still too early for the visitors to arrive. Maddie turned her attention back to Ray. She moved her left hand over to her right and slowly removed her wedding band from her finger. She held it in her fingertips and watched the light reflect from it. Tentatively, she lowered her hand into the casket and moved his jacket over enough so that she could slip the ring in the shirt's front pocket. She adjusted the jacket so it was straight again. She shuddered at the stiffness of his body. Maddie felt as if she should say something to him. She collected her thoughts for a moment, then again checked to make sure she was alone. She spoke in a soft whisper.

"Ray, I'm sorry that you had to die alone. I'm sorry for what happened to us. I feel I have already mourned the loss of the husband I used to love. You have not been that man in such a long time. I wish I could cry tears for you. Maybe I will someday. Right now, I am crying for myself—for all you put me through and for all I've lost and will lose because of you. You can have your ring back. I have no use for it now. I thank you for the freedom your death has afforded me. It has come at a great cost and I am prepared for that. Rest in peace, for I know you were not at peace here with me."

Maddie heard the sound of voices and walked towards the foyer to see who had arrived. She found Lisa and her family there with her dad. People slowly started flowing in. Ray's elderly Aunt Bonnie was the only one, besides his cousin Doug, to come representing his family. There were not many left in the area, and Bonnie was the last to keep in contact with Ray. She was Ray's mother's sister and, despite his rude ways, she loved him like her own. Maddie gave her a hug and escorted her to the casket.

Maddie mingled with the guests and tried her best to be cordial. She noticed the gang from Smitty's had congregated in the corner. They had been somber at first but were now joking around amongst themselves. She said hello to the hired hands and their wives, and then she spotted Johnny, Randall, and their mother, Lynn, entering the room. She made her way through the crowd and greeted the boys. She gave them each a hug and shook Lynn's hand. The two women were acquaintances but were not exactly friends. Lynn had called the farm on occasion to speak to the boys, and Maddie had always thought she sounded nice. She was tall and thin with blonde hair. Maddie knew she was probably around the same age as her but thought Lynn looked a lot older. She had the look of a woman with a hard life. Maddie politely excused herself and stepped out of the room to get a glass of water. When she returned, she noticed the three were standing beside the casket. Randall was at his mother's side and he was holding her hand. They stayed there for what seemed like a long time. Maddie watched Lynn reach out and touch Ray's chest. Then something happened that made Maddie stop and stare in puzzlement. She saw Lynn's shoulders droop and then she began to sob. Randall took her in his arms and hugged her. He wiped tears from his eyes and looked over to see Maddie watching them. He smiled weakly, then escorted his mother away from the casket. She watched them until they were out of her sight, then slowly put her head down. Maddie was acutely aware that people were watching her and she felt a slight panic as to what she should do. She felt awkward standing there alone. She was grateful that Lisa's arm encircled hers and then led her out of the room. Maddie was still trying to process what she had just witnessed but couldn't seem to grasp it.

Lisa led her to a back room and had her sit down on the couch.

"You okay?" Lisa asked.

"I don't know. What happened back there?" Maddie was puzzled.

"I'm not sure."

"Did you see what I saw?" Maddie asked her sister.

"Yeah, and I don't know what to make of it," Lisa said.

"Could things get any worse for me?" Maddie questioned.

"Oh, Maddie," Lisa said and gave her sister a hug. "It's all going to be okay. I promise." Just then, Gina entered the room looking equally as confused. After inquiring about what was going on, she informed them that the director was about to say a few words and wrap things up. He had sent Gina to find Maddie and bring her back. Fortunately for Maddie, it took only a few minutes and people began filing out of the funeral home. Tomorrow would be easier. Only family and a few friends were going to the graveside service.

* * *

A dozen folding chairs had been placed under a blue tent by the gravesite. Maddie took her place in the center and folded her hands in her lap. Ray was being laid to rest beside Matt, and it comforted Maddie that her son was now beside his father and no longer there alone. The site to the right of Matt was waiting for her. In her heart, she knew she would be joining them soon.

The minister had arrived before them and patiently waited until everyone took their seats. "Ray's family and I thank you for coming today. We are witnesses to the final step to lay Ray to his eternal rest. This man spent his life working the soil of his land and it seems very symbolic that he returns to it now." He paused for dramatic effect. "Taken too young, he leaves behind his wife, Maddie. In death, he is joined by his son, Matt, who passed on from this life when he was just eighteen." At the mention of Matt, Maddie's eyes welled with tears. She glanced over at her son's headstone. The minister continued speaking, and Maddie's mind wandered to thoughts of her son but then jerked back into the present with the minister's next words, "Ray was a good father to his sons and a good boss to his hired hands. They all spoke well of him at the viewing last night . . ." The minister then began to read from the Bible. Maddie's mouth went dry, and her heart began to race.

The minister continued as if nothing he said was out of order. Maddie struggled to decipher if what she had just heard was actually spoken or if her mind was playing tricks on her. She lifted her head and looked slowly at the people around her. *"Did anyone else hear that?"* she thought to herself. No one else around her showed any signs indicating that they had. She turned to look at the boys and noticed Lynn was with them. Again she looked visibly shaken. She was obviously very upset about Ray's death. She then looked at Randall's face. His eyes were red and puffy. He kept wiping his nose with the sleeve of his shirt. He ran his hands through his hair and it was the way he held his head to the side that made Maddie think of Ray. She gasped.

Suddenly, she knew she had to get out of there immediately. She stood up and apologized, then quickly walked from the site. She trotted away as fast as she could in her heels. "Oh . . . how could I have missed this all this time? How could I have not noticed the similarities?" She stopped to catch her breath. Her mind was racing. She knelt down on the grass, looking back to see Lisa slowly coming towards her. Lisa stopped when she saw Maddie raise her hand up.

She sat staring at the ground and began to put the pieces together. What facts did she know for certain? Maddie knew that Johnny and Randall had the same mother but different fathers. Johnny only talked about his dad to bad mouth him, but Randall never mentioned his father. Maddie had never asked him about it. She just assumed it was a sore subject and none of her business. Lynn was known around town to be a bit promiscuous, so it was not a surprise when she became pregnant with Randall out of wedlock. She worked as a waitress at the local tavern and made enough to support herself and the boys. Despite her rough appearance, she was a good mom and did her best to give them a stable home.

Maddie thought of the many late nights Ray stayed away from home over the course of their marriage. He could have done anything without her knowing about it.

She would have to find out for sure, but she just knew in her heart of hearts that Randall was Ray's son.

Maddie picked herself up and walked toward her sister. She and Lisa walked in silence back to the others. Maddie went over to the boys and gave them each a hug. She told them she'd like them to stop by the house the next day, as there were a few things she wanted to talk to them about. They told her they would be there. She then turned to Lynn and looked her in the eyes with scorn and disgust. Maddie could sense by Lynn's body language that she was uncomfortable around her. The secret was out. Maddie didn't speak to her. She was at a loss for words and couldn't capture what she was feeling. Maddie held Lynn's gaze for a moment before she turned and walked away.

—Chapter Nineteen —

After the burial, Maddie's dad drove her back to the church where the ladies had prepared a lunch for everyone. Maddie ate very little and mostly sat quietly at the table. Lisa encouraged Maddie to come and spend the night at her house. It would give them a chance to talk. Maddie knew Lisa would not permit her to refuse, so she went willingly. They stopped by the farm briefly so Maddie could get a few things and also pick up Sarah to bring her along. Maddie didn't want to leave the dog alone for the night.

Around ten o'clock, Doug took Lisa's cue and had the boys go to bed. He then headed over to Maddie's farm to help with the last of the nightly chores. Lisa put on some tea and sat with Maddie at the kitchen table. They quietly sipped their tea and munched on some cookies left over from the church. It was Lisa who began the conversation.

"So, that was really strange today at the gravesite," she started. Maddie didn't feel like talking but it was unavoidable. She wanted to forget the day. "What are you thinking?" Lisa softly inquired.

Maddie sighed. "To be honest, what has happened these last two days has me really confused."

"Maddie, did you ever suspect Ray was having an affair?" Lisa asked. There had been several rumors spread around town about him, not many of them favorable. Ray had spent many nights at Jay's, the local tavern. Not much good came out of his late nights there. Lisa didn't mention what she knew.

Maddie was silent for a moment. Even though she was with her sister, with whom she could talk freely, Maddie felt uncomfortable. She was a private person, never one to showcase the intimacies of her marriage. "At first, I never would have thought it was possible," Maddie said.

"Maybe I was just extremely naïve. As we drifted apart, I figured there was a good possibility he was having sex with someone else. We hadn't had sex in a really long time. I think he had lost any attraction he ever had for me."

"Did you ever confront him with your suspicions?" Lisa inquired.

"I wouldn't have dared," Maddie said. Her sister had no idea how bad it had become for her at home. Maddie had been very careful to give them the impression that Ray had an attitude, nothing more. If she knew Maddie was being abused, she would have dragged her from the farm. "Ray was very temperamental. He would have become very angry and, in the end, he would have blamed it all on me," Maddie said. "It was just easier not to think about it."

"I despise that man," Lisa said. She was restless in her chair so she got up and poured herself another cup of tea. "It upsets me that you put up with him for so long." She sat back down again. "I couldn't do it."

"It wasn't always bad," Maddie commented, thinking back to the early years of her marriage to Ray.

"If Doug ever treated me like that, I'd be out the door," Lisa said.

Easier said than done, Maddie thought to herself. Maddie knew it wasn't that cut and dried. A failed marriage develops slowly. Like a garden left unattended, the weeds begin to creep in, gradually strangling the beauty from it.

Lisa continued, "Don't get me wrong, we've had our fair share of tough times. When the boys were babies and had colic really bad, Doug would stay in the barn for hours. It infuriated me. I would lash out at him when he finally came in. I thought I was going to lose my mind. This went on for a couple of months, until I finally couldn't take it anymore. One day, I brought all three kids into the barn, left them at his feet, and went into town. I watched two

124

movies back to back, stuffed my face with popcorn and malted milk balls. I drove home in tears, half from stress and the other from missing my babies—hoping Doug had remembered to feed them. From that moment on, Doug came in several times during the day to give me a break. He didn't want me to have a nervous breakdown, because that meant he would have to take care of the kids all on his own." Lisa chuckled and sighed.

"I don't remember you ever telling me that story," Maddie said.

"I didn't. I wanted everyone to think I had my act together, that I could do it all and Doug was the perfect husband."

"We're both good at hiding things," Maddie admitted.

"I guess you're right. Maybe it's in the genes," Lisa said, half smiling.

"Doug is pretty great, Lisa," Maddie stated.

"You're right, he is. I just wish you could have had what we have."

"Me, too. It all fell completely apart when Matt died. We just couldn't cope. We had grown apart over the years. When the accident occurred, there was no real relationship left to cling to. You can't comfort someone if you are afraid of them." Maddie stopped herself. It was the first time she had admitted this to Lisa.

"Did he ever hurt you physically?" Lisa asked quietly.

Maddie tried to keep herself from crying. "He came very close at times. It was one thing Ray swore he would never do. His dad used to knock around his mother when he was young. I think it really messed up his idea of marriage," Maddie said. Even with him dead, she was still making excuses for Ray.

"That is still not an excuse for him to mistreat you, Maddie. A lot of people go through dysfunctional child-hoods but don't end up abusing their wives and children."

"He was never cruel with Matt. He was very good with Johnny and Randall. With me, it seemed to be only when he was drinking . . . at least in the beginning," Maddie admitted.

"I could tell something was different after Matt died. At first, I thought it was all because you were mourning him. You were more than sad, though. You became paranoid, jumpy, like you were trying to hide something."

"I was."

"I wish you would have told me what was going on," Lisa said

"How do you tell someone that your husband terrifies you?" Maddie said, voice cracking.

"I don't know, Maddie. I'm going to start crying."

"Me, too," Maddie said, letting the tears flow. She looked into her sister's eyes. This was the time, the moment she had been dreading. "Lisa, there is something else I need to tell you," Maddie began.

"You're scaring me, Maddie," Lisa said nervously.

"Things got really bad between Ray and me. I was so scared, so alone. I just wanted to escape, to get away from the pain. I was too weak to ask for help, too afraid of Ray to make a false move. Lisa, I let myself get sick. I've been sick for a very long time."

"I don't understand," Lisa said, brows furrowed.

"I have cancer, just like Mom," Maddie said nervously, bracing for an emotional reaction from her sister.

"What?" Lisa said with sudden anxiety.

"I've been sick for a long time. I realized I was not well months ago and let myself get sick so I could get away from Ray. I wanted to die. I needed to end the pain."

"Maddie . . . what have you done, sweetheart. Are you going to be okay?" Lisa rested her face in her hands. Maddie rested her hand on Lisa's shoulder. After a few moments,

Lisa raised her head and looked at her sister. "The hospital . . . you knew then, didn't you?" Lisa asked.

"I did. I'm so sorry, Lisa." Maddie was now crying uncontrollably. "I didn't know he was going to die. How could I know that?" Maddie sobbed.

"You couldn't, sweetie. It's just a cruel twist of fate."

"I don't know what to do now, Lisa. I've avoided all my doctors and didn't go for the treatments I should have. They probably all hate me. What if it's too late? I don't want to die now. I'm so scared to die," Maddie said.

"I know, I know. It's going to be alright. We'll get through this together." Lisa stroked her sister's back and they held each other close.

They talked for another hour about Maddie's last two years living with Ray. When Johnny and Randall became part of the conversation, Maddie was embarrassed that she had never made the connection between Randall and Ray. It all seemed so obvious now. It infuriated Maddie to think that Ray had been so cocky to parade the boy right under her nose. How could she have been so clueless? Maddie knew the answer. She didn't want to know. It was easier to close everything off and live in denial. She was dying now, so it was no use getting any more worked up about it. It wouldn't be long and none of it would matter anymore. Maddie and Lisa decided to get some rest and continue to talk in the morning. They needed to form a plan as to what to do next. There was so much to think about. Lisa made her take one of her sleeping pills and Maddie didn't refuse.

When she woke, it was nearly ten o'clock in the morning. Maddie felt groggy from the medicine and the fact that she had slept so late. The house was quiet. She changed her clothes and went down to the kitchen to find Lisa already in the kitchen. She poured Maddie a cup of coffee and sat at the table with her. One look at her sister made Maddie's eyes tear up and she began to cry.

"I'm so sorry, Lisa. I should have told you a long time ago. You've always been so good to me." She wiped her eyes. "I hope you can forgive me."

"Oh, Maddie, of course I forgive you. I love you. I can't judge you and your decisions because I am not the one who was in that situation. You must have been miserable to have wanted to die to escape it," Lisa stated and wiped a stray tear from her eye.

"I was," Maddie replied. "Thank you, Lisa, for everything."

Lisa smiled. "What we need to concentrate on now is getting you better. I think the first thing we need to do is get an appointment with your doctor. I'll go with you."

Maddie immediately felt uncomfortable. "I don't have a right to call her. She's already done so much to try to help me and I walked away from her."

"I'm sure she'd understand if she knew the whole story. She seems really nice."

"She is, but what if it's too late for me? I've let it go for so long."

"What have you got to lose? I mean, think about it, Maddie. You might still have a chance. But you have to act now," Lisa insisted.

"I'm scared," Maddie said.

"Me, too," Lisa replied, "but what scares me more is the thought of losing you without trying to save you."

Maddie knew what she had to do. At Lisa's gentle urging, she phoned Dr. Brown's office and made an appointment for the following day. It would be hard to face her and even harder to tell the story again. She was already feeling nervous about it. It was now close to eleven and she figured she'd better clean up and head over to the farm. The boys were supposed to be there around one. They had wanted to come in the morning as usual but she told them it wasn't necessary. The other hired hands could handle the morning chores.

She brought Sarah along. Maddie figured her faithful dog would like to be back where she belonged. When Maddie pulled in the drive, she noticed Randall and Johnny were already there and were sitting side by side on the steps of the front porch. She greeted them and asked them to follow her into the house. They did as she requested and took a seat at the kitchen table. Maddie poured some fresh water in Sarah's bowl and gave her some rawhide to chew on. That would keep her occupied while they talked. She poured the boys a soda and set a bowl of chips on the table. She was stalling and she hoped they didn't notice. When she had calmed her nerves sufficiently, Maddie sat down beside them.

"Quite a day yesterday, huh boys?" Maddie said awkwardly.

"One I don't want to repeat anytime soon," said Johnny. Randall sat quietly, picking at his fingernails.

"Are you boys holding up okay? I know it was hard for you to see Ray like that," she paused. "You've both been very brave."

"Thanks," was all Johnny said.

Maddie toyed with how to phrase what she wanted to ask the boys. They were young and she needed to be sure not to offend or get too detailed in her questioning.

"Boys, a lot has happened, and I've had time to think about things. You know I think the world of you both. I can't begin to tell you how proud I am of the work you do here and of your dedication to the farm."

"We love it here, Mrs. Stevens. To be honest, I can't think of another place I'd rather be. Randy and I have been talking and we both don't know what we're gonna do now. Farming's the only skill we've got."

"Don't worry yourselves about that right now. I do, however, have something very important to talk to you about. It has to do with something I saw at the viewing for Ray and with a comment the pastor said at his funeral." Maddie watched as Randall raised his eyes to meet hers. She continued as both boys looked pensive as if holding their breath. "Am I right to conclude that your Mom and Ray had a romantic relationship?"

"Yes, ma'am," Randall said in a voice slightly louder than a whisper. Maddie felt sorry for him. He should never have been put in this situation.

"It's alright. This is not your fault, sweetie," Maddie said and placed her hand on his. "Randall, honey, is Ray your father?" She let her question sink in and watched as Randall put his head down.

Unable to control his emotions, Randall let out a choked, "Yes," and then with shoulders shaking began to cry. Maddie instinctively got up from her chair and went over to embrace the boy.

"It's okay, it's okay," Maddie said as she stroked his back. "I want you to look at me." Randall obeyed her and tried to stifle his cries. "This was never your fault. What an awful place to put a boy. Shame on Ray. You deserved more than that from your Dad."

Johnny felt the need to defend Ray. "He thought it was the best way to not hurt anybody. It's hard to make sense of it now, but we understood at the time. We'd do anything for Ray. He was good to us."

She learned from the boys that Ray had had an affair with their mother years ago and had fathered Randall as a result of it. Over the years, he would come around once a week, and their mother would go outside for a while with him. When they were old enough to be left alone, she would be gone for a few hours with Ray, returning home alone. He would give their Mom money for groceries or bills. They came to look forward to his visits because that meant their Mom would be in a good mood. She would usually take them to the store the next day and would let them get a treat. At first, they didn't know who he was. He was referred to as Mr. Ray. It wasn't until after Matt died that Lynn decided to let the boys know who he really was. They still had to keep it a secret and that was okay with them. Ray kept their Mom happy. He eased the burden of providing for the boys. He had even given Johnny steady work.

"I'm glad he was good to you, boys. I just wish you could have had a real dad whom you didn't have to hide from the rest of the world. It's so unfair. Ray should have owned up to his son—been a man and faced the consequences of having an affair."

"Mrs. Stevens, my real dad left when I was born. I never knew him and, given the chance, I'd never want to. Ray was enough for me, and he was everything to Randy." With that statement, Randall began to cry again.

"I'm sorry, boys. I didn't bring you here to get you all upset. I'm just trying to figure things out. It's all still so confusing."

"I'm sorry we kept this secret from you, Mrs. Stevens. Mom and Ray thought it best to keep things quiet. It had worked for years. I guess we just got used to it. Would it help if you talked to my Mom?" Johnny asked.

"No, no. I don't think so. I'm not in the right place to talk to her now. Maybe someday, just not now."

"Mrs. Stevens, I hope we can still be friends," Randall said weakly.

"Of course we can, sweetie, of course we can." Maddie smiled warmly at them.

She knew that they were innocent in the situation and she couldn't be upset with them. How confusing it must have been to grow up like that. If only Ray had been honest with her. It would have saved a lot of heartache for so many people. She was partly to blame for the situation as well. If she had been strong enough to stand up to her suspicions . . . it would have changed a lot of things. She apologized to Randall for the way Ray had handled things. He should have owned up to his son and shown them how to be a man by facing the consequences of his decisions.

Maddie then brought up something that had been on her mind since Ray had died. She knew she could no longer live at the farm. It held too many bad memories, and she needed to move on, especially if she was going to begin treatment. She explained to the boys what she was thinking. "I want to make you boys an offer. I know you love the farm. You are very hardworking and responsible." She turned to Randall and spoke to him directly. "Randall, I've been thinking of who should run the farm now that Ray is gone. I know that I can't do it, nor do I want to. You and Johnny know this place inside and out. I trust you more than anybody with the farm. I am planning on moving to town as soon as possible. Once I get a place, I will no longer be staying at the house. I was wondering if you two would like to move in and take over the farm."

Randall and Johnny looked at each other. She could tell they were shocked. They didn't respond. "I know you are both young, and I expect you to keep up with school, Randy. Ray wasn't that much older than you, Johnny, when he took over for his own family," Maddie said.

"I don't know what to say, Mrs. Stevens. It hardly seems right considering all you know now about Mom and Ray," Johnny replied.

"Actually, my decision has a lot to do with that very thing. Randall has a right to this farm. He is a Stevens, regardless of what name he may have now. He is Ray's son and he's entitled to this land. It is rightfully his."

The boys slowly processed what she was saying. She

explained that she would share the profits with them and that they could stay at the house free of charge. She would have enough money from Ray's life insurance to be able to rent a small place in town and support herself. If she ever needed extra money, she could always sell some of the vast farmland they owned. She didn't plan on doing that though. She didn't think she would be alive long enough to need any more money. She told Randall that when he turned twenty-one, she would transfer ownership of the farm to him and Johnny. They would be partners. She felt Johnny deserved the same as Randall and knew Ray would have wanted it that way.

The boys thanked her for being so generous. Maddie promised Randall and Johnny she would talk to them again soon and reminded them that they needed to talk to their mother about her offer. Maddie knew as a responsible adult she should have talked to their mother first but knew she could not face Lynn right now. She didn't owe Lynn anything, let alone respect. She walked the boys out to their truck and watched them drive away, knowing she had made the right decision. This place needed a heart. Hers was dying.

– CHAPTER TWENTY –

Maddie sat in Dr. Brown's waiting room, listening for her name to be called. She was fifteen minutes early and already had been told the doctor was running behind. She tried looking at an outdated copy of a gossip magazine but couldn't concentrate on what she was reading. She scanned the room to see who else had the pleasure of seeing their gynecologist that day. There was a well-dressed lady in her mid-seventies sitting next to the door. Across from her was a young girl, maybe thirteen or fourteen. Her mother was sitting beside her and was balancing her checkbook. Maddie smiled at the girl. She imagined what must be going through her mind. That first visit is a scary and awkward thing. The entry door opened and a woman with two small children came in. *"She couldn't find a sitter,"* Maddie thought to herself. She watched the woman juggle her diaper bag and the child in her arms while she signed in.

The door to the interior office opened, a name was called, and the older woman got up and followed the nurse. Maddie was surprised that the woman had a slight limp in her walk. She had looked so graceful sitting in her chair. Maddie closed the magazine and placed it back on the coffee table before her. As she sat back, Lisa put her arm around her. She had been sitting quietly next to Maddie, reading the newest book club selection. Maddie rested her head back and closed her eyes. She was so thankful for her sister.

Thirty minutes after her original appointment time had lapsed, a nurse finally called her name. Maddie and Lisa followed the nurse down the hall. Per routine, Maddie stepped on the scale, and then the nurse led her to an examination room. She took Maddie's blood pressure and asked a few questions about why she was there. Fifteen more minutes passed after the nurse left before Dr. Brown finally entered the room. She greeted Maddie and Lisa with a smile. Maddie figured she was happy to see that she had brought Lisa with her.

"Hello, Maddie. It's good to see you." It sounded cliché but Maddie knew that she meant it. "So tell me how you have been."

"I'm hanging in there," Maddie replied.

"I heard about your husband. I'm really sorry, Maddie."

"Thank you. It was a shock to say the least." She turned to where Lisa was sitting. "Have you met my sister, Lisa?"

"Yes. Hi, Lisa." She went over and shook Lisa's hand. "I remember meeting you when Maddie was in the hospital." Dr. Brown took a seat on the rolling stool by the exam table. She opened Maddie's chart and took out her pen. "So fill me in on what's happened since we last talked. It's been a long time."

"About eight or nine months," Maddie said.

"That long? Wow," Dr. Brown replied, glancing down at Maddie's chart.

Maddie felt embarrassed and ashamed. She felt flushed. "I've been feeling pretty good to tell you the truth. I was surprised at how quickly I bounced back after the surgery. The bleeding stopped, as well as the cramping. I started walking again these last few months and that has made me stronger."

"Good . . . good. So what do you want to talk to me about today?"

Maddie paused for a moment, cleared her throat, and then apologized. "First, I want you to know that I've told my family about the cancer. I don't know if you knew I didn't go for treatment after the surgery. I couldn't do it then, but I want to try it now."

Dr. Brown looked at her with empathy. "Oh Maddie, what took you so long? I've been waiting for months to hear that you'd changed your mind. I ask Dr. Dillon every time I see him and am disappointed each time he tells me no." The tone of her voice was that of a mother exasperated with her child but loving her at the same time. "Help me understand what has brought you to this place?"

Maddie tried as best as she could to describe the dynamics of her marriage to Ray, Matt's death, and her life since then. She explained how she had viewed her illness as her way out of a hopeless situation. When Maddie finished, Dr. Brown stood and embraced her.

"I'm sorry for all that you have had to endure and that you have kept it secret for so long," Dr. Brown said sincerely.

When Maddie had collected herself, Dr. Brown continued, "It's delayed but still a good idea to follow through with the treatments. I think we need to get a few tests to see where we stand. I want you to get an MRI and a CAT scan. I want to see if the cancer has spread to other areas. I was pretty confident we got it all with your surgery but it's never guaranteed. I'd also like to have one of the nurses do some blood-work today. We need to have a baseline to work from once your therapy starts. We may be looking at chemotherapy this time around. It will be rough, but I'm confident you're strong enough to get through it. If it's okay with you, I'll talk with Dr. Dillon and bring him up to date on everything."

"I'll do whatever you want me to do." Maddie felt afraid but she was glad she had come. It was good to have everything out in the open. She knew she no longer wanted to die. She was ready to face the battle she had been avoiding for so long. Dr. Brown set up an appointment with an oncologist and a radiologist for the following week. She would still be involved in Maddie's care but would take her place on the sidelines. She reminded Maddie that her follow-up treatment was beyond her scope of practice.

After meeting them, Maddie was pleased with the specialists Dr. Brown had recommended. They were nonjudgmental, at least when talking to her, about how she had delayed her cancer treatments. They were frank about her odds and were not surprised to see that the cancer had metastasized to her liver. They reassured her that the chemo and radiation would target that area as well as the initial site of her cancer. The plan was to have all of her treatments as an outpatient. Maddie was thankful for that. She wanted to stay out of the hospital as much as possible. They scheduled a simple procedure to have a med port placed in her right upper chest. They explained the medication port would enable them to give her the chemotherapy and to draw blood without having to start a new IV every time she came in. They scheduled the surgery to have the port put in her chest for the following week. When that time came, the procedure only took an hour and she was able to go home the same day of her surgery.

Lisa was Maddie's ever-present support through it all. She came to her appointments with her whenever her schedule permitted. She called Maddie every night before going to bed to check in on her and to see how she was doing. Maddie's dad, however, took the news hard when she told him. He said it was as if he was losing her mom all over again. Maddie felt ashamed. She was sorry and didn't know how she would ever make it up to him. She reassured her dad that she would be okay.

Maddie was grateful that Gina had entered her dad's life. She was able to comfort him in ways Maddie couldn't. Once he got over the shock of the news, her dad told her that he would be by her side, for whatever might happen.

He was not angry, just sad that she hadn't trusted him before this with the truth. Even at Maddie's age, it was hard to face the fact that she had disappointed her father. She hated the way that made her feel.

– Chapter Twenty-One –

Maddie's first and second rounds of chemotherapy went well. She was surprised at how well her body tolerated the powerful chemicals that seeped through it. She spent her weekdays in either the doctor's office or the hospital's outpatient radiation department. It was embarrassing to get the radiation treatments. The area they had to treat meant she had to be in some awkward positions and she had to do some uncomfortable things. The technician was very nice and always remained very professional. Maddie appreciated that the hospital scheduled her treatments on the same days each week. That way, the same person worked with her all the time, and it got easier each time she went.

Her third round of chemo was a different story. Toward the end of it, she was feeling worn down. Maddie was thankful that she had made the move from the farm into her new apartment in town. She had been fortunate that an apartment had opened up in her dad's building. The units went fast and her dad had asked a personal favor of the owner to let her have a look at it first. After hearing of Maddie's story, the owner couldn't refuse and Maddie put money down on it the same day. Everyone chipped in and helped her move before her third round would start. It was going to be a very different way of life from that of the farm, but Maddie welcomed it. She left all the furniture for the boys, wanting everything for her apartment to be new. A fresh start was what she needed to face the new life she was going to be leading.

It had been ten days since her last chemo treatment, and Maddie woke up feeling very tired. She sat up in bed and a wave of nausea hit her. Slowly, she sank back into the covers and decided to try to fall back to sleep. Maddie hoped a little more rest was all she really needed. Two hours later, she woke and this time was able to get up. She made some coffee and poured herself a bowl of cereal. With the first bite, however, her stomach turned. She couldn't even swallow what was in her mouth. She knew if she did she would throw up. She emptied the half-chewed cereal into her napkin and lifted her mug to take a drink. The smell of the coffee was different from before. She hesitantly took a drink. At first, it tasted normal, but a metallic aftertaste followed. Another drink provided the same results. She took the mug to the sink and dumped the coffee down the drain. After she rinsed the mug out, she filled it with water. It didn't taste much better than the coffee but she forced herself to drink it anyway.

She headed back to her room to take a shower. The warm water felt good streaming down her back. She lathered the soap and smoothed it on her arms. As she rinsed the soap off, she noticed some small red dots on her arms. It looked like a rash. She then examined her stomach and thought she saw some dots there, too. It was hard to see because the lighting was poor in the bathroom and the air was filled with steam. She finished her shower, dried off, and put on her robe. Maddie walked toward the window of her room and pulled up the blinds to let in some natural light. Pulling her robe open a little to expose her legs, she noticed the red dots there as well. They were all over her body. "I must be allergic to something," she thought to herself. She tried to think if she'd eaten anything new lately but couldn't come up with anything. She hadn't tried any new detergents or soap. It was odd.

Maddie sat on the side of her bed to gather her thoughts. She remembered the doctor telling her about the side effects of her treatment and what things to look for. All of them seemed to escape her mind at the moment. She lay back on the bed and stared at the ceiling. She was unsure what she should do. Was a rash something she should be worried about? Her doctor did say to look for anything unusual. She looked at her arms again. The rash definitely was unusual. She rolled over and reached for the phone on her bedside table. It wouldn't hurt to give her oncologist a call.

She was put on hold, which made her second guess the decision to call. She was about to hang up when her doctor answered the phone.

"This is Dr. Dillon."

"Hi Dr. Dillon, I'm sorry to bother you. This is Maddie Stevens." She hadn't realized the nurse was going to go get the doctor. She figured she could just call to report the symptom and hopefully be told it was normal and she would go on with her day. Not so today.

"No problem. How can I help you?" Dr. Dillon asked.

"I have noticed a few things and I wanted to talk to you about them."

"Okay."

"Um . . . well, I've felt really run down lately, which I guess is to be expected. I'm having some nausea and, when I try to eat, things taste different from normal. I taste metal."

"Uh-huh," her doctor said in a way that Maddie took to say continue.

"—and I noticed this morning a strange red rash all over my body."

"Can you describe this rash?"

"It's red and scattered all over my body. It's not raised and it doesn't itch."

"Does it look fine? Like small pin pricks?"

She looked down at her legs again. "Yeah, I guess you could say that. I've never had a rash like this before."

Her doctor paused for a moment. "I tell you what. If you can, I'd like you to swing by the hospital and have some blood-work done. I'll call in the order. Do you have someone who can take you there?"

"I guess I could ask my dad. I feel fine though. I could drive myself."

"I think it would be better if he took you. I don't think you should be driving if you're not feeling well."

"Okay," she said, feeling a little nervous.

"Good. I'm going to have them process the results right away. Would you be able to stick around and wait there at the hospital?" he asked.

"If you want me to, I will," Maddie replied, fearful of what that meant.

"I'll have them page you after I get the results, then we can talk. Can you do me another favor?"

"Uh . . . sure." This was the longest she'd ever talked to a doctor on the phone before.

"I want you to take your temperature, then call the office back and tell one of the nurses. I need to get off the phone, so I'll talk to you in a little while."

"Alright. Thank you, doctor."

"No problem," he said and hung up the phone. Maddie placed the receiver in its holder and headed back to the bathroom. She hoped she still knew where she had placed the thermometer. With a little searching, she found it. She put it in her mouth and waited for the results. After it beeped, she took it out and read the results. It read 101.6 degrees. This really surprised Maddie since she didn't feel like she had a fever. Her body was definitely going through something. She dialed the doctor's number and told the nurse who answered the phone what her temperature was. The nurse promised to let the doctor know. She hung up the phone and decided to get ready. When she finished dressing, she put on a little make-up and grabbed a sweater and her purse. Maddie locked the door behind her and walked the short distance to her dad's apartment. She knocked on his door but there was no answer. It was around ten-thirty and usually he was home at this time. She waited and knocked one more time. She thought about calling Lisa but decided that she didn't want to bother her. This was something she could do on her own; she was fine.

She drove to the hospital and, once inside, found her way to the outpatient lab. The technician took four tubes of blood without difficulty.

"Dr. Dillon told me to wait for the results. I'd like to head to the cafeteria for a little while and then come back it that's okay," Maddie said.

"That will be just fine. We can page you over the intercom when the results are in," the technician replied. It was after eleven so she decided she should try again to eat something. Nothing looked good, so Maddie decided to try some soup and crackers. She passed over the coffee and got a bottle of water instead. After paying the cashier, she sat down in a booth. The soup was tolerable, and she sipped on it and slowly ate her crackers. Maddie felt a tap on her shoulder. Looking up, she was surprised to see Kevin Brewster standing there. The mere sight of him stirred her, just like before, a kind of youthful giddiness she had forgotten existed.

"Hi, Kevin," she replied, thinking about how she always ran into him at the strangest times. He looked good, and the way he looked at her made her feel nervous.

"Hello, Maddie," he said, smiling at her warmly. "It's good to see you."

"What are you doing at the hospital on such a nice day?" Maddie asked.

"I brought Dad over to have his pacemaker checked. He loves the muffins in here so we had to stop and get one before we headed home. It's his reward for going out to see the doctor. It takes a lot to get him out of the house these days." Maddie looked beyond where Kevin was standing and saw the elder Mr. Brewster sitting at a table. She hadn't seen him in a long time. He looked really frail and she could tell he had lost some weight.

"Mind if I sit for a moment?" Kevin asked.

"Please do," Maddie replied, moving her things from the center of the table to make room for him.

"So how are you? What brings you to the hospital all by yourself?" he inquired.

"I needed to have some blood-work done. I'm just hanging around to get the results."

"Is everything okay?" He wore a look of concern on his face.

"I'm fine. I've been just a bit rundown lately. I might be a little anemic." She tried to make it sound like it was no big deal, although she knew it very much was.

"You've been through a lot lately. It was a shock to hear of Ray's death. Had he been ill?" Kevin asked.

"No, Ray was hardly ever sick. It was just as much of a shock to me as to everyone else. The doctor said he went fast and did not suffer. I'm glad for that. I never would have guessed I'd end up a widow. Life's full of surprises." Maddie gave him a half smile and shrugged her shoulders.

"It sure is." He fixed his eyes with hers again as if wanting to say much more than he did. "So, I hear you're living in town these days. Are you enjoying city life?" Kevin joked.

"It's definitely less complicated. I've enjoyed spending more time with my dad." She looked over at Kevin's father. "Speaking of dads, I should let you get back to yours."

Kevin looked over at his father. "I'm surprised he didn't take the opportunity to snag another muffin while I wasn't watching," he laughed and then stood. "It was good to see you, Maddie. I hope your tests come out okay and that I'm able to run into you again soon. Take care of yourself." He briefly touched her shoulder.

"Thanks, see you later." She watched as Kevin helped his dad up from the table. He offered his arm and the elder Mr. Brewster took it. As they were walking towards the door, Kevin turned to look once more at Maddie. He looked pleased to see that she was watching him leave. He met her eyes and they both smiled.

– Chapter Twenty-Two –

The test results were far from good. Maddie's blood counts were dangerously low. Her platelets were down to 100, and Dr. Dillon expected them to keep dropping. The red blood count was teetering on emergency levels. Her white blood count was high, indicating Maddie was fighting an infection. All of these results pointed toward a very tenuous time for Maddie's health. The doctor was insistent that she stay at the hospital so she could be admitted immediately. Maddie was upset that she wasn't able to run home to get some of her personal items. But she trusted her doctor and was a bit alarmed by his tone and urgency. She decided to stay.

The staff insisted Maddie sit in a wheelchair as they wheeled her to the oncology department. They gave her a private room and asked her to change into a gown. She did as she was told and then climbed into the bed. She draped the cold covers over her and waited for the nurse to return. When she did, she was wearing a mask. This puzzled Maddie. The nurse explained that the mask was to protect her from them and not the opposite. The nurse told her that her immune system was weakened and it would be hard for her to fight off the slightest infection. The nurses and doctors wanted to protect her. They put her in what was called either "protective isolation" or "reverse isolation." It didn't matter what it was called, it still made Maddie feel nervous. She watched the nurse prepare the items needed to start the IV fluids her body desperately needed.

"Alright Maddie, I need you to lie down on your back and turn your head toward the wall, away from me," the nurse said. Maddie did as she was instructed. "You're going to feel something cold on your skin. It's just the alcohol

I'm using to clean your skin. Now you are going to feel a little prick as I insert the needle. Ready? Here we go . . ."

Maddie winced as she felt the needle inserted into the raised bump in her chest. She tried to remember what she had been told to expect after they inserted the medicine port, but it was all a blur now. The nurse applied a clear dressing over the needle and the tubing attached to her chest.

"Are we all done?" Maddie asked.

"Yes, you can relax and turn your head back now. You did well," the nurse said, smiling with her eyes. "I'm just going to hook up your IV so I can start giving you fluids."

"Am I dehydrated?" Maddie asked

"I haven't seen your lab-work yet, but I suspect you are. You have a fever and that's enough to get the ball rolling," the nurse said empathetically.

Maddie watched as the nurse programmed the machine beside her. The fluid dripped in at a fast rate. The nurse pulled up a chair next to her bed and took a seat. She asked what seemed like an endless number of questions about Maddie's health history and seemed to have too many papers to fill out. Maddie was overwhelmed.

"I'm going to give you some Tylenol for the fever. I'll come back to check on you once I get your chart together and put your orders in the computer. The doctor ordered antibiotics, but I'll have to wait until they come up from the pharmacy. Can I get you anything?" the nice nurse asked.

"No, I think I'm okay right now," Maddie said.

"Okay, just use your call light right here if you think of something." The nurse showed Maddie the various buttons on the side rail of the bed.

"Thank you," Maddie said. Once her nurse left, Maddie decided she should call Lisa to tell her what was going on. She had promised her sister that she would not keep anything from her and she was going to keep her promise. Maddie used the phone by her bed to dial Lisa's number.

"Hey, Lisa, its Maddie."

"Hi sweetie, what's up?" Maddie could hear the TV in the background and the boys laughing.

"I just wanted to give you a call to let you know I'm in the hospital," Maddie said, anticipating a big reaction from her sister.

"Hold on a minute," Lisa replied, the alarm in her voice noticeable now. "Boys, be quiet and turn down the TV—I can't hear your aunt on the phone." The phone rattled as Lisa talked to the boys. "Okay, I'm sorry, Maddie, I couldn't hear you very well. Did you say something about the hospital?"

"I did. Lisa, I don't want you to panic, but they admitted me to the hospital today—"

"—Maddie!" Lisa blurted out, interrupting her sister. "You promised me you'd let me know what's going on!"

"That's why I'm calling you now, Lisa. I wanted to wait to see what happened first so I wouldn't worry you."

"What's going on?" Lisa asked. "Knock it off, boys! I said to keep it down. Go into the kitchen and get a snack." Lisa then directed her attention back to the phone conversation.

Maddie recapped the day's events and tried to convince her sister not to come to the hospital. After failing this attempt, Maddie asked Lisa to drive carefully and take her time. Maddie returned the phone to the receiver on her bedside table and then rested her head on the pillow. It comforted Maddie to know that her older sister would be there with her soon.

* * *

It was unnerving to see Lisa enter her room wearing a mask. Even though she understood the reason for the mask, Maddie couldn't help but feel like she had the plague. Had the circumstances been different, Maddie would have laughed and made fun of her sister's appearance, but this was not a costume. It was real, and Lisa was concerned when she saw Maddie. They had both been optimistic, perhaps even a bit delusional, when the first rounds went so well. They hoped round three would go likewise. Maddie filled Lisa in on the events of the day and of what she knew of the current situation. Of course, Lisa was frustrated that she hadn't been called earlier and that Maddie had come to the hospital alone. The sisters decided to make a list of things she would need for her stay. The staff had told Maddie she would be staying at least a week, if not two. Lisa put the list in her purse, took Maddie's apartment key, and hugged her goodbye. She would return in the morning with the things Maddie had requested. Lisa reassured Maddie that she would also fill in the rest of the family. Maddie asked that she try to convince their dad not to come until the next day. For now, Maddie just wanted to get some rest. Feeling relieved with Lisa's help, she drifted off to sleep.

— CHAPTER TWENTY-THREE —

Lisa finished getting the kids' breakfast and made sure they were on their way before she headed to Maddie's place. She found an overnight bag and packed pajamas, socks, underwear, and a lightweight robe. She added some make-up, shampoo, and Maddie's toothbrush. After looking around to see if she'd forgotten anything, Lisa locked the door and headed to the grocery store. A few magazines and some crossword puzzles would be a good distraction for Maddie. She pulled into Brewster's and grabbed a cart. Browsing through the book display, she found an intriguing mystery novel, loaded up some magazines, then headed to get some gum and mints. Maddie wanted some bottled water, so Lisa put a large case in her cart. She found some pudding and Jell-O cups and thought those might taste good. She was studying the large selection of crackers when she heard her name.

"Hi, Lisa. Is there something I can help you find?" Kevin said as he walked from the other end of the dry goods aisle.

"Hello, Kevin. How are you?" Lisa put the box of crackers she had been holding into her cart.

"I'm real good, thanks." He looked in her cart to see what she was buying. "It looks like you're preparing for a road trip."

"Oh, no." She understood what it looked like. "This is for Maddie." When Lisa said her sister's name, she wished she could take it back. Maddie didn't want people to know she was sick, let alone in the hospital.

"Really? I just saw her yesterday," Kevin replied, seeming confused.

"Oh yeah? Where?" Lisa needed to stall because she didn't know how to dig herself out of the hole she had created.

"I ran into her over at the hospital, in the cafeteria. I was there with my dad."

"Oh. How's your dad?" Lisa tried to think quickly and turn the conversation somewhere else.

"He's doing pretty well; thanks for asking. Maddie told me she was having some tests done. I hope everything is okay."

The dilemma. Should she lie or just come out with the truth? She was a terrible liar. Kevin waited for an answer. She decided she couldn't do it. She'd have to tell him the truth. She could tell he was concerned. Lisa liked Kevin and knew he really cared about her sister. Maddie would just have to be mad at her. She took a deep breath, then started. "Kevin, I hope I can trust you with what I am about to tell you." She saw the features of his face change. He looked at her intently. Lisa continued, "Maddie is very sick. I'm not sure what she told you yesterday, but she is not well. She has cancer and has been receiving chemotherapy and radiation treatments. Her blood counts are low and they put her in the hospital yesterday. I'm just here getting a few things for her."

"Wow . . ." he said as he ran his hand through his hair. She could tell he was shocked at what she had just told him. "I don't know what to say. Is she going to be okay?"

"I hope so. She has an infection so they are treating her with antibiotics."

"I'm in a bit of shock here. She looked fine yesterday. I wish I would have known she was sick. I would have stayed with her."

"I know. Believe me, she's really good at hiding things. Maddie doesn't want to burden anyone. She's always been that way. She keeps a lot to herself. She's suffered so much. You have no idea," Lisa said, careful not to divulge even more than she already had.

"Your family must be so upset. Your mom died from cancer, didn't she?"

"Yes, she did. It's been a big blow to find out Maddie's sick. We're still trying to process it all."

"Is there anything I can do?" Kevin asked. "I'd love to drive over there right now to see her, to make sure she's okay. Maddie's such a special person. I can't stand to think of her sick or hurting . . ." Kevin sighed as if to stave off any more show of emotion.

"You can pray for her," Lisa said.

"I will." He looked down at her cart again. "Hey, this stuff's on me. You get Maddie whatever she needs."

"Oh, Kevin, you don't have to do that," Lisa said.

"I want to. Please, let me do this much." By his tone, Lisa knew he wouldn't take no for an answer.

"Okay. Thank you, Kevin."

"Anytime. If there is anything your family needs, let me know," Kevin said with sincerity.

"I will. Thanks again." She started to move her cart.

"Please tell Maddie I'm thinking of her."

"I will." Lisa watched as he walked up to the cashier and spoke with her. He turned and pointed at Lisa and the cashier nodded in understanding. Kevin waved at Lisa. She smiled back at him. She could tell he was upset.

— CHAPTER TWENTY-FOUR —

After five days in the hospital, Maddie felt ten times worse than when she came in. She was shocked at how weak she had become in such a short period of time. All she wanted to do was sleep. The first couple of days, she had enough strength to get up on her own and walk around the room or use the bathroom. As she became weaker, she used her IV pole to steady herself as she walked. After she nearly fell trying to get into the bathroom, the nurse insisted they put a bedside commode in her room. After that, they no longer allowed her to get up on her own because she was so unsteady on her feet. The thought of the device grossed her out but she did admit it was a lot easier than going all the way into the bathroom. The distance from her bed to there now seemed daunting to her. Now all she had to do was stand and turn to sit down on the commode. She was thankful she could still do that. She cringed when she thought about having to use a bedpan.

Her doctor had come in earlier that morning and talked to Maddie about needing another blood transfusion and more platelets. She had already had two units of blood and three separate platelet infusions. It no longer freaked her out to receive someone else's blood products. She told her doctor she would agree to whatever he wanted. Dr. Dillon talked with her about starting intravenous feedings, where she would receive nutrients and fats through her veins instead of by eating normally. He had reviewed her morning lab results and was not happy with what he was seeing. He asked Maddie to try to eat a little more if possible and told her that she had to start drinking more. She had lost her appetite since being hospitalized and her mouth had become sore. Even drinking water bothered her. She felt better if she avoided eating or drinking altogether.

The doctor said he would check the results the next morning and, if they didn't improve, they would start the infusions. He encouraged her to take the medication he had prescribed for nausea, and Maddie had been doing so. She said she would. It helped to make her sleep but she always woke up feeling nauseated again. Maddie was taking more medication now than she had in her lifetime. She no longer could remember what normal felt like. With so much being pumped into her body, she felt like she was an experiment. Maddie wondered how they knew if anything was working or not. She was sure some things must counteract others. Everything they gave her had the potential of side effects. It was all so confusing. Maybe it was good she was too miserable to care.

Day seven peaked as her worst day. The massive quantities of antibiotics took a toll on her. She had relentless diarrhea that made her even more dehydrated. They increased the volume of intravenous fluids, which meant she had to get up to use the bathroom more often. She was also on the TPN and lipid feedings that her doctor had decided she needed. Her energy was at an all-time low. She was mortified when she woke up from a nap and found she had wet herself. Maddie cried when the nurse had to change her gown and the sheets. All she could do was lay there while the nurse bathed her, and she even needed help turning from side to side. Seeing how weak Maddie had become, the nurse spoke to her about having a catheter placed. She gently explained that it would help her so she wouldn't have to worry about going to the bathroom. She agreed. Anything would be better than wetting the bed again.

She rested for most of the afternoon. When Maddie woke up, she noticed that Lisa was sitting at her bedside.

"When did you get here?" Maddie said hoarsely.

"I've been here for about a half an hour."

"You should have woken me up."

"Don't be silly. It was nice to see you rest peacefully for a little while." She reached for Maddie's hand and held it.

"It's been quite a day, Lisa." Maddie said to her sister.

"What happened?" She sat forward and stroked Maddie's hand.

"Well, between the vomiting, endless diarrhea, and wetting my bed . . ."

"Oh, Maddie, you poor thing," Lisa said empathetically.

"Did you see my latest addition?" She pulled back the cover to expose the clear tube that was coming from under her gown. Lisa looked down at the bag hanging from her bed. She hadn't noticed it before now.

"Another catheter?" she sighed. "I'm sorry, Maddie."

"Me, too."

"When can they take it out?" Lisa asked.

"This one's staying for awhile," Maddie said with resignation.

"Can they do anything else to make you *more* miserable?" Lisa was agitated at Maddie's ongoing discomfort.

"They are going to put in a rectal tube in a few minutes for the diarrhea," Maddie said, trying to keep a straight face.

"They are not!" Lisa exclaimed. Maddie started laughing. It hurt to laugh but it felt good at the same time. It was nice that she could still keep her sense of humor through this ordeal.

"I'm kidding. They really do have those though. The nurse told me all about it. She says they are horrible and don't really work. Can you imagine?" Maddie said scrunching her face in disgust.

"No! That sounds horrible. I think I'd rather poop the bed," Lisa said and then laughed.

"I'm not so sure about that. Let's just hope my diarrhea stops. I think these guys could talk me into almost anything." They heard a soft knock at the door and Maddie's nurse walked in. She told Maddie that she had a visitor waiting at the front desk. She had him wait there so she could check with her to see if it was okay to send him down. The nurse said he said his name was Kevin Brewster. Maddie looked at Lisa but didn't say anything in front of the nurse. They already had talked about Lisa running into Kevin at the store. Maddie wasn't mad at Lisa; just embarrassed for some reason now that he knew. She knew she shouldn't be but she was. Maddie didn't want him to see her at her worst. Lisa rose from her chair. "I'll go out and talk to him. Thank you," she said to the nurse.

"I don't want to see him," Maddie insisted.

"I know. I'll tell him you don't feel up to visitors today. Don't worry," Lisa reassured her sister.

Lisa removed her mask when she entered the hall. Kevin watched as Lisa approached. He appeared to be nervous with his shifting stance.

"Thanks for coming, Kevin. Unfortunately, Maddie isn't up for visitors right now. Would you take a little walk with me?" Lisa asked.

"Sure," Kevin replied, still perplexed. "What should I do with these flowers?"

"That is so sweet of you, but Maddie can't have flowers in her room right now. They could have organisms or bacteria on them that could make her sick. Her immune system is really suppressed right now," Lisa explained.

"I had no idea. I feel foolish for bringing them. You can see how much I know about cancer patients."

"Let's see if we can find someone who could enjoy them in their room," Lisa suggested.

That is what she had been doing with the other flowers Maddie had received. It had been Maddie's idea. Lisa and

Kevin walked by a few rooms and stopped at the door where they could hear a soft humming. There wasn't a sign stating that a mask was required so they knocked and entered. The owner of the beautiful voice was a frail-looking woman, they guessed to be in her eighties, sitting in a chair by the window. She wore a bright, floral robe, and a homemade throw blanketed her lap. When she heard the knock, she slowed her singing. The flowers inspired a bright smile that shone against her wrinkled, ebony skin.

"My, my, my . . . will you look at those," she said as she shook her head from side to side. "Now let me take a closer look. Come on over here." Kevin came closer to the woman and knelt down so she could smell the flowers.

"Hello, ma'am. My name is Kevin and this is Lisa," Kevin said as he walked towards her. The woman smiled at them.

"Nice to meet you folks. My name is Delores Jackson." She extended her hand out to them. Lisa reached for it and the woman held onto it for a few moments. She commented on how pretty Lisa was.

"It's nice to meet you, too, Ms. Jackson. My sister, Maddie, is the patient in room 212. She's not well enough to have flowers in her room, so she wanted us to find someone who would enjoy them."

"Well, bless her heart. My, they sure are beautiful." Delores bent her head down towards the flowers so she could smell them.

"I'm glad you like them," Kevin commented.

"My, yes, I sure do. And how is your sister fairing?" She directed her question to Lisa.

"She's having a hard time," Lisa said softly.

"I'm sure she is. She wouldn't be here if she wasn't. You tell her I'll be praying for her," Delores said.

"I will. She'd appreciate that. You're very sweet."

"As well are both of you for brightening my day. I'll

say some prayers for you, too." She smiled at them. "Thank you for stopping by."

"You're welcome," Lisa said.

"Have a good day," Kevin added as he escorted Lisa out of the room. They walked down the hall to the family lounge. Lisa explained to Kevin just how sick Maddie was and all that had been going on with her. Kevin understood why Maddie didn't want visitors right now. He told her to reassure Maddie that he was fine with that and to not feel bad about anything. When they had finished talking, Kevin left, heading towards the elevator that would take him back down to the main lobby on the first floor. Lisa walked back to Maddie's room and found her asleep. She decided to leave her a note, telling her to call her later that evening when she was up for talking. She knew Maddie would be interested to hear what Kevin had to say.

—Chapter Twenty-Five —

It was the twelfth day of her hospital stay, and Maddie had gained some of her strength back. It appeared the antibiotics finally were working. Slowly, she had begun eating again and, thankfully, the catheter had been removed from her bladder. Although still weak, Maddie insisted on getting up on her own. When she made it to the bathroom that first time, she was startled to see what she looked like. She had lost quite a bit of weight. Her face looked sunken and her color was pale. Her lips were still dry and chafed. Gradually, she had begun losing her hair and now her head was mostly bald. She had patches of hair and knew she needed to just shave the rest off. She put on the polka-dotted headscarf she had been given the day she came in. She decided then and there she would not look in the mirror again for the rest of her hospital stay. It was too depressing.

The doctors gave her the okay to take short walks in the hall. It was liberating to be out of her room. She had to wear a mask while she was out of her room to protect herself. She was glad for the IV pole she wheeled beside her as she walked. It gave the illusion she was stronger than she felt, keeping her weak legs steady. As she pushed it with her left hand, she was able to hold onto the wall rail with her right. As she walked by the patient rooms, she couldn't help but glance in. She was curious to see those who were sharing her plight. Maybe she could match a face to the coughing or crying she heard late at night. It was the soft singing that stopped her and drew her into a room not far from hers. She remembered Lisa telling her about the nice woman to whom they had given Kevin's flowers. This must be her, she thought. Maddie knocked on the door and a tall woman got up from her seat and walked to the door.

"Hello," the woman said. "May I help you with something?"

"Who is it, Lorna?" a voice called from inside the room.

Maddie felt embarrassed for stopping. She had no right to bother someone who may be as sick as she was. "I'm sorry to intrude. My name is Maddie . . . Maddie Stevens. My sister stopped a few days ago and brought some flowers."

The lady motioned her into the room. "Mom, the nice lady who gave you the flowers the other day is here to see you."

"Oh my, well send her in here. Let me get my eyes on that dear soul."

Maddie walked into the room. She saw the bright smile that Lisa had described to her. It was a warm, welcoming smile; like that smile had been waiting just for her to come in and see it.

"Here, child, you sit yourself down now. You needn't be wastin' all the strength you've saved up for your walk." Maddie took a seat beside her bed. The older woman pulled herself up a bit in bed, straightened her nightgown, and repositioned a bobby pin she had stuck in her peppered hair. "Now I suppose a proper greeting is in order." She winked at Maddie. "My name is Delores Jackson and this here is my youngest daughter, Lorna." Her daughter smiled and said hello.

"It's nice to meet you both."

"It's a pleasure to meet you, too. It was nice to see your family as well the other day." Maddie didn't have the heart to correct her about Kevin, so she just let her assume he was family.

"I hope you enjoyed the flowers," Maddie said.

"Oh yes, they were beautiful. It's a shame those doctors don't let you keep them in a time when your spirits are so low," Delores said with a scowl on her face.

"I know. I've just got to trust that they know what they're doing. I try to be a good patient and do what they say."

"That's good, honey. You know, your attitude about all this is just as important as the medicine they're giving you. We gotta have hope or else there's no use fightin'," Delores said with determination.

"I'll remember that. Thank you," Maddie said.

"Mom's living proof that you never give up no matter what they tell you," Lorna said as she took a seat on the end of her mother's bed, stroking her leg. "We thought we'd only have a few months with her and here we are going on over a year now." She smiled at her mother.

Maddie watched them with a bit of sadness. Seeing the two of them look at each other made her miss her own mother. She missed not having a grown-up relationship with her. "Do you mind if I ask what kind of cancer you have, Miss Jackson?" For a moment, Maddie wondered if she was being rude asking such a personal question. It was too late now, she already had asked.

"It's my pancreas. And you can call me Delores," she said, smiling. "It's a mystery to me really. I never drank or smoked. I haven't even had a touch of the diabetes. My mother died of that, you know? Terrible disease, just terrible," Delores said as she shook her head back and forth.

"I'm sorry to hear that," Maddie sympathized.

"Yes, it was hard on her. She suffered for years." She said this in a faraway voice. "She even lost her leg over it."

"Oh, my." Maddie didn't know what else to say.

"The cancer has been rough but nothing like what she went through. I can still have my sweet potato pie and not bat an eye at it," she said, grinning at Maddie. Lorna laughed at her mother and shook her head. "So tell me about yourself, Miss Maddie. Don't be shy." Maddie could tell Delores was the type of woman who liked a good story.

"There's not much to say, really. I guess I could start with why I am here. I've got endometrial cancer. Or I guess I did before they took it out. Now I'm getting treatment because it's spread to other parts of my body." She was starting to feel self-conscious. Her face felt warm under the mask she was wearing.

"Go on, dear. It's alright," Delores coaxed her on.

"Okay. Well, I've been receiving chemotherapy and I got really sick this time around," Maddie continued.

"And do you have a husband?" Delores inquired.

"I did. I'm a recent widow. He died a few months ago."

"I'm so sorry," Lorna said and gave Maddie a look of pity.

"It's okay. I'm alright. He wasn't a very nice man." She was surprised she was being so candid with people she'd just met. Usually, she tried to hide everything but for some reason she felt comfortable with them. She trusted that they would listen and care about what she had to say. "I have a great sister and my dad to look after me."

"How about children?" Delores asked.

"I did have a son but he died when he was eighteen. He was in an accident at a pond near our home," Maddie added quietly.

Delores reached over and took Maddie's hand in hers. "You poor child. My, my, my. Now where's your Mama? Is she around to comfort you?"

"No, she died when I was young. She had cancer, too." Maddie couldn't help but laugh through the tears that had formed as she told them about her life. "It's pitiful to hear this story out loud. It sounds awful when you put everything together. I guess I never really did that before," Maddie said, wiping the tears from her eyes.

"That's quite a bit of heartache for one soul to bear," Lorna said sympathetically.

"The good Lord doesn't give us more than we can bear. He knew you could handle it. You're a strong one, Maddie." Delores looked directly in her eyes and Maddie could see the wisdom in them. "You keep up the good fight."

"Believe me, I don't feel very strong now," Maddie confided to them.

"Keep the faith, child. He'll see you through this. He's gotten you this far. He won't leave you now," she said and squeezed Maddie's hand. For some reason, Maddie believed her.

"Thank you both for your kindness and for listening. I needed that." Maddie stood from her chair. "I should let you rest."

"Okay, dear. You come back to see me, okay?" Delores said.

"I will. It was nice to meet you both." Maddie smiled at them from under her mask.

"The pleasure was ours," Lorna said and walked Maddie to the door of the room. Maddie wrapped her hand around the IV pole, said goodbye to the two ladies, and walked herself back to her room. She crawled into her bed and thought through the conversation she had just experienced. Delores was facing death and she had such a peace. Maddie wondered where that faith came from. How does a person die with grace? Maybe it was her age. Delores had lived a long life. Maddie imagined she had touched many people with her life. It struck Maddie that, when it came her time, her life may not leave much of a mark. She had no living children to impact now, and her husband was gone. Maybe God was allowing her to die because He saw no more purpose for her life or else He loved her enough to answer her prayer for death to spare her from more suffering. What was the purpose of Ray's death? The timing was horrible. If God was in control, couldn't he have let her die before him? She wouldn't have to question the purpose of her suffering. She'd just be gone.

Maddie had held back from really crying, but now the tears could not be stopped. She had lived through so much pain and sorrow. She allowed herself to feel sorry for herself for a few moments but then remembered the wisdom of her new friend. Maddie was a strong woman. She wouldn't still be alive if she weren't.

CHAPTER TWENTY-SIX

Following another visit with Delores, Maddie returned to her room. While up and walking around, she had stopped several times over the last few days to see her. Maddie's blood counts finally started moving in the right direction, which meant she no longer needed to wear the mask. The visits with Delores had done wonders for her spirit. She learned that Delores had lost her husband just a month before she was diagnosed with cancer. He had congestive heart failure and his body finally gave up on him. His name was Ezzie, they had been married for fifty-one years, and they had three daughters. Lorna was the youngest and was with her mother the majority of the time. The other two, Dee-Dee and Crystal, usually stopped by at night. When all four of them were there together, you could hear the hooting of their laughter clear down the hall. It was a joyous sound, Maddie thought. She could tell they were a close family. Their joy was infectious.

Delores loved to talk about herself and her family. She was a proud woman but not in a bad way. She was sure of herself and had raised three grounded and strong women. It was in one of her conversations with Maddie that she described her role in the church choir. She talked of how she started singing in front of the congregation when she was just five years old.

"Oh, yes," Delores began, "I remember the first time I was brought forward to sing in front of the church. My mama dressed me special that morning. She braided my hair as tight as she could and polished my black patent leather shoes until they shined." Delores smiled as she talked. "I wore the prettiest white dress with lace that trimmed the sleeves and hem. Mama used that same lace to trim my bobby socks. Whoo-whee, I was a sight, let me tell you." Delores paused and laughed with her daughter. "I wasn't nervous one bit, if you can believe that. I'd been singin' since I was born, my Mama used to tell me. Even my cries had a melody about them." Delores laughed again, then placed her hand to her cheek.

"Do you remember the song you sang that day?" Maddie asked.

"Why, of course I do! It was 'Amazing Grace.' I'll never forget the look on my Mama's face and the sight of all my aunties crying. It was in that moment that I made the decision that I wanted to sing every Sunday of my life."

"Did you?" Maddie asked.

"I wish, child. In our church, there were plenty of girls like me, anxious to be on stage belting out a hymn. Most of them ended up being part of the most powerful choir I had ever witnessed. I was invited to be a part of that choir when I was fifteen," Delores said proudly.

"Wow," Maddie commented.

"When I was forty, I was elected choir leader and led them for close to thirty-five years. Oh, we could sing. I had a ball, Miss Maddie." Delores paused and became a bit despondent. "That's what I miss the most. I felt it was my calling."

"I'm sure you were wonderful," Maddie said, her heart going out to this new friend.

"She was," Lorna said as she put her arm around her mother. "She still is."

"I haven't been to church in so long. It's just too hard for me to sit that long," Delores said. Their service didn't last just an hour as most churches do. It was not uncommon for it to run two to three hours. They would sing and praise God until they felt satisfied. Then they would gather the family and eat all afternoon. Delores sighed at the good old days. Now she took comfort in the gentle humming she could still do. She was a hospice patient now and it was only a matter of time until she would slip away. She told Maddie that she was not afraid and that she was ready. She looked forward to singing with the angels and seeing her Mama again.

As she had been sitting and listening to Delores talk, an idea formed in Maddie's mind that excited her. It was a good feeling because nothing had excited her in a very long time. As she was leaving the room, Maddie asked to speak with Lorna in the hall. She agreed and followed Maddie out into the hallway.

"Lorna, I was wondering if you had a picture of your Mom singing in the choir?" Maddie asked with anticipation.

Lorna thought for a moment. "I'm sure I do somewhere. What do you need it for?" She was intrigued by Maddie's request.

"I have an idea, but it's a surprise. Is there any way you could look for the picture and bring it to me tomorrow?"

"Sure. I'll stop by Mom's place in the morning. She has several albums and I know for sure there's some pictures from church in there." She smiled at Maddie.

"Great, I'm excited." She smiled back.

"Are you sure you can't tell me what you're up to?" Lorna prodded.

"I'd like to keep it a secret if you don't mind."

"Okay, but you know it's gonna drive me crazy. And how do you suppose I get around all the questions that Miss Nosey in there is going to nail me with when I go back in the room?" Lorna had her hands on her hips and was smirking at Maddie.

"I'm sure you'll think of something. I have one last question. What color was the choir robe she wore?"

"Well they have worn several colors over the years, but the blue ones were her favorite. They were a rich, royal blue."

"Perfect. Thanks!" Maddie had a hard time containing her excitement. "I'll see you tomorrow."

Back in her room, Maddie went to the closet and pulled out a flower-printed gift bag with pink tissue paper peeking out of the top. She carried it over to her bed and slowly began to pull out the contents of the bag, laying them neatly on the mattress. There was a sketchpad, two charcoal pencils, and an eraser. In patterned tissue paper, there was a beautiful set of pastels. She ran her fingers slowly over them and picked up one with her hand. It had been so long since she had held one and it felt good. There were also several tubes of oil paints and a set of brushes. A white, plastic paint tray was taped to two small canvas boards. The last item in the bag was a light that attached to the canvas board.

He had thought of everything. It was such a thoughtful gift. When she had received it several days ago, she had glanced in the bag but hadn't taken anything out. She was so sick at the time that she hadn't taken an interest in it. She knew it was from Kevin but didn't bother to read the card that was attached to it. Looking at everything before her now, she was ashamed at how she had behaved. She hadn't called him or sent him a thank-you note. After she had received the gift, she had asked Lisa to put it in the closet. She was grateful Kevin hadn't presented it in person. The gift represented something she wasn't ready to deal with. She searched the bottom of the bag and found the card that had come with the gift. She slowly removed the card from the envelope. It had a picture of a woman in a flowing, white dress walking barefoot on a beach. The colors were soft and the sun was setting, which made the water behind the woman glisten. Inside was a handwritten note:

Maddie,

I hope you are doing well and are getting better with each passing day. I want to apologize for stopping by unannounced the other day. I wasn't thinking and I hope I didn't make you feel uncomfortable. About the flowers, who knew? I am a novice when it comes to medical matters. I want you to know that I totally understand why you didn't want any visitors. I would have felt the same way. No one wants an audience when you're feeling sick. I've learned my lesson. I have had you on my mind so much lately and I wanted to do something that might bring you a little joy. Since the flowers were a flop, I decided to stick with something I knew you would like. I even checked it out with the nurses and they seemed to think it was okay. I hope you enjoy everything. May it bring you a little escape from your current situation. I wish you a speedy recovery and renewed health.

Your friend,

Kevin

Maddie read it again, and then, instead of putting it back in the envelope, she got up and placed it on the windowsill with the rest of the cards she had received from family and a few friends. She left her art supplies on the bed and went into the bathroom. She brushed her teeth, washed her face, and then hung up her robe. Now in her pajamas, she crawled into bed. She reached for the CD player on her bedside table and put the headphones on. With the music flowing in her ears, she took the sketchpad and the charcoal pencil. She attached the light to the top of the pad and positioned herself so she could work comfortably. Without thinking out any clear strategy, she began to draw. Two hours had passed with only one small interruption from the nurse. She had just finished working when she received her nightly phone call from Lisa.

"Hello," Maddie answered casually.

"Hey, Maddie, how are you doing tonight?" Lisa asked.

"I'm good. I've had a good day."

"You sound excited. Did something happen?"

"Do you remember that gift from Kevin?"

"Yeah," Lisa said.

"Well, I got it out today and really looked at it. I was so touched by what he had done. I started to sketch and before I knew it, two hours passed. It was wonderful."

"Good for you, honey. What did you draw?" Lisa asked.

"That's a surprise. I need a favor, Lisa."

"Will you tell me what you are doing?" Lisa teased.

"No. That would ruin the fun."

"Yes, of course I'll do you a favor. What do you need?"

"I want you to go to the Craft House tomorrow to see if you can find a large canvas for me. If you go to the back of the store on the left hand side there should be a bunch of them. Look for one that's, oh, maybe 3 feet by 5 feet. Anything close to that size should work," Maddie said with excitement in her voice.

"Okay, I'll go in the morning, then swing by to see you and drop it off."

"Thanks, Lisa. You're the best! See you tomorrow." Maddie carefully laid the phone back in the receiver. For the first time in a long time, she felt excited about something. It felt good.

In the morning, Maddie's oncologist stopped by and talked with her about being discharged in the next couple of days. Maddie was grateful to be leaving but was more excited about her new project. She hoped she would have enough time to complete it before she went home. As promised, Lorna stopped by after lunch with a beautiful picture of Delores. She wore the royal blue robe that Lorna had described yesterday. It had white satin that ran from the collar down the entire length of the zipper where it ended below her knees. She was standing at the front of the church and the stained glass windows glowed behind her. Maddie studied the details of the picture, especially the expression on Delores' face. Lisa had already been by in the morning and had dropped off the canvas. She was anxious to get started.

Maddie propped the canvas on a chair and secured it with towels rolled on each side. She clipped the light in the center and the picture in the upper right-hand corner of the canvas. She would need to refer to it often. Delores looked to be in her prime. She must have been in her mid-fifties. Her smooth, brown skin was free of the wrinkles that now graced her face. She had her hair done in the style of the time and her bold, gold earrings matched the sparkle in her eyes. Her arms were raised in worship and a bright, wide smile shone as she sang. Maddie could almost hear the music as she looked at her and wished she could. She escaped for a moment into the scene of the picture and imagined herself sitting in the church pew, watching the woman of God sway and clap her hands to the rhythm of the hymns. She could hear the crowd sporadically saying, "Praise the Lord," "Amen," or "Hallelujah" as the music moved them.

Delores would have been inspiring to watch, Maddie thought to herself. After she had painted for over an hour, she sat back to examine what she had accomplished. She had a good framework but had a lot more detail to complete. The nurse came in with her antibiotic, so Maddie decided to take a break. Lying back in bed, she studied her work as the medicine flowed in. She contemplated her next stroke, color choices, and then felt herself drift to sleep. She awoke two hours later. Feeling refreshed, she decided to do a little more work on the portrait. She worked again for a couple hours, until it was close to dinnertime. Lisa soon would be coming with some take-out food. Maddie's appetite had improved and she was tired of the bland hospital fare.

Lisa entered the room and began talking about the kids and her husband and what had happened during the day. She unpacked the food as she talked, and then got settled into a chair beside Maddie's bed. She was in the middle of a story when she noticed the painting propped against the wall in the corner of the room. She stopped mid-sentence.

"Oh, Maddie," she gasped, "it's absolutely beautiful!" Lisa put down her food, stood, and walked over to the painting.

"You think so?" Maddie asked. She wanted her sister's opinion but deep down she knew that it was really good.

"It's amazing!" she exclaimed again, turning to Maddie. "I can't believe you did all this since this morning!"

"I know. I just got into a groove and this is what came out of it. I surprised myself. It has been a long time but it all came back so quickly. It's hard to explain, but it feels like I've come alive again. When I paint I feel liberated. For the first time in a long time, I feel like I have hope," Maddie said as her eyes began to well with tears.

"Oh, sweetie," Lisa said as she hugged her sister. "You need to have hope. You've fought so hard and you are doing so well. You do have a future and you need to embrace it. You are so talented, Maddie. I had forgotten how good you are."

"Thank you," she said as she wiped her eyes. They stood looking at the portrait. Lisa put her arm around Maddie and rested her head on her shoulder. "Lisa, I need you to do me another favor."

"What do you need?" Lisa said without moving.

"I need you to go somewhere tomorrow and see if you can get this matted and framed. She loves the color purple, so maybe you could find matting that would go well with the blue. I know it's a lot to ask and I'll pay for everything. I'd like to be able to give it to her before I leave the day after tomorrow."

"I'll do my best. I'm sure I can pull a few strings—especially under the circumstances," Lisa said.

"Thank you so much. It would mean so much to me," Maddie said, holding back tears.

Lisa stayed for another hour. They watched the nightly news and she left about seven-thirty. The next day, Maddie took it easy and spent some time with Delores and her family. Maddie knew her time with her new friend was limited and she felt sad that she would have to say goodbye the next day. She enjoyed listening to them tell stories and sing together. It was touching. Lisa visited later that day and told Maddie everything should be ready by tomorrow morning. She planned on going to the framing store when it opened to pick up the picture. Lisa had promised that she would bring it over as soon as she could. Maddie had a hard time sleeping that last night. So much was going through her head. She felt like she was a different person from the one who had entered the hospital. She had faced death and her own mortality in a very real way. Now she felt she could endure almost anything. She had renewed strength to live. She wanted to keep alive the feeling she had experienced these last two days. She was ready to live but scared at the same time. It was a frightening thought to be out in the real world and no longer under the gentle care of the nurses. Again, Maddie would be responsible to track her own symptoms and her disease. She felt well but knew she was not well. Her battle with cancer was ongoing. The treatment course was not complete and this worried her. Maddie was unsure if her body could sustain another bad infection. She would find out soon enough. Her doctor was already talking about scheduling her next round of chemotherapy.

* * *

In the morning, Maddie was up early and showered. She ate a decent amount of her breakfast. The nurse drew blood from her and gave her the antibiotics she needed in pill form. She wanted to make sure Maddie could tolerate them before she went home. Maddie would be taking them at home and couldn't afford to throw them up. The nurse said the doctor wouldn't be making rounds until that afternoon. This was fine with Maddie. It would give her plenty of time to deliver the portrait to Delores. Maddie had walked down to Delores' room earlier in the morning to tell Lorna that her mother's surprise would be delivered later that morning. Lorna was very excited for her mother and could hardly wait to see what it would be. Lisa arrived around eleven and unveiled the finished product for Maddie's inspection. Maddie was so pleased with what she saw. The framers had done a beautiful job. They had showcased the portrait in a gold, filigree frame that brought out the sparkle of Delores' earrings. The matting was a delicate, jewel-toned, speckle print. The mixture of purple, green, and blue complimented the color of her choir gown. Lisa helped her wrap it in pretty, purple paper. They carried it down the hall, aware that everyone was watching them. The nurses were beside themselves with anticipation of Delores' reaction. They also had bonded to both women and had gotten a sneak peek of the portrait when Lisa had passed the nurses' station on her way to see Maddie.

Maddie knocked on the door and walked in. She was surprised to see Dee-Dee and Crystal had joined Lorna and Delores. Lorna must have called them after Maddie talked to her that morning. "Well, hello, ladies. I'm surprised to see you all here," Maddie said and placed the package on a chair with Lisa's help.

"Child, you don't think we'd sit by and let Lorna have all the fun do ya?" Dee-Dee said with a smile. "We just love surprises."

"You come over here, Miss Maddie, and show me what you've got," Delores said, motioning to Maddie. Delores sat in a recliner by the window. "Lift up the package and put it where I can open it, sweetie," Delores requested with child-like excitement. Lorna and Dee-Dee held the package up so their mother could reach it. "Okay . . . let me see here," she said out loud as she contemplated where to tear the paper. As she unwrapped the picture, Delores began to shake her head back and forth. "Oh, my . . . oh, my . . . girls, would you take a look at that!" She scanned the picture with her eyes. Lorna and her sisters moved around so they could get a good look at the portrait. They all gasped at what they saw as Delores finished peeling away the paper. The picture of their young mother glowed. It was so lifelike. Maddie had beautifully captured the grace and spirit of their mother.

"Oh, Miss Maddie. You are precious, child. I don't know what to say . . ." Delores choked up and began to cry. "It's the most beautiful gift I've ever received. Thank you . . . thank you so much." She trembled as she cried, and her daughters embraced her. Maddie felt for a moment that she should leave them alone, but she knew they would have no part of that. Lisa reached for and held Maddie's hand at their reaction. They both squeezed their hands in response to the emotion they witnessed and echoed what the women felt. Lisa and Maddie had the same bond. The ladies came over and each hugged Maddie. They realized, as Maddie had hoped, that the portrait was a gift for them as much as it was for their mother. They would always have the picture by which to remember her. Maddie gave Delores a kiss and told her to look at the picture whenever she felt down or sad. She hoped it would bring her comfort in the days to come.

"Maddie, you've given me a taste of heaven. I feel a peace come over me when I look at it. Everything is gonna be just fine . . . it is . . . just fine," Delores said.

"I'm so glad you like it, Delores. I thoroughly enjoyed every minute of creating it for you. It was so good for me." Maddie let them know she would be leaving later that day. Tearfully, they said their goodbyes and promised to keep in touch. As she left the room, she looked back to see Delores and her daughters gazing at the picture. A healing had taken place within Maddie. Her body may have been broken, but she was leaving with her heart intact.

– CHAPTER TWENTY-SEVEN –

Maddie had been home for a little over a week when she received news of Delores' death. Lorna had called, explaining that her Mom began to decline a couple days after Maddie went home. She was sleeping more during the day and had lost interest in eating. Delores started complaining of more pain than usual, and they eventually had to put her on a morphine drip. It quieted her and slowly she began to slip into a coma. The day she died, she didn't wake up at all, and finally she just stopped breathing. Lorna said it was a peaceful death and Delores seemed comfortable.

Maddie called Lisa and told her. The funeral would be in two days and she wanted to attend. They decided to go shopping the next day to find something for Maddie to wear. She had lost so much weight that nothing fit anymore. Even the suit she had worn for Ray's funeral hung loosely on her thin frame. She found a simple, black dress with a flowing skirt. While looking for earrings, she noticed a gold pin shaped as a musical note. It was studded with tiny crystals and sparkled when she moved it from side to side. She decided it would be the perfect memorial to wear in honor of her friend since Delores loved music. Maddie bought it without thinking twice.

Simple, gold hoops matched the pin perfectly and would detract away from her wig. It had been delivered to Maddie's home while she was still in the hospital. Lisa brought the wig to the hospital so Maddie wouldn't have to leave the hospital without hair. Maddie was starting to get used to how she looked with it on.

On the ride home from shopping, Lisa stopped by Brewster's to pick up a few things for home. Maddie decided to go in. She was nervous thinking about running into Kevin but at the same time hoping to. She had yet to thank him for the gift. As they walked through the aisles, she started thinking of Delores and how attached she had become to her in such a short period of time. It saddened her to think of her daughters mourning her. Maddie then thought about Kevin and the fact that if it hadn't been for the flowers he brought, she may never have met Delores. It was funny how life worked; a gentle balance of cause and effect. Maddie felt like wandering around the store and told Lisa she would catch up with her in a few minutes. She made her way to the service desk and, before she could think through what she was doing, she asked if Mr. Brewster was in. Glancing at her watch, she noticed that it was now four-thirty. She hoped maybe he was already home and she would be off the hook. She was suddenly nervous about seeing him. Scanning the store, Maddie tried to see if she could locate Lisa. She turned back to the desk and listened to the woman talk on the phone. The woman told Maddie he should be down from his office in a few minutes. Maddie waited. With each passing minute, she regretted she had asked for him. Seeing Kevin walk towards the desk, she turned so he couldn't see her face, pretending to be looking for something in her purse.

Maddie could sense Kevin approaching her and was unsure what she should do. Fortunately, he addressed the woman at the desk first. She pointed at Maddie and he walked toward her. He was noticeably surprised when he saw her. He reached out to gently touch her arm and asked how she was feeling.

"I'm doing fine, thank you," Maddie said quietly.

"I'm glad. How long have you been home?" He reached out to touch her frail arm but stopped himself.

"About a week or so. It's been nice to be home." Maddie was still nervous talking to him, but she was starting to relax. His reaction to seeing her had been so warm. She could tell he was genuinely concerned about her.

"I'm sure it is. There's nothing like being at home, sleeping in your own bed . . ." Maddie watched him as he spoke and was almost sure he started blushing. "Brenda said you wanted to talk to me. Is there something I can help you with?"

"Oh yeah. I was just wondering what the specials are for today?" He looked at her with a puzzled look on his face. She laughed and realized how cheesy the comment was. "I'm just kidding. Seriously though, I wanted to thank you in person for the gift you sent to me. It was so thoughtful. I feel bad that I haven't thanked you sooner."

"Don't worry about it. That should be the least of your concerns. Have you had the chance to use them yet?" He asked with a tone of anticipation.

"I have. I used them in the hospital. Do you remember the woman to whom you and Lisa delivered the flowers you brought for me?"

He thought for a second. "Oh yeah, I do. She was nice and was really grateful for the flowers. It was the only good point of that embarrassing evening." He smiled at her.

Maddie smiled back. "You shouldn't be embarrassed at all. I was touched. It was very sweet of you to bring them in for me. I wish I could have enjoyed them," she said, pausing as she thought of the flowers. "Well, I ended up becoming friends with that lady during my stay there. I visited her often and became quite fond of her. I ended up painting a portrait of her."

"Wow, that's great. I'm sure it was beautiful." He had a look of satisfaction on his face. Not one of arrogance but a look of someone who had found the perfect gift to give. "I was pleased with it," Maddie said. "Do you know that was the first thing I have painted since I graduated high school?" Maddie was embarrassed to admit that. She

183

couldn't believe it had been that long and that she had been able to give it up so easily. It was an even bigger contrast when she thought of how much she had enjoyed painting the portrait.

"You're kidding me, right?"

"No. I'm serious. That summer, I got married to Ray and put my art supplies away. Ray never understood why I liked art so much and never encouraged me to do it. I'm just as much to blame. I got all caught up in married life and devoted my time to making Ray happy. It wasn't until I painted that picture of Delores that I realized how much I had given up, how much I missed that feeling of creating something beautiful. My mind has been going a mile a minute since then. I have you to thank for that. It's been a blessing, Kevin, and I can't thank you enough."

"I had no idea," Kevin said. "I was trying to think of something you'd like. It's been so long since I've spent time with you, real quality time. I had to reach back to when we were friends in high school. I remembered how your face would light up when you talked about your art. I figured I couldn't go wrong with art supplies," Kevin said as he smiled at her warmly. Maddie blushed.

"Well, *there* you are!" Lisa blurted out as she walked toward where they were standing. "I thought you fell into a display or something."

"Not funny, Lisa," Maddie said jokingly, thinking about the last time she had made a scene at the store.

"So how are you, Kevin?" Lisa asked.

"I'm good, thanks."

She smiled. "So what are you two talking about without me?" she teased.

"I was just thanking Kevin for the flowers and the art supplies," Maddie said.

"Oh, Kevin, you should have seen the portrait Maddie painted," Lisa gushed. "It was amazing. I know Delores's family will cherish it now that she's gone." Kevin looked confused. He looked at Maddie for the answer.

"We recently found out she passed away," Maddie said.

"Oh . . . I'm sorry to hear that," Kevin replied.

"Me, too," Maddie said. "She was a lovely woman. Delores was a great comfort to me when I was in the hospital."

"I'm glad. It bothered me to think of you sad and alone there. It must have been so hard for you," Kevin said.

"It's one of the scariest things I've ever had to go through. I'm better now. I'm getting stronger everyday."

"I'm happy to hear that," Kevin said, briefly touching her arm with his hand. Just then the produce manager summoned him. "It was so good to see you, Maddie. I hope to cross your path again soon." He winked, then said goodbye.

On the drive home, there was a comfortable silence until Lisa burst out, "I think he likes you, Maddie."

"He's just an old friend, Lisa."

"You can't see the way he looks at you?" Lisa laughed. "I think it's obvious. It was like I was hardly there. He couldn't take his eyes off you."

"I don't know," Maddie said, feeling embarrassed. "Maybe he was just being nice."

"Call it what you want," Lisa teased.

Maddie laughed and then looked out the window. Maddie thought back on the conversation and the touch of his hand on her skin. It made her feel warm. She looked to see if Lisa was watching her, thankful that she wasn't. She was embarrassed to admit that thoughts of him made her blush. Lisa helped Maddie carry the packages inside and then hugged her goodbye. They made plans for Lisa to pick her up in the morning. Maddie felt strong enough to drive but Lisa insisted.

*   *   *

Maddie woke on her own around eight and was surprised when the phone rang at eight-fifteen. It was Lisa, calling to say that she couldn't come to the funeral. The boys had been roughhousing that morning and Trevor had landed on his arm. She wasn't sure if it was broken, but they were on their way to the emergency room to find out. She apologized to Maddie for leaving her high and dry, but duty called. Maddie reassured her that she would be fine and that she was looking forward to driving the car again. After a short safety lecture, Lisa said she would call her later and hung up the phone. Maddie got up and showered. She donned the specially made wig and applied some make-up. At first, she had felt ridiculous in the wig, but the more she wore it the more comfortable she became with it. She had thought she might just go bald from the get-go and not bother with a wig. After thinking it through, she knew she wasn't strong enough for that yet and needed the security of the wig. It made her feel a little more normal and would not draw as much attention as a bald head. It was styled nicely and Maddie had to admit it was well made and flattered her. She examined herself in the mirror. What a drastic change from her condition in the hospital. Her color had returned and she had gained around five pounds. She still had more to gain and was working to add extra calories to her diet. It was amazing to her what a difference five pounds made in her appearance.

A benefit of living in town was that she was only ten minutes from the church. She had never been in Delores's church before, even though she had lived in the same town her whole life. Once inside, she realized she was definitely the minority but they welcomed her with open arms. She was taken aback by how friendly and loving everyone was to each other. Dee-Dee had spotted her almost immediately and brought her over to where the family sat.

"Maddie, hello!" Dee-Dee exclaimed, then tucked her arm around Maddie's waist. "Come say hello to everyone." Maddie followed Dee-Dee's lead.

"Maddie," Lorna said and embraced her. "I'm so glad you could make it. How are you feeling, dear? You look well. I want you to meet my husband, Ron, and these are my boys, Sean, Derrick, and Anthony." Maddie shook hands with the tall gentleman dressed in a stylish, black suit and waved a hello to the three young men sitting in the pew. Lorna turned to address the ladies seated behind them. "This is my Auntie Faye; she's mother's sister." Maddie shook her hand. She could see the resemblance in the warm eyes of the elderly woman. They sparkled just like Delores's had.

Dee-Dee led her towards another group of people, all members from the church, where she introduced her as Delores's friend—and the artist behind the portrait. They showered Maddie with praise, hugs, and kisses. Lorna directed Maddie's attention to the front of the church where they had displayed Delores's portrait. They had arranged flowers around it and had placed soft lighting above it. Maddie was pleased at what she saw. It made her proud. She then noticed the choir softly humming and swaying back and forth to the organ music. Tears welled in her eyes. If they only knew how much meeting Delores had affected her. She felt like Delores had been placed in her path for a reason. It was more than a mere coincidence that she had become friends with her. Maddie knew there was a higher purpose in all that had happened during her hospital stay. It was only in hindsight that she could put all the pieces together and recognize that God had brought her healing through the whole ordeal. Delores had been meant to cross paths with Maddie.

The service was more a celebration of life than a funeral. The members expressed much emotion and Maddie found herself tearful several times. After the service, Lorna asked Maddie to stay behind and meet the pastor. He praised Maddie's work, then led her to the altar and gestured for her to kneel. He stood before Maddie and motioned Delores' daughters to stand behind her. Maddie felt the women's hands on her shoulders and, as she bowed her head, the pastor placed his hand on the top of it. He began to pray for Maddie's strength and for her survival.

The tone of his voice was mild and smooth. "We pray, Lord, that you give our sister, Maddie, peace and comfort during her time of need. Give her wisdom, we pray, and courage to face the road You've laid before her. May she feel your Spirit beside her every step of the way. We pray for renewed health and healing. Please bless her and keep her in Your tender care, in Jesus' name, Amen."

Never before had she felt a prayer more real and true than at that moment. Maddie was deeply touched and had a hard time controlling her emotions. She had grown up going to church but had never felt any true emotions when she was there. The message of her church never seemed relevant to her life. Maddie had gone to her own church out of routine. She went because it was what she thought she should do, not so much what she wanted to do. Delores' church was different. The people here really believed. She could see it and she could feel it. She realized that these people had tapped into something to which she was not even close. They had genuine faith.

When the pastor finished his prayer, they all remained in silence with their heads down. She felt Lorna's hand on her shoulder and felt comforted. Maddie was unsure as to what to do next. Something deep inside her nudged her to pray silently. "God, I know I have no right to ask this of you . . . especially after all that I have done. Give me a faith like these people. Give me Your peace. A chance is what I ask. Forgive me, please, and give me one more chance to live . . ."

Maddie rose, shared several loving embraces, and returned to her seat. She dabbed her eyes with a tissue and reached for her purse and her sweater. When she looked towards the back of the church, she noticed a man sitting alone in the last pew. She recognized immediately that it was Kevin. He stood as she walked towards him. Kevin looked unsure as to whether he should hug her and was hesitant at first. When she drew near, he reached out to comfort her. She welcomed his embrace and rested her head on his chest. He stroked her back gently. As they parted, he kept hold of her hand, and she didn't pull away.

"Thank you," Maddie said and looked warmly into his eyes.

"Are you okay?"

"Yeah, I think so. What just happened was unexpected but good." She felt his thumb stroke the top of her hand.

"Did you come alone?" Kevin asked, looking around as he spoke.

"Yes. Lisa was supposed to come, but one of her boys got hurt this morning. She had to cancel at the last minute."

"I wish I had known. I would have picked you up."

"Thanks, but I did just fine. It felt good to do something on my own for a change. Anyway, I didn't know you were coming." She released her hand and dabbed her eyes again. She watched as he put his hands in his pockets and hoped that she had not offended him.

"I wasn't planning on it but for some reason, when I woke up this morning, I changed my mind. I had a feeling you might be here and figured you could use a friend today." Kevin looked up toward the front of the church.

"Do you think the family would mind if you took me up to see the painting?"

"Oh, not at all. They are such a lovely family. Come on, I'll take you up." Surprising herself, she reached for his hand and led him to the painting.

When Kevin reached the portrait, he leaned in close to get a good look. She could tell by his reaction that he was impressed. He then stood back as if to take it all in. Maddie watched his face carefully to capture his reaction to the portrait. She had hoped he would get to see what she had done. It was all because of him.

"Wow, Maddie. This is amazing. It's really beautiful."

"Thank you, Kevin, I'm so glad you got to see it."

"It looks so real, like she could start talking or something." He had his arms crossed over his chest and continued to study it.

"I would have loved to hear her sing," Maddie said softly.

"If she was anything like those ladies singing today, then I'd be blown away. They were incredible."

"They were." She sighed. "Delores used to be the choir director before she got sick," Maddie added.

"Really?" Kevin said.

"Her daughters said she could really belt it out." She looked around the church, now almost empty. "Speaking of them, I should probably get to the cemetery. Are you planning on going?"

"I hadn't made up my mind yet. It felt kind of awkward being here for the service. I really didn't know her."

"You could come with me if you'd like to," Maddie proposed.

"Well . . . okay. I guess I could. Would you mind if I drove us there?"

"I've got my car here," Maddie said.

"Why don't you leave it here, and I'll bring you back

when the service is over." She thought for a moment and decided. "Alright, that sounds good to me."

Kevin escorted her out of the church and they were on their way.

– Chapter Twenty-Eight –

As Kevin drove the car along the winding road that lead to the cemetery, Maddie was thankful for the music playing on the radio. It was a good distraction and she felt like being quiet. She also felt confused. She was unsure of what was happening between them. It was hard to tell if her emotions were clouded by the somber day or if she had true feelings for Kevin. They had always referred to each other as old friends but today things were different. The touch of his hand and the attention he had given her lately made her stop and wonder. It was strange that, after all the years of having no contact with him, she found herself with him at the funeral of someone they had both just met. Again, as she had about meeting Delores, she felt as if there was another force working in her life. Kevin was here for a reason and she didn't quite understand what it was.

They arrived at the cemetery, parked the car, and slowly walked to the gravesite. Maddie led them toward the back of the gathering crowd. She was grateful she didn't have to come alone. There must have been at least a hundred people there. She had never been to a funeral like this before. The pastor placed himself in front of the casket, thanked everyone for coming, and bowed his head in prayer. As he spoke, a soft humming began. Being a curious soul, Maddie looked up to see five women holding hands standing to the right of the pastor. They were beautifully dressed and all wore fancy hats that matched their suits. Their eyes were closed and they swayed back and forth in unison. Fearful that someone would catch her peeking at them, Maddie closed her eyes and bowed her head. As the pastor continued, the women intensified and matched his rhythm. When he ended with a distinct "Amen," the ladies began a sorrowful song that made the hairs on Maddie's arms rise. The emotion of their singing brought soft whimpers from the crowd that escalated into wails from the family. It was as if all the struggles and heartache had broken free at that moment. Maddie's heart went out to them. What a life Delores must have led. As she stood and watched those around her mourn, she felt Kevin's hand move slowly and softly across her back. He then rested his hand on her shoulder and pulled Maddie in beside him. She rested her head against his shoulder and listened to the rhythm of his breathing. She matched hers with his. It was comforting to be steadied by him. For those few moments, Maddie felt safe and calm.

After the service, Maddie and Kevin made their way through the crowd to the family. Maddie had to wait a few moments until the crowd thinned before she could reach Lorna. She hugged each of the daughters and paid her respects to their mother. They thanked her again for the portrait and told her to stay in touch. Kevin and Maddie politely declined the offer to return to the church for a meal. She was exhausted and just wanted to go home. Kevin offered his arm and led Maddie to the car. He opened the door for her and made sure she was comfortable before closing it. Maddie felt emotionally drained. She must have looked the part because, when they reached the church, he was hesitant about letting her drive home alone. They sat in Kevin's parked car.

"Are you sure you don't want to go inside and get a little something to eat? You are looking a little pale and I noticed your hands are a bit shaky."

Maddie folded her hands in her lap to steady them. She wasn't sure what she wanted to do. She thought for a moment and decided she really should try to eat something. She hadn't had much to eat that morning and knew, if she went home, more than likely she would just crawl into bed and fall asleep. She really couldn't risk getting weak again.

"Okay, I guess I could eat a little something."

"Great," Kevin said with restrained excitement. Maddie once again left her car at the church, and Kevin drove them out of the parking lot and towards the center of town. She was surprised when he pulled into Lily's Tea Room. It was definitely not what she had expected.

"You come here often?" she managed to joke with him.

"Actually, I do." He smiled at her. "My Mom loves this place. She always wants to go here when I take her out. It's actually pretty good. They have really good soup."

"I haven't been here in forever," she said and allowed him to hold the door open for her. They entered the restaurant and the hostess led them to a small table near the window. It had a delicate, lace tablecloth with a small vase of miniature roses in the center. Floral-patterned china was set along with polished silverware. Two small, votive candles were lit and placed on either side of the vase. It was a beautiful table setting. Kevin pulled her chair back as she went to sit down.

"It's my treat so eat as much and whatever you want," he said, handing her a menu and opening one for himself.

"I'm a cheap date these days. My appetite still hasn't returned to normal," Maddie said, wondering if "date" was a wrong choice of word for what they were doing. She wished she'd said something else. She watched Kevin closely. He seemed to be studying the menu and didn't react to the comment.

"So what looks good to you?" he said as he laid down his menu and looked warmly into her eyes. She looked back down at the menu, feeling a bit uncomfortable.

"I think I'll just have the French onion soup and a cup of tea," Maddie decided.

"Sounds good." Kevin motioned for the waitress and they placed their order. He focused his attention back on

Maddie. "Besides feeling exhausted from today, how have you been feeling?"

"Oh, it's getting better everyday. I try not to overdo it so I've been sticking close to home . . . I mean the apartment. I need to build myself back up for another round of chemo. Fortunately, I'm done with the radiation so I won't have to worry about that anymore." When she finished talking, she noticed the smile had left Kevin's face and his demeanor had changed.

"You have to go through more chemotherapy?" He seemed shocked by the idea.

"Unfortunately, I do. My oncologist thinks it's best if I complete at least another round." She tried to sound upbeat about it, but the thought of more chemotherapy was daunting.

Kevin leaned forward in his chair. "But you were so sick. Do you really think it's a safe thing to do?"

"My doctor said it will give me the best chance at survival. It's better than the alternative." She tried to joke but it wasn't funny. Kevin just looked at her and took in what she had just said.

"It scares me to think of you back in the hospital," Kevin admitted. He reached over and covered her hand with his.

"Me, too," she said and sighed.

The waitress came to the table and brought their drinks. Soon the food followed, and they ate quietly. He talked her into a piece of apple pie but she could only take a few bites. She was stuffed but was glad she had finished her soup. Kevin paid for the meal and they walked out to the car. He drove back to the church and parked beside Maddie's car. Kevin helped her out and walked her to her door. They stood looking at each other, searching for something to say. Maddie reached into her purse and retrieved her keys. She looked up again at Kevin. He had stepped closer to her while she was distracted. He looked as if he would lean in and kiss her. The mere thought of it both thrilled and terrified her. Maddie didn't know if she was ready for this.

"Thanks so much for everything." She initiated a hug and Kevin held her close, waiting for her to end the embrace instead of him. He rested his head against hers and she felt his cheek against hers. After a moment, they slowly parted. His embrace was strong and safe. She could linger there for hours. "I guess I should get home," Maddie said. Kevin caught her hand as they parted and held it in his.

"Are you sure you aren't too tired to drive? Would you like me to follow you?" he asked.

"Oh, no, I'll be fine. I feel refreshed now, thanks to you," she said, winking at him.

"Alright, well until next time," he said a little nervously.

"Have a good night, Kevin."

"You, too." Kevin gave her hand a soft squeeze, released it, then turned and walked to his car. Before Maddie could close her door, he turned and said her name. She stuck her head out. "Yes?" she said.

"Would you mind if I called you sometime to check on how you are doing?"

"That would be nice."

"Well, then, I guess I'll talk to you soon."

She smiled at him. "Bye, Kevin."

"Bye," he said and opened his car door. Kevin closed it and pretended to be looking at something in the passenger seat as she backed up her car. Maddie looked in her rearview mirror and caught his image watching her. A fleeting impulse made her want to turn around and go to him, but instead, she drove on.

– CHAPTER TWENTY-NINE –

Maddie spent the remainder of the week cleaning her apartment and organizing things. Her doctor's appointment was on Monday morning, and she felt she should get done what she needed to before then. She knew the doctor would bring up the subject of when he wanted her to start chemotherapy again, and she was not looking forward to it. Because her last experience scared her, she was more on edge than before. Dr. Dillon had reassured her that the reason she got so sick with her last round was because she developed an infection somehow and had a hard time fighting it. He had said they would be on guard for signs of infection and would treat her symptoms immediately if they occurred. At least this time she knew what to look for, and she wouldn't delay calling the doctor if something wasn't right.

It felt good to get her place really clean and to have accomplished it herself. It definitely took longer than it used to, but she made sure she rested when she felt tired. Maddie had yet to hear from Kevin since the day of the funeral. It had only been three days but she had hoped he might call. She thought about the weekend ahead. It was Friday and she had nothing else planned. She thought through her options and decided it would be good to drive out to the farm and check on things. She had only been out twice since she had moved out of the house. The boys were doing well and seemed to have matured quickly. She still felt the need to guide them on the big decisions, so she had made sure to call them every two weeks to see if they had any concerns. She picked up the phone and dialed the familiar number. She spoke with Johnny and made plans to drive out the next afternoon.

Feeling tired from the work of the day, she settled on the couch and turned on the television. In a matter of minutes, she was asleep and woke to find that two hours had passed. As the tea-kettle warmed, she changed into her pajamas and settled back on the couch. She looked forward to a quiet night at home. She flipped through the channels of the TV to see if anything caught her interest. In the midst of her search, the phone rang, and Maddie figured it was Lisa. She was surprised to hear Kevin's voice.

"Hi, Maddie. How are you?" Kevin said.

"I'm good, thanks. How are you?" Maddie sat down on the couch and turned the volume down on the TV so she could hear him better.

"I'm good as well. I just got home from work a little while ago and thought I'd give you a call. So what are you up to tonight?" There was a hint of nervousness in his voice.

"Well, I'm just trying to find something decent on the tube but am not getting very far."

"Good luck. There isn't much on that's worth watching these days."

"So, how was work today?" she asked. He told her about a few irate customers and how he remedied their problems. They talked freely for over an hour. Toward the end of the conversation, Kevin asked if she would like to do something together the next day.

"I'm sorry," Maddie apologized, "I already made plans to go out to the farm."

"It's no big deal, maybe we could do something another time," Kevin replied. Maddie thought for a few moments and decided to go out on a limb.

"Would you like to drive out with me?" she asked.

"I'd love to. I could use a little country air. How about I pick you up at your place at one?" he said, more than pleased with the offer.

*　*　*

Kevin was on time, and she gave him a quick tour of her apartment. It was small, but she was proud of what she had done with it. It was the first time she had been on her own, and she was really enjoying it. She locked up the apartment and got into his car. It was a sunny afternoon, and the warmth of the sun felt good on her skin. Kevin pulled in the long gravel drive of the farm and parked the car. Sarah came running out to greet them, barking excitedly when she saw Maddie get out of the car. Maddie knelt down and stroked her old companion. Sarah panted and licked Maddie's face. The dog followed as Maddie and Kevin walked up to the house. Maddie knocked on the door and waited for someone to answer. She could have gone right in but felt it would be a rude thing to do. Randall opened the door and welcomed them. Maddie introduced Kevin as her friend, and he shook hands with the boys. Maddie looked around the kitchen and noticed the small changes that had been made. It made her happy that they were making the place their own.

Kevin and Maddie took a seat at the table and chatted with the boys. They filled Maddie in on how business was going, and she helped them troubleshoot a couple of minor problems. Her brother-in-law, Doug, had been coming down to the farm three times a week as a favor to Maddie. He made sure the boys weren't overwhelmed with their new responsibilities. Johnny told Maddie he was going to take a couple of classes at the community college. He wanted to know more about running the farm from the business end of things. Maddie was very proud of him. She was glad she had made the decision to turn things over to Johnny and Randall. The boys had done a fine job, and Maddie was very proud of them.

They carried on their conversation while walking out to the barn. Maddie inspected everything and was pleased that the barn was neat and tidy. She could tell by what she saw that they had been working hard. She made sure they knew how proud she was of how they had taken on the responsibilities of the farm. Some of the hired hands were in the barn, and Maddie chatted with them for a few minutes. She could tell they were uncomfortable with her new appearance, so she tried to make them at ease by keeping the conversation light.

"Ma'am, we sure do appreciate you keeping us on after Ray's death, and we hope you're feeling better yourself," one of the hands said sheepishly.

Maddie wondered how many other people knew the details of her illness. It was easy to be caught up in her life and not realize the community around her.

"Thank you for your concern. I'll let you get back to your work," Maddie replied.

As they walked back outside, Johnny asked Maddie if he could talk to her alone. Maddie followed him back towards the house. Kevin watched as they took a seat on the porch. "Randall, will you show me around the fields?" Kevin asked.

"Be glad to," Randall answered, proud to have the chance to show off the hard work he and his brother had accomplished on the farm. Kevin started walking with the boy and took one look back at Maddie. He noticed she was listening intently to Johnny.

"Mrs. Stevens, I think there are some unresolved things that came out after Ray died. I've thought about it a lot, and I guess I have always wondered what you thought about things now." Maddie listened quietly to him. She thought she knew what he was talking about but wasn't sure.

"I guess what I'm getting at is that I'm sorry for the way things came out. It was terrible timing," Johnny said. What he said next took her aback. "I hope you don't mind, but I called my Mom and told her you were coming out today. She would really like to talk to you." Maddie instantly felt uncomfortable. She hated confrontation and would do anything not to face an uncomfortable situation. She now regretted coming out to the farm. She remained silent and knew that Johnny was nervous about her answer. He continued. "Mom is here at the house. She's been back in the living room the whole time but didn't want to come out if you didn't want to talk to her."

Maddie looked out to where Kevin's car was parked and noticed a blue car parked beside the boys' truck. She hadn't paid any attention to it before then. It must be Lynn's car. Maddie felt a knot in her throat. She looked back at Johnny. What was she supposed to do? She had been put in a terrible position. If she decided to talk to her, it could be very upsetting and, on the other hand, if she didn't, she could miss the opportunity to find out the whole story. It was a difficult decision to make, a no-win situation.

Johnny told Maddie that his Mom had wanted to talk to her since the day of the funeral but felt it was not her place to call. "It's my fault that she's here," Johnny said. "She was afraid to come, but I talked her into it. She needs to make amends with you. She feels terrible about you being sick and wants to apologize for hurting you. It's been tearing her apart, and I just want her to be happy again." Johnny continued that he knew he was being selfish but thought it would do them both good. Maddie contemplated what he had said for a few moments and then reluctantly agreed. Johnny went back in the house and returned in a few minutes with Lynn. She offered her hand, but Maddie couldn't bring herself to shake it. She knew it was immature but she didn't care. She didn't owe anything to this woman. Maddie was surprised at how angry she suddenly felt. Seeing Lynn, Ray's lover, walk out of *her* house was unnerving. She felt little sympathy for Lynn's suffering. Had she not been involved with a married man, Lynn wouldn't be hurting now. Maddie was bitter.

Lynn drew her hand back and nervously looked at Johnny. He suggested they take a walk. Without a word, Maddie started walking, and Lynn followed. Maddie was grateful to be outside. If they were in the house, she would feel that the walls were closing in on her. They walked in silence for a good ten minutes. Neither one of them knew where to start. Maddie held her ground and let Lynn go first. She was the guilty one, for heaven's sake.

"Maddie, to start I want to thank you for speaking with me. I've gone over a thousand times what I would say to you if I got the chance. Now that I'm here, I'm not sure what I should say or where I should start."

"Why don't you just start at the beginning?" Maddie was surprised by the biting tone of her voice. She had fooled herself into believing she could move on from her past. She still faced many demons, and Lynn represented one of them.

Maddie's one comment had voiced a million, and Lynn treaded lightly. "I first met Ray when he used to come into the bar a couple times a week with his buddy. They used to just drink beer and play pool. I think you two were only married a few months. As with most patrons who came in a lot, I became friends with him and Dale. They were a lot of fun. It was just a friendship for a couple years. I was involved with different guys and I had Johnny at home. He was a little one then." She smiled nervously at the memory. Maddie still remained silent and let her continue. "I noticed that, after you all had Matt, Ray came in a little more frequently and more times alone. He'd sit at the bar and wait for me to go on break so he could talk to me. I want you to know that he talked to me about you most of the time. He needed to confide in someone, and I was there to listen."

They continued to walk and had made their way onto Maddie's favorite path. "Ray had a hard time adjusting to having a baby around. He loved Matt but felt like he was coming between the two of you. Ray admitted that he was jealous of the attention you gave to the baby. Being a mother myself, I tried to make him understand that a mother's love for her child is different from the love she has for her husband. I told him it was in a different category, but I don't think he fully understood that. Time went on, and he began to resent any attention you gave to the baby when he was around. He just wanted things to go back to the way they were before you got pregnant. He said it was good then and feared it would never be good again. I told him to be patient, and he said he would try. He continued to come in over the next year or so, until one night when things changed between us. I came in late to work one night and wasn't myself. It took all I had just to get through the night, and Ray wouldn't let me be. He knew something was wrong, and it was driving him crazy. I avoided talking to him until my shift was over, and he walked me out to my car. He pressed me to tell him what was wrong. Maddie, I want you to know that I counted him as my friend at this point. Had I known what would happen next, I never would have told him, but I did."

Maddie remained silent, trying to understand what she was hearing. Lynn tentatively continued. "Earlier that night, I had gotten into a nasty fight with my live-in boyfriend, Russ. We were fighting about something stupid, and he became irrational. He started accusing me of all kinds of things, and one thing led to another. He ended up knocking me around and ended up taking off in his car. I didn't know what to do. The first thing I thought was that I needed to get my baby out of there. I packed up a few things and took him over to my mom's. I knew he would be safe there, because Russ had never met my mom and didn't know where she lived. I couldn't afford to miss work, so I got myself together as best I could and drove to the bar. Ray was really angry when I finished telling him what had happened. He said I shouldn't go back home. I didn't want to go back to my mom's in case Russ was watching me, so I let Ray take me to a motel nearby, and he said he would stay out in his car and stand guard. I took him up on his offer because I was scared. I trusted Ray.

They continued to walk, and Maddie could tell that Lynn was really nervous and seemed to be rambling on. Lynn was giving way too many details for Maddie's comfort level, but she wasn't about to stop her. It was like watching a horror movie. You were terrified to watch but couldn't pull your eyes away from it. Maddie needed closure on this part of her life, and she was willing to endure Lynn to get it.

"Ray stayed there for an hour and then called his buddy Dale from the payphone outside. About a half hour later, Dale was there, and Ray came up to tell me that he'd be gone for a little while and that Dale would keep watch. By now, it was around four in the morning. Ray told me he would be back. I learned later that Ray had driven out to my place and found Russ sleeping on the couch. With the advantage of having my keys, he went in and caught Russ off guard. He proceeded to beat the tar out of him, made him pack his things, and told him not to even think of coming back. Surprisingly, Russ did just that. When Ray returned to the motel, he said I should stay there. I was scared, so I did. Ray insisted he stay to make sure I was okay. I think we were both vulnerable at the moment, and one thing led to another. I'm sorry for telling you all these details, but I want you to know that it wasn't planned. We didn't mean to hurt you. It just happened. He went home quickly after. He felt very guilty for having cheated on you. Ray felt even worse when he found out I had gotten pregnant."

Lynn paused. Maddie's head felt like it was spinning. It seemed as if she had been living in a hole somewhere while the world was going on around her. How could she have lived in the same town all these years and no one had ever told her about what was going on? She wondered if she was the only one who didn't know what had gone on between Lynn and her husband.

"Maddie, I want you to know I'm really sorry for all that has happened. I didn't intentionally get pregnant. When Ray found out, he was really shocked. He questioned who the father was, but I knew without a doubt that it had to be Ray. All you have to do is look at Randy and you can see the resemblance."

"I never did," Maddie said flatly.

"I told Ray that I could manage on my own because I'd done it before with Johnny," Lynn continued. "Ray said that was out of the question. He made sure I went to the doctor, and he paid for everything."

"You mean *we* paid for everything," Maddie couldn't help but comment.

"You're absolutely right. You and Ray paid for it. I am forever grateful for the help I received. I never would have been able to provide for my boys if it hadn't been for his kindness. Ray tried to see Randy when he could, and we never told Randy that Ray was his daddy until after your son died. Ray felt the need to bond with Randy after that. He needed to feel like a father again. He was really hurting. Maddie, even with all that was going on, I want you to know that Ray still loved you. He just forgot how to show you. He knew things weren't right between you, but he couldn't let you go."

"He could have saved me a lot of heartache if he had just been man enough to tell me the truth," Maddie said.

"He was a selfish man, Maddie, and a jealous man. He couldn't stand the thought of losing you. You were his prize," Lynn said.

"I find that hard to believe," Maddie said sarcastically.

"It's true. He didn't care if you both were miserable. At least he had you. He was frustrated that he couldn't get through to you or help you with your grief. He needed comfort and I gave it to him. I loved him for all those years, but out of respect for you and your family I kept my feelings inside until I couldn't any longer."

"Hold on a minute. I can't stand this anymore. What do you mean 'Out of respect for me'? Are you kidding me? Do you actually believe that? Am I supposed to feel sorry for you?" Maddie was seething.

Lynn stepped back away from Maddie. "It sounds awful the way it's coming out. I guess I shouldn't expect you to understand, but I loved him and he loved me. He loved my boys, too," Lynn said a bit defensively.

Maddie tried to compose herself. "Lynn, do you feel at all guilty?" Maddie asked. "I mean in one sense you are apologizing but, in another, you are not. Do you realize what you did to my family? You make it sound like you were the one who lost out as if it's my fault this all happened to you." Maddie now stood face to face with Lynn. "I'm the one who lost everything! I don't have a son, Lynn. I no longer have a husband or a family. I am sick and will more than likely die before the year's out. I have nothing!" She took a few steps back. "I need to go now. I can't listen to anymore of this. I'm so tired of being the one to blame for everyone else's unhappiness. It's not my fault."

"Maddie, I never meant to imply that. You are misunderstanding me," Lynn said.

"If you are looking for me to tell you it's okay what you did, well, I can't. It was selfish, and it was wrong."

"I know," was all Lynn could say. Maddie turned and began walking back. She stopped and spoke to Lynn for the last time. "I want you to know that I have no hard feelings toward the boys. I'm very fond of them and always will be."

"Thank you," Lynn said and watched Maddie walk away. She stayed behind and allowed Maddie to disappear from her sight. Maddie walked the remainder of the path alone. Upon reaching the house, she saw Kevin and the boys sitting on the porch. Kevin stood when he saw Maddie. Johnny had given Kevin a few details of what the women were talking about. Kevin walked out to meet Maddie. After making sure she was okay, Kevin took the hint that Maddie wanted to leave right away. Maddie gave the boys a hug goodbye. She told them she would be in touch. As they were pulling out of the driveway, Maddie could see Johnny and Randall heading down the path to look for their mother. They were good boys.

The ride back to Maddie's place was quiet. She was lost in her thoughts and appreciated that Kevin didn't probe her with questions. He played soft music, and Maddie gazed out the window. When they got to her apartment, he walked her to her door and gave her a warm hug goodbye. She didn't want to let go of him. Maddie pondered briefly on inviting him in but felt it would not be right since she was in such a vulnerable state.

Her interaction with Lynn left her sad and disappointed in herself. She had been so far removed from reality all those years that she had not seen the writing on the wall. Ray had cheated on her, but she had cheated him as well. She hadn't needed him like she did before she had Matt. She had preferred to spend her energy on their child instead of Ray. It was so much easier since Matt's love was unconditional. It was pure. When Matt died, she consciously closed herself off emotionally, especially to Ray. She didn't want anyone to comfort her, especially not Ray.

"Are you going to be alright?" Kevin asked.

"I'll be okay. I'm sorry the day turned out the way it did. I hope you don't think I'm rude for not wanting to talk about everything. I haven't said more than two sentences on the way home. I just need time to sort everything through." Maddie looked up at him. "I appreciate you, Kevin. You are very patient with me."

"It's because I care about you," he said and drew her back into his embrace. His mouth was close to her ear. He whispered, "You can talk to me about anything. I hope you know that," he said and kissed her cheek softly.

"I do," she whispered back, then tilted her head so she could look in his eyes. "You are a good man, Kevin."

He cradled her face in his hands and kissed her forehead. "I know," he teased. His kisses thrilled Maddie and she wanted more, but she felt cautious and not ready to dive right in.

"I'll give you a call when I'm feeling more like myself."

"Okay. Get some rest, and try not to be too hard on yourself."

After saying goodbye to Kevin, Maddie closed the front door. She locked it and, out of the window to the side of the door, she watched Kevin get into his car and drive away. She felt grateful he had once again entered her life.

– CHAPTER THIRTY –

Maddie slept in until ten o'clock the next morning. What an emotional day the previous one had been. It was Sunday, and she was planning to stay home and take it easy. She wanted to relax and think of nothing. She knew tomorrow would be a whole new ballgame.

Maddie spent the day taking catnaps and reading the book she had started months ago but had never finished. By evening, she was hungry, so she ordered a pizza. It smelled wonderful, but she could only finish one piece. She placed the rest in the refrigerator. She thought she would try to eat some of it tomorrow if she had the appetite. After a long, hot, bubble bath, she decided to call Lisa. They talked for over an hour and, when she hung up the phone, it rang immediately. Answering, Maddie was pleased to hear Kevin's voice.

"I'm just calling to see how you're feeling," Kevin explained. "I've been thinking about you all day." His voice was full of concern. Maddie decided to share with Kevin the details of her conversation with Lynn. He listened intently and appeared as shocked as she had been at the details of the affair. It was good to be able to talk freely with him.

"How was *your* day?" Maddie asked, hoping to move the conversation to a lighter note.

"I normally have Sundays off, but today I got a call from one of my managers who told me that the cooling system for the main freezer case was malfunctioning and that he needed me to come in. We had to give away most of the frozen foods by the day's end. They were unsure of how long the unit had been malfunctioning, so I decided to give the food away to anyone who wanted it. I didn't want to sell any of it and be liable for food that had not been kept at the proper temperature." Kevin was laughing about it as he told her the story but, at the time, it had been very stressful.

"You'd think we were giving away gold the way these people were rushing to fill up their carts. It was unbelievable. You say the word 'free' and people go crazy," Kevin said. Maddie laughed at the thought of old ladies fighting over who would get the frozen pies.

"Then," Kevin continued between laughs, "they started calling their friends and relatives and, before I knew it, the place was swarming with people. We had to use tickets from the deli counter so that people would wait their turn."

"You're kidding me," Maddie said.

"I wish I was. Everything was cleaned out in under an hour." Kevin sighed. "At least my employees left happy. I let them take whatever they wanted." Kevin had brought food to his parents' house and had stocked his deep freezer at home. He offered Maddie her pick from his loot.

"I'm okay, but thank you. I don't eat much these days," she said.

"You can always use a chicken pot pie. Come on . . ." he teased.

"I haven't had one in years," Maddie said.

"I can set you up. How about I bring a few around tomorrow?"

Maddie thought for a moment. "I guess that would be okay." She tried to think about her schedule for the next day. "I have a doctor's appointment in the morning, then lunch with Lisa. So, maybe sometime after that?"

"Sure. How about you call me after you get back from lunch and we'll set something up?"

"Okay. Should I call you at work or home?" Maddie asked.

"Home. After the episode today, I decided I could use a day off tomorrow," he said, then warmly added, "I'd enjoy seeing you."

"You, too. I guess I'll call you tomorrow then," Maddie said.

"Sounds good and, hey, I hope it goes well at the doctor's."

"Thanks, Kevin." Maddie smiled to herself as she hung up the phone.

*   *   *

Maddie arrived at her doctor's appointment the next day as scheduled. The nurse checked her in and then left her alone in the exam room to wait for the doctor. She studied the posters on the wall and the brochures for different medications hanging in a rack next to the sink. She noticed the border hanging around the ceiling of the room. It was of sailboats on blue water with sand in the background. The exam table and the cabinets in the room matched the same blue of the wallpaper. On the counter were the customary clear glass jars of cotton balls, swabs, and a box of tissues. Never had she ever seen a doctor reach in the glass jar in need of a cotton ball. She studied her hands as she sat on the exam table. They were dry and desperately in need of some lotion. She no longer wore her wedding ring, so her fingers were bare. She placed them under her thighs and sat in a slumped position. The exam table offered no back support, so she had to sit there with legs dangling and her back feeling uncomfortable. The table paper crinkled when she switched positions, and she wondered why the room had to be so cold. It's like they wanted to make you as uncomfortable as possible before the doctor sees you, she thought. She straightened when she heard the quick knock on the door and saw her oncologist, Dr Dillon, enter the room.

"Hello, Maddie," the doctor said, giving her a quick hug. "How are you? You look good." Dr. Dillon took a seat on the wheeled stool and opened her chart onto his lap.

"Thanks, I'm doing alright. I feel so much better now that I am home," Maddie admitted.

"Everyone always does. Let's see here, it's been a month since your last treatment. Your hospital stay delayed things a bit, but I think we are ready to get back on track. You gave me quite a good scare there for awhile," Dr. Dillon said honestly.

"You and me both," Maddie said.

"It's not uncommon to end up in the hospital during treatment. The human body can only take so much. How have you been eating lately? Do you have your appetite back?" the doctor questioned.

"It's okay. I find I can just eat one meal a day. I snack the rest of the time."

"Make sure you make good food choices. You need to build yourself up as much as possible. You look like you might have gained a couple of pounds since I discharged you."

"Five," Maddie said, happy that she had been able to accomplish such a great feat.

"Excellent! Keep it up. How would you feel about starting another round next week?" Dr. Dillon asked.

"To be honest, it scares me a lot."

"I know. We'll keep a close eye on you. I'm going to ask you to be very diligent to wash your hands often, get plenty of rest, and limit your exposure to large crowds."

"I will," Maddie said, already nervous about what lie ahead.

"I'll let them know upfront to get you scheduled. Any other questions for me today?" Dr. Dillon said as he stood to leave.

"Do you think this could be my last round of chemotherapy?" Maddie asked, not really wanting to know the answer.

"Maybe . . . I'll see you next week."

Maddie was satisfied with the visit. She already had assumed what he would tell her and, for the most part, she was right. She left the office feeling a bit scared but comfortable with the decision. Maybe this would be her last round. She prayed that it would.

She drove to Lisa's house, and they had a relaxing lunch together. Maddie told her everything that the doctor had said. Lisa seemed surprised for some reason. She had been harboring false hopes that the doctor would say Maddie was done with treatment, and everything would be fine. She was scared to think of Maddie getting sick again. Lisa had really thought she was going to lose her. They had a nice visit, and Maddie got home around three o'clock. She checked her messages, and no one had called. She decided to call Kevin as she had said she would.

"Hello," Kevin answered on the third ring.

"Hi, Kevin, it's Maddie."

"Hey. It's good to hear your voice. How was your appointment?"

"It was fine. I had a nice visit and lunch with Lisa. She always makes me laugh and feel better."

"I'm curious about what the doctor had to say."

"We just talked about what to plan for next. I'll see him again next week." Maddie didn't feel like getting into the details with him. "So what have you been up to today?" She hoped he took the cue and he did.

"Oh, I've just been tooling around the house. I sat down to do something quick on the computer, and two hours slipped away. Your call rescued me from possible irreversible eye strain."

"You're funny," Maddie replied.

"Now that you are back, can I sway you to come over for dinner and a movie at my place?"

Maddie was torn about what she wanted to do. She was exhausted, but the thought of spending time with Kevin made her want to ignore her fatigue.

"I'd love to come over but, to be honest with you, I'm so tired from my day. I'm afraid I'd be worse company than the other day, if that's possible. I hope I'm not disappointing you."

"I'd be a liar if I said I wasn't. I understand you need to rest. It's hard to remember sometimes that you are sick. I have this urge to be near you, and I don't mean to come on too strong. I'd love a rain-check. Deal?"

"Deal. I'll talk to you later."

After she hung up the phone, Maddie felt bad that she had cut things so short. She hadn't meant to. Maddie went back to the bedroom and turned down the covers of her bed. She got in and closed her eyes. She started thinking of Kevin and the conversation they had. She was worried and was having trouble relaxing. After tossing and turning several times, she opened her eyes and stared at the ceiling. Driving home from Lisa's, she had felt drowsy, but now she was wide awake. She sat up in bed and looked over at her alarm clock. It was four o'clock. She didn't know what she should do. Maddie wanted to talk to Kevin again but felt foolish calling him saying she couldn't sleep. After thinking for a few moments, she had an idea. She got up and remade the bed. She freshened up her make-up and changed her clothes. She drove to the grocery and bought ingredients for a salad and homemade dressing. She found some marinated chicken and some fresh bread. Before checking out, she looked around the bakery section for dessert and decided on a peach pie. Maddie loaded the car and drove over to the quaint bungalow where Kevin lived. Taking a chance that he was still there, Maddie was relieved to see that his car was in the driveway. She hoped he didn't mind her stopping by without calling first. With the groceries in both arms, she walked to the front door and struggled to ring the doorbell. She felt nervous as she waited for him to answer. Kevin opened the door, obviously surprised to see her. He looked happy at the sight of her, and that made her feel much better.

"Got a grill we could heat up?" she asked tentatively.

"As a matter of fact, I do. Here, let me take those for you." He took the bags from her. "Come on in." She followed him inside the door and into the foyer. "Well, that was a short nap," he said. Maddie smiled.

He led her into the living area, which opened into the kitchen. She couldn't help noticing how tastefully decorated his home was. The dark brown, leather couches looked rich against the mocha-colored walls of the room. She watched as he unpacked the groceries and carefully folded the paper bag that held them.

"Well, after I hung up the phone with you, I tried to lie down, but I couldn't fall asleep," Maddie explained.

"Oh, I hate it when that happens. It seems there's nothing you can do at that point other than get up and try again later. It's frustrating isn't it?"

"You have a lovely home," Maddie said.

"Thank you. I've been working really hard on the place. It's been a lot more work than I originally planned but fun," Kevin said as he leaned against the counter. He had on loose fitting jeans and a short-sleeved polo shirt. Maddie was very aware of how attractive he looked.

"The kitchen is beautiful. I love the tile and these counters are lovely, so smooth," she said as she slid her hand along the cool, black granite. Kevin smiled at her reaction to his handiwork.

"You're too cute, do you know that?" Kevin said.

Maddie blushed. "I've just never seen a kitchen this fancy," she said playfully. "I'd love to see the rest of the house."

"Really?" Kevin said. He was excited to show her his home.

"Definitely. I had no idea you were this talented. You have really good taste," Maddie said.

"Thank you." He motioned her to follow him. They walked into the living room, and he explained how he had pulled up the carpet and found hardwood floors. He had refinished them to a golden brown. He had restored the fireplace and added built-in bookshelves. Maddie bent down to scan some of the book titles that filled them. She was interested to see what kind of books he liked to read. She read them to herself, *Devil in the White City, The Five People You Meet in Heaven, A Tree Grows in Brooklyn.* The last title peaked her interest. It was the story of a poor, twelve-year-old girl, growing up in Brooklyn. She had read it three times and counted it as one of her favorites.

They took a quick look at the bathroom, then headed upstairs. Maddie paused to look at the pictures hanging on the walls of the hallway. She studied them, smiling at the ones where Kevin looked young. There were pictures of his children in their youth as well as some Maddie thought were more recent. A graduation picture captured the whole family. She focused in on Kevin's ex-wife. She was very pretty. The kids resembled her. Maddie thought they made a lovely family. Kevin noticed her studying the picture.

"Those were the old days," Kevin said.

"Your wife was beautiful," Maddie commented honestly.

"Yes, she was," he said, shifting his gaze to a picture of a landscape. She followed his cue.

"So what's this a picture of?" Maddie moved closer to where he was standing. She studied the picture as Kevin studied her. They were barely touching and she could feel the warmth of his body next to her.

"That is a picture from a trip I took to Colorado. It's breath-taking country out there." Maddie nodded in response as he described the scene. She could feel the lightest touch of his arm against hers. She didn't want to move. It felt good and exciting to be so close to him. It had been a very long time since she had felt attracted to a man.

"It looks lovely," she said. Maddie felt his hand brush hers and was pleasantly surprised when he interlocked his fingers with hers. She felt flushed by his touch.

"Let me show you the rest of the upstairs, then I'll start dinner." Kevin led her along gently, and she saw his office, guest room, and finally his bedroom. She was thankful he didn't linger there. At the landing of the stairs, he released her hand and followed Maddie downstairs.

When they reached the kitchen, Maddie took a seat at the island in the center of the room. Kevin took a bowl out of a cupboard and placed it by the sink. As they talked, he began washing the vegetables and placed them on a cutting board. He then excused himself, indicating that he would be right back. He went outside to light the grill so they could cook the chicken. Kevin came back in the house and found Maddie standing by the counter, slicing the ingredients for the salad. He stopped before she could see him, watching her work in his kitchen. She looked comfortable and moved easily in the space. Without saying anything, he went to the refrigerator and took out a bottle of wine. He placed it on the counter and opened a drawer and found the corkscrew. She was aware of his every movement but was not directly looking at him. He walked into his dining room and came back with two wineglasses. He turned on his CD player and selected one of his favorites, *The Dave Matthew's Band*. He walked over to where she was standing and opened the wine, pouring them both a glass. She accepted it with a soft thank you. There was a quiet rhythm to their preparation of the meal. A slow tension had developed, and they were both aware of it. Maddie brought the glass, half-full with a deep red wine, to her lips. From the corner of her eye, she could see Kevin watching her. She allowed the warm wine to settle in her mouth and, when she swallowed, the full-bodied flavor lingered on her tongue.

"So how do you like it?" he asked, already knowing the answer.

"It's wonderful." The wine warmed Maddie immediately.

"I bought this bottle on my last trip to San Francisco. They have the best wineries out there."

"You sure do travel a lot. I wish I could say the same for myself. I've never left Ohio."

"I'd love to broaden your horizons," Kevin replied. Maddie smiled at him coyly.

When he finished grilling the chicken, they dined el fresco, enjoying the cool evening air. Maddie hadn't eaten much all day and was pleased that she nearly finished her meal. It was a small victory, for her doctors comments weren't far from her mind. Kevin made her laugh often, telling her stories from their past and his own. She was glad she had gone against her better judgment and come over. It felt good to do something out of character for her.

When they reached a comfortable pause in conversation, they decided to clear the table and head back inside. Kevin ground fresh coffee and poured them each a cup. As he was getting the coffee ready, Maddie had made herself comfortable on the couch in the living room. She was drowsy from the long day but didn't want to leave just yet. She watched Kevin working in the kitchen. She felt very comfortable being there with him.

He made his way to the couch and took a seat close to her. "Are you warm enough? I can get you a blanket."

"I'm fine, thank you. I was just thinking to myself about how comfortable I feel being here with you," Maddie said.

"I'm really happy to hear you say that," he said, leaning in closer to her. He traced his index finger along the top of her hand. She watched his gentle gesture and languished in the warmth of his touch. She wanted to lose herself in the moment.

"Maddie," he said, almost in a whisper. "You haven't mentioned your doctor's appointment at all tonight, and I am hoping that means everything is okay. I've tried not to think about it, but I'm worried about you. I really care for you." He brought her hand to his lips and gently kissed it. Afterward, he continued to hold her hand in his.

Maddie looked up at him and saw the apprehension in his face. She wanted to confide in him about everything she had bottled up inside, but she was afraid. She didn't want to spoil the evening. She was having such a good time. Maddie straightened herself on the couch and briefly let go of his hand but quickly found it again once she had repositioned herself. She liked the feel of him. He made her feel safe. She began, "It was a good visit. I'm so fortunate to have such a caring doctor. He answered all my questions just like I thought he would. I have to go through another round of chemotherapy, and he was pretty sure I'd likely need another when this one's finished. He said we would wait and see how I did with this one to see if I could tolerate any more . . . or to see if I died first." She knew that was a bad joke and she shouldn't have said it. Not with what she now wanted to tell him.

"Please, don't say that." He looked at her with concern and some confusion. "When did he say you have to start?"

"I have a week. He wants me to start a week from today."

"Wow . . . that was quick. You just got out of the hospital a little while ago. It seems like they're rushing things a bit, don't you think?"

"My doctor assured me that this was the normal treatment course, especially considering my situation," Maddie replied. Kevin looked puzzled. Maddie was afraid to continue, but she knew she had to. She had developed feelings for Kevin and needed to be honest with him. From his behavior tonight, she knew he wanted more than just a friendship. It was not fair to allow things to progress without him knowing the truth.

Maddie released her hand from his and turned to face him. "There's a big piece of the story you are missing that I need to tell you. Please hear me out before you say anything. The person sitting next to you is much different from the one I was not too long ago. I have not been the same person you knew from our high school days. That person had been long gone until recently. Actually, until you re-entered my life." She smiled at him. He was hanging on her every word. "When Ray and I got married, I was happy and I loved him." Kevin let out a sigh. Just the mention of Ray's name made him uneasy.

"My marriage was good, for awhile. After I had Matt, I was complete. He fulfilled me, and I spent most of my time and attention on him. I can see now how that put a strain on our marriage, but I was young then and just figured that's what happened once you had a baby. The years passed and I couldn't have any more children, so that made my attachment to Matt even stronger. Ray and I slowly drifted apart but still loved each other, or so I thought. We pretty much did our own thing unless it was time for a meal or we needed to work together on the farm. Ray could always be temperamental, but we would work through it. I had resigned myself to the fact that we probably would never get back to what we had when we were young. I thought that was okay. I had Matt then." Talking about Matt always made Maddie teary-eyed, and she wiped her eyes. Kevin remained silent as she had asked him to.

"Everything changed when Matt died. Ray and I didn't know what to do or how to relate to each other. I didn't want him to comfort me. I became very depressed. Ray dealt with his grief by drinking. He had always had a beer or two most nights, but he started drinking heavily after Matt was gone. He would be gone all night sometimes. I didn't mind most nights, although sometimes I felt scared being alone. Mostly I was scared of him. He got very mean when he drank like that."

Kevin's face began to change and she could tell he was bothered by what she was saying. "Ray started verbally abusing me and, in the state of depression I was in, I allowed him to do it. I was in a very vulnerable place, and he had me convinced I was worthless. I felt helpless, like there was nothing I could do, except continue on doing what I did on the farm. I felt I had no way of escaping, and I feared leaving. He did that to me and, now that I think back, I'm shocked at how easy it happened. I never thought I would get to such a low place. He made my life miserable."

"Did he ever physically hurt you?" Kevin spoke with restrained anger.

"Almost, but luckily that never happened. I'm sad to say that I probably would have stayed for that, too. I had no strength to defend myself, especially when I started getting sick." Again, Kevin looked puzzled by what she was saying. "Kevin . . . I knew I was not well long before I ever sought treatment." Maddie cringed a bit at the look on his face.

"What do you mean? I'm not sure I understand." He was looking at her with his brows furrowed.

"What I mean is I started having symptoms that I ignored at first as being nothing. After awhile, I realized that what was happening to me was not normal. Something else very real was going on. I started losing weight without trying. I began to have a lot of bleeding, and my stomach began to feel firm." She could tell Kevin was still confused. "It dawned on me one day that I might have cancer. Knowing that my Mom had died from it strengthened my belief that I did. What I decided next will shock you, I'm sure. Instead of seeking a cause of my symptoms, I began to embrace them. I knew that whatever was happening was getting worse and not better. I let it get bad because I wanted to die." She paused to let what she had just revealed sink in. He looked away from her and stared at the floor. He couldn't believe what he was hearing.

"I can't expect you to understand but, at the time, all I wanted was an escape from the pain. I welcomed the thought of death. I decided I could endure any kind of physical pain if I could finally get rid of the emotional pain that suffocated my every waking moment." Maddie felt like she was hurting him with each new detail but knew she had to get it all out. She needed to be completely honest with him. "I couldn't endure years of living with Ray the way we were. I felt I had no other options. I decided to let myself die and prayed for God to take me. Everything was going as planned until I collapsed in your store."

"Thank God you did," he said, exasperated at what she had just confessed. Maddie couldn't read his tone. For a moment, she regretted saying anything to him. There was no turning back now. She continued but was a little guarded now.

"At the hospital, I learned that I had a large cancerous tumor, and I allowed my doctor to remove it. At the time, I was unsure as to what to do next. I questioned my decision and what to do until Ray reaffirmed it. He did some things that broke my heart and my spirit. From that point, I decided I didn't want any cancer treatments. I stuck with my plan until that fateful day when I found Ray dead, and that changed everything."

Kevin paused for a few moments and then spoke. "Maddie, to tell you the truth, I'm at a loss for words. You're right, I don't understand. How could you do that when so many people love you? Didn't you think of your family? Your sister, your dad?"

She immediately felt defensive. How dare he judge her? He had no idea of the pain she had endured. "Like I said before," she spoke defensively, "I don't expect you or anyone else to understand what I did. You have no idea what I've been through and never will. Right now, I don't need anyone to judge me, especially you, Kevin. I count you as a friend and felt it would be best to be honest with you. Maybe I was wrong to say anything."

"No, Maddie, I'm glad you did," he said, changing to a softer tone of voice. There was a silence between them. Maddie got up and walked over to where she had left her purse and jacket. She put it on and turned to face Kevin. He was now standing near the couch, a few feet away from her.

She felt like crying and just wanted to run away. She had hoped this would have gone smoother. "I'm going to be fine no matter what happens. Like I said, I am not afraid to die. I don't want to, but I'll be okay if that's what ensues." She reached in her purse and found her keys. "I should go. It's getting late and I'm feeling really tired all of the sudden. Thank you for dinner. It was really nice." Kevin walked closer to her.

"Would you like me to follow you home?" Kevin offered.

"No thanks." She was being short with him and had trouble looking him in the eye.

"Well, at least let me walk you out to your car," Kevin said.

"I'm fine." She walked to the door and opened it. "I just want to go home."

"Suit yourself," he said, exasperated. He held the door open and watched her walk down the sidewalk towards her car. Pride made him want to stay, but his heart made him follow her. She was almost at her car when he called her name. It was dark, and only the soft glow of the streetlights illuminated her small frame. Hearing her name, she stopped and turned to see Kevin walking towards her. When he reached her, he stopped only inches from her face. Her lower lip had a slight quiver. Tears stained her cheeks.

"Maddie, I'm sorry for the way I reacted back there. I was insensitive and I had no right to be. I didn't know how to react to what you told me. I'm still in shock over it. You have been through so much and I'm so sorry if I hurt you. It's the last thing I would ever want do," Kevin said, placing his hands on her shoulders.

Maddie started to cry. "I never meant to hurt anyone. I . . . I . . . I didn't know what else to do. I was so lost. If I could take it back, I would. I'm so sorry. I didn't know Ray would die. How could I have known he would die first? It's just so unfair." She hung her head down and let the tears flow. He held her head in his hands and drew her into himself. He felt her sobs and was moved to tears himself. She slowly raised her head so they again faced each other.

"Maddie, I'm just so scared. I don't want to lose you. All I've ever wanted to do is love you. You can't die. You just can't." He was crying as much as she was.

"Oh, Kevin," Maddie said, her heart going out to him.

"It's not fair, Maddie. I've waited so long for you, and to think you could be taken away . . . I couldn't handle that. I need you, Maddie. From the moment I saw you again, I have longed for you. All these years, you've not been far from my mind. You don't know how many times I've wanted to kiss you and hold you. I love you." He continued crying as he spoke. Maddie reached for him and took his face in her hands. She guided him towards her, their lips meeting in a soft kiss. His arms circled her waist, and he pulled her even closer. She could feel the suppressed passion he felt for her as his kisses deepened. He had waited an eternity for this moment and was empowered by the return of affection from her. He needed her to love him.

He gently parted his lips from hers so he could see her face. He wanted her to reassure him that what he thought he felt from her was real. She rested her hands on his chest. "Oh Kevin, if only my eyes could have been opened such a long time ago. What a foolish girl I was not to see the man I do before me. Things could have been so different." She began crying again. She couldn't help it. "What have I done to deserve your affection? Why do I deserve to have your love after such a long time? You deserve so much more, Kevin. You don't need someone who's broken, who's sick. After all I've done . . ."

"It doesn't matter what has happened up until this moment, Maddie. I love you, and that's all that matters. I will always love you, no matter what." She leaned in again and kissed him gently. Maddie then whispered the words he had been waiting forever to hear. "I love you, Kevin. I love you so much," she said breathlessly.

– Chapter Thirty-One –

Fearful that what had happened to them the night before was just a dream, Kevin called Maddie the next morning. The sweet, sleepy voice he heard warmed him. "A week," he remembered her saying to him. He had one week before she again would enter that scary world of cancer treatment. He had been laying awake in bed for what seemed hours after Maddie left his home the previous night. He replayed their conversations, the way she looked at him, her kisses. Kevin was still reeling from Maddie's declaration of love for him. It was unexpected and delightful. As he listened to her soft voice on the line, Kevin decided he would make that week one she would remember. He wanted to give her something to look back on when she wasn't feeling well again. Kevin called work early that morning and told his assistant manager he would not be in for the rest of the week. It was liberating. He was taking a gamble that Maddie would want to spend more time with him. He hoped he could see her every day. He didn't want her to second-guess her feelings for him. Kevin knew he would not be able to face being rejected by her again, especially now that she said she loved him.

Maddie was flattered when Kevin told her that he had called off work to spend time with her. She, too, had been replaying their evening and needed reassurance that it really happened. She hadn't planned on telling him that she was in love with him last night. Until that moment, she hadn't defined her feelings toward him. It was in that vulnerable moment, however, that she was able to let go and allow her emotions to reveal themselves. This was big for Maddie. Her fragile heart was his for the taking. As she lay in her bed listening to Kevin's excited chatter, she felt a rush of emotion. She wanted to be near him again, to touch him, to smell him.

On their first day together, he took her to Cincinnati, and they toured the art museum. Maddie was in her element. She lingered at the paintings and entered into a world of which she so much wanted to be a part. They walked hand in hand, resting at times on the benches that were scattered throughout the museum. Afterwards, they stopped at a coffee shop and talked for hours about the past, their interests, and future dreams. The next day, he took her on a traditional date consisting of dinner and a movie. Kevin asked Maddie to pick the movie, and he chose the restaurant. As a joke, he pulled into Red Lobster and she smiled at him. "Just kidding," he said through his laughter. He drove them to a family-owned, Italian restaurant that was low lit and romantic.

The next day, Maddie eagerly anticipated where he would take her for their Friday night date. When he pulled up in front of Smitty's, she again thought he was joking. He remembered her commenting on how she detested that place. When Maddie realized he was serious, she tried to not look disappointed. She hadn't set foot in the restaurant in years. She immediately thought of Ray, and her excitement about dinner faded. He took her hand and said, "Trust me." She followed him in and was surprised that the place had changed so much. It had been repainted, and there were new tables and chairs. Gone was the musty, smoky smell. The lighting was brighter, and her heart skipped a beat when she saw her dad and Gina waving to her from a distant booth. Kevin led her over to where they were sitting. Kevin had arranged for them to meet there for dinner. The foursome chatted and laughed over several plates of Smitty's famous, all-you-can-eat, fish fry. Maddie was very touched by what Kevin had arranged. As they sat side-by-side in the booth, she rested her hand on his thigh. He placed his on top of hers and gave it a light squeeze from time to time. On their way out, they said their goodbyes to Maddie's dad and Gina.

As they walked back to the car, Kevin had asked Maddie if she was up for doing one more thing. Maddie indicated that she was game, now very interested in what he had in mind. He drove over to the high school football field. She was puzzled and smiled at him shyly. He took her hand, and they walked to the gate. It was locked, but he fished a key from his pocket. Kevin unlocked the gate, and Maddie wondered how he had the key in his possession. Picking up on her inquisitive look, Kevin explained that he knew the maintenance guy for the school. His name was Paul, and he also had a job at his store. Paul had given Kevin the key as a favor. No school activities were scheduled that night, so the place was deserted.

"Isn't this kind of illegal?" Maddie asked as she looked across the field at the dark school in the distance.

"Probably. I'll make a big donation to the booster's if we get caught." She gave him a nervous smile. "Don't worry," he said. "We pay taxes for the school and we are alumni, so I think we have the right to come here and enjoy the stadium anytime we want."

She shook her head at him. "You are something else."

"I know." He led her though the gate toward the bleachers. They climbed to the top and sat with their backs against the press box. She hadn't noticed that he was carrying a small pack in his other hand. He unzipped it and took out a thermos and two mugs. He poured them a cup of hot chocolate. She sipped on the warm, sweet liquid and snuggled in close to him. He put his arm around her and held her close.

"That was really fun tonight at Smitty's," Maddie said.

"I'm glad you had fun. Do you know why I took you there?" he asked.

She thought for a moment. "Not really. At first, I thought you were joking again."

"I figured you would be surprised." He turned to look her in the eyes. "Maddie, I wanted you to see that you can make new memories. You can go to places that were once linked to Ray and make them something completely different. I want you to let go of all the negative reminders of your past with him. I thought by taking you back to Smitty's with your dad and Gina, you could see that it's not the place you detest but the feeling you have connected with. Do you understand what I'm trying to say?"

Maddie contemplated what he had just said. "Yes, I do. I have never thought of it that way." Kevin continued to amaze her. He always seemed to have her best interests in mind.

"Did the fish taste better this time?" he asked.

"Not really," she laughed.

"I didn't think so either. Your dad and Gina sure put it away though."

"Tell me about it." She looked at him, and her eyes were soft with the love she felt for him. "Thank you, Kevin. This week has been just what I needed. You are what I have needed." He leaned over and gave her a soft kiss on the lips.

Kevin lingered for a moment and then said softly, "Do you want to see why I brought you to this place?"

"Okay," Maddie said, feeling warmed by his kiss.

Kevin packed up their mugs and gently led her down the bleachers onto the track. They walked to the side of the bleachers, and he guided her underneath them to the middle where there was space enough for them to stand facing each other. Still puzzled, she watched his every move.

Kevin wore a sly grin. He looked very proud of himself for pulling this off. "I have a confession to make. When we were in high school, I used to come to the football games just so I could watch you cheer. The way you moved around in your little skirt drove me crazy," he said with a laugh.

"Kevin!" she said a bit embarrassed. He continued.

"Those nights were the most tantalizing and frustrating," he said as he placed his hands on her hips. "I used to fantasize that, during half-time, you would sneak under the bleachers to meet me, and we would make out until a minute before the game would start for the second half. Then you would go back in front of the crowd and cheer, directing your motions toward me." He laughed sheepishly.

"You're naughty," she said playfully.

"You have no idea what goes through a seventeen year-old boy's mind..."

"So this part of the date is purely selfish on your part. You were hoping to wine and dine me at Smitty's, and then get me to make out with you," she teased.

"It would be a fantasy realized." He moved his hands up her back and she rested hers on his chest. "You are just as desirable as you were back then," he said and leaned in to gently kiss her. She closed her eyes and allowed herself to be transformed back in time to the carefree days of her youth. She was but a frail shadow of the girl she had once been, but Kevin made her feel young and alive again.

*   *   *

It was as if she floated home. Maddie rested alone in her bed, thinking again of this wonderful man who was now the one for whom she lived. Maybe God wanted her to be happy after all.

Their Saturday date was one about which Kevin thought the most. They had grown close in their week together. She had shared more with him than with anyone in her life. Kevin had listened carefully and thoughtfully to each new thing she revealed. He had opened up as well and shared the pain of his divorce and how lonely it had made him feel. Kevin had told Maddie he could tell her anything, and she would understand. She had always been his friend and now she was his love.

The day he planned would be a hard one for her but one that he thought they needed to work through together. It was a bright, sunny day, and for that Kevin was grateful. He picked her up at ten am, and they drove to a nearby nursery.

"Are you curious?" Kevin teased.

"Yes, I am," Maddie said playfully.

"Well, this is all I'm going to tell you. I want you to walk around, take your time, and look at trees."

"Trees?" Maddie asked skeptically.

"Yes, trees," he said smiling. "I'd like to buy you a tree today."

"Okay, and what am I to do with this tree we buy? Remember, I live in an apartment."

"I remember. You'll just have to trust me," Kevin said and smiled.

"Alright then, let's get looking." Maddie walked slowly down each aisle of the nursery. She paused to inspect leaves and read the tags attached to the trees. Kevin looked around and periodically would come over to check on Maddie's progress. An hour passed, and Maddie finally picked what she wanted.

"I think this Weeping Cherry tree is beautiful," Maddie said.

"Is this the one you want?" Kevin asked, putting his arm around her waist.

"Yes, I really like it."

"I think you made a perfect choice." Kevin lifted up the tree and led them to the checkout. After securing the tree in the back of his truck, they drove out of the nursery. Kevin drove at a leisurely pace along the familiar country roads. Maddie surveyed the farmland that dipped and curved, dotted occasionally yet regularly with barns and houses. They had both traveled these roads for years, but that day they held a new beauty. The rich, green landscape, freshly tilled earth, and bright, blue sky tickled her senses. When they neared the turn-off to Johnson's pond, it didn't register at first what they were doing. In only a few moments, Maddie became filled with dread. She looked at Kevin, a terrible feeling of panic now beginning to rise.

"Kevin, I can't do this. I can't go here." She felt the need to get out of the truck and run. She had never gone to Johnson's pond again after Matt's death. It was too painful.

"Maddie, you need to trust me. Do you trust me?" Kevin asked intently.

"I do. I really do, but I don't think I can handle this. It's too much, Kevin. It will hurt too much." Maddie was terrified. This was like a bad dream from which she couldn't escape. The thought of what had happened there made her recoil. She had thought of the accident many times over the years but had never attempted to come in person to see where it happened. The image of a broken rope hanging from the old tree had haunted her. She felt sick.

"Honey, there is nothing I would do to intentionally harm you. I think you need closure on what happened with your son. Remember how you told me that Ray never let you go to the pond when Matt died? How you just needed to go to him?" She nodded her head and tried to fight off tears. "You have never been back here since the accident. You have never visited this place and it haunts you. I'm here to help you. I thought we could find a peaceful place, away from the accident, and plant this tree in memory of Matt. I know it may sound stupid, but it would grow and live on and represent your love for him." He waited, and finally she nodded in agreement. She stayed silent as they walked along the path that led to the water. Kevin led her over to the bank, and she forced herself to look into the water. It was a peaceful, beautiful place. The blue-green water was calm but for a faint ripple from a playful fish. She could imagine the sound of kids laughing and splashing in the water. She turned to Kevin.

"Can you give me a few moments?" she asked. Kevin backed away.

"Take as long as you need," Kevin replied.

Maddie walked along the perimeter of the pond. She inhaled slowly and methodically, trying to stave off the tears that were about to flow. She finally made it to the place she had feared. It was the old tree with its branches reaching out towards the water. She noticed a new rope had been attached, and suddenly she was filled with dread as she imagined how many children had tempted fate to swing from these branches. She had the urge to climb the tree and cut the rope down. Maddie knew it wouldn't do any good. Someone would come and hang a new one. How could she have known that this childhood place, a place with so many happy memories, would one day take her child? It was cruel to think about. The way nature held such beauty and so much danger at the same time. The dark water, so cool and inviting, could swallow you up in one quick moment.

She sat down and drifted in her thoughts of Matt. How much she still missed him, and how she loved him, as much now as she ever did. Not knowing what to do, she bowed her head and said a quiet prayer, that God would help her work through her unresolved grief and that she would one day be able to think of Matt with peace in her heart. Maddie looked up to see Kevin on the far bank helping two young boys with their fishing line. She knew Kevin was a great dad by the way he interacted with children. He had such a big heart. He looked up at her and waved, saying goodbye to the boys as he began walking around the pond toward Maddie. Before Kevin reached her, she stood and said softly, "I'm sorry I was not here for you, baby. I will never forget you Matt. I love you." She wiped a stray tear from her eye and welcomed Kevin's embrace. He comforted her and, when she was ready, he asked her where she would like the tree planted. She decided that the spot where she was standing was as good as any. Her tree would overlook where Matt spent his last living moments. Mother and son would be connected in this little way. She knew that she probably would never come here again, but the thought of the tree in that place would be comforting to her.

— Chapter Thirty-Two —

Maddie and Kevin settled into a comfortable routine. She started her chemotherapy treatments but decided to do things differently this time around. Her doctor encouraged her to stay away from big crowds, so Maddie limited her outings to the doctor's office, her sister's, and home. She allowed herself walks outside but didn't go into restaurants. It sounded extreme, but it was cold and flu season, and she didn't want to take any chances of getting even the common cold. She knew that could be enough to do her in. Kevin's new occupation was a perfect fit for her plan. He did her shopping for her and delivered the groceries himself. He called her each night to check on her, hoping each night that she needed him to come over. Often, he would end up making her dinner or bring dessert, and they would snuggle on the couch watching TV or a movie. Her fondness for him grew more with each passing day. He saw her through the early symptoms of nausea, and she was surprised at how she seemed to tolerate it better than the last time around. Kevin was a good distraction. She never thought she would again feel the fluttering of her stomach that only happens during the glorious stages of new love. She felt warm when she thought of him and felt safe when she was near him. Kevin was attentive to her needs and cautious not to stay too late so she wouldn't get too tired. Maddie enjoyed the attention he lavished on her and found some humor in his overprotective behavior. Maddie stayed very optimistic about her prognosis. Kevin was more reserved and didn't bring up the fact that he was on the internet every night visiting medical websites to try to predict her prognosis. He called every evening to say goodnight, secretly needing the reassurance of her voice before he could rest. She was thankful for the slow pace of their courtship, especially since she was not feeling herself.

Thankfully, her treatment course went well, and Maddie was able to stay home for the entire time without returning for a hospital admission. That was a huge victory for her. She was on antibiotics for part of the time and had to have a transfusion once but, other than that, it was smooth sailing as far as the chemotherapy was concerned. Her doctor had said that all looked well and that, after some follow-up tests, they might be done with her cancer treatment. Maddie and Kevin were elated. Kevin wanted to celebrate right away, but Maddie was reluctant until they got all her test results back. She didn't want to get all excited, only to be crushed later with bad news. The doctor scheduled her for an appointment to go over the results of the testing, and Kevin accompanied her for the appointment. It had been three weeks since she took her last dose of chemotherapy, and she was starting to feel pretty good. Her appetite was returning and, fortunately, no fevers had begun.

Kevin followed Maddie back to the treatment room. It was comforting to have him there. They had fallen in love, and she could no longer picture her life without him. He had become her strength through this last stage of her battle. He stood beside her and held her hand. They felt uneasy but managed to smile. Kevin kissed the top of her head and told her to hang in there. They'd have the news soon. It was hard not to feel nervous. Their future was riding on what the doctor had to say.

Dr. Dillon entered the room. He placed Maddie's chart on the counter and greeted them. "You are looking well, Maddie. How have you been feeling?"

"Really good. I'm surprised how I've bounced back so quickly," she replied.

"Well, let me get right to what you have been waiting to hear. I'm pleased with all your test results. The last round of chemotherapy went better than I had hoped. I think we are able to hold off on another round for now." He paused as Maddie let out a sigh of relief. "I'm happy to say I don't need to see you for a while. I was thinking we could shoot for around three months and see how you are faring."

"Wow, I don't know what to say. I'm so relieved to hear that!" She turned to Kevin and saw the relief on his face as well. He had feared they would hear bad news. He wanted her to be well. He wanted a lifetime with her. Kevin and Maddie thanked the doctor and made sure to heed the advice he gave for her next three months. They would do everything recommended in order to ensure that she would be okay. As they walked out of the office and into the parking lot, Kevin couldn't help but lift her up and swing her around. He didn't care that he looked foolish. He was so happy she was okay.

They were both elated as Kevin drove her home. They had a light lunch at Maddie's place, and he left shortly after they had finished eating. He planned to pick her up later for dinner and suggested that she wear something nice. Maddie was happy that she had been able to maintain her weight throughout the last treatment and could wear a dress without looking lost in it. After she finished getting ready, she was pleased with herself, wig and all. Kevin picked her up at six. He told her she looked beautiful and that he was really looking forward to their night together.

Without telling Maddie where they were going, he drove them about forty-five minutes out into the country. They reached a vineyard and pulled onto a long, curving drive. Rows and rows of grapevines lined the path and, in the distance, they could see the large, stone house that was in the center of the small, rolling hills of the vineyard. He parked the car and escorted her out. She surveyed the beautiful landscape that surrounded the restaurant. There were people gathered in a gazebo in the distance, and Maddie could hear their distant laughter. By way of a pebbled walkway lined with ivy, Kevin led her to the front door of the house. Candles were lit in old-fashioned, lantern sconces on each side of the doorway. Inside, there was a roaring fire and small tables where a few couples and one larger group chatted and sipped wine. There was a small bar set up in the corner of the room, and the walls were lined with wine bottles. The room was awash in a soft glow, and she could smell the scent of fresh herbs and cedar. She had never experienced anything like it. Kevin had her sit down at a table, and she watched as he went over to the bar. He spoke to the lady behind it, and she left briefly, returning with a platter of cheese, fresh fruit, and bread. Kevin brought it over to the table, and the lady from the bar followed with a bottle of wine and two glasses. Maddie and Kevin conversed quietly, enjoying the fare before them. He stroked her back, and she felt the warmth of his gaze upon her. Leaning towards her, Kevin placed a light kiss on her lips. The effects of the wine and the romance of being there with him were almost too much for her to handle. Holding hands, they watched the flames of the fire flicker before them.

A short while later, the hostess called Kevin's name, then a waiter led them through the dining area towards a room at the far end of the house. As they walked through the doorway, they could see two tables, but only the far one was set. There were candles lit around a bouquet of flowers in the center of the table. The waiter explained to them that this room was the original breakfast room of the house and that it had a secret door that led to the kitchen. The walls featured floor-to-ceiling windows and, in the morning, the room glowed with the first of the sun's rays. Since it was evening, they could see softly glowing lanterns romantically hanging from the trees outside the house. After seating them, the waiter appeared a few moments later with a cart containing the ingredients for Caesar salad. Except for his polished explanation of the ingredients, he prepared the dish silently. Maddie was fascinated. She hadn't realized all that went into the salad, especially the anchovy. They enjoyed more bread, and then the entrée arrived. Kevin had ordered for both of them the same entrée of grilled salmon and fresh asparagus. Dessert was a berry tart with fresh cream.

After enjoying their feast, they lingered over coffee and savored the moment. Maddie was aglow with happiness. It was a perfect evening. She gazed over at Kevin and couldn't keep from smiling. Kevin had arranged the entire evening himself. No wonder he wanted to celebrate right away. Had she known this is what she would be getting, she would have taken him up on it. Kevin slowly rose from his chair, and Maddie started to do the same when Kevin said, "Please, allow me." He motioned that he was going to pull back her chair but instead knelt down beside her.

He cradled her hands in his and took a slow deep breath. Maddie looked down at him and felt herself start to tremble ever so slightly. She smiled at him. Immediately, her heart began to race because she realized what he was about to do.

"Can I kiss you first?" he said as he leaned toward her. She bent down and their lips met. He softly kissed her, then pulled away gently so he could look into her eyes.

"Maddie," he said softly. "I can't remember the last time I've felt this good. I have been completely mesmerized by you. Deep in my soul, I have always believed that we were meant to be together. I felt it when we were teenagers, and there is no denying my feelings for you now."

Maddie blushed. He continued, "I've often thought, over the years, of what I would say to you if I ever had this opportunity. It's here now, and I feel like there are no words brilliant enough to capture my emotions when it comes

243

to you. I love you. I love the way you laugh, your wise eyes, and your amazing inner strength." He paused. "To have gone through all you have and still be the wonderful person you are . . . I think you are amazing! I can't imagine my life now without you in it. Maddie, I would be honored if you would accept this proposal and become my beloved, my wife."

Maddie didn't hesitate with her reply. "Of course I would, Kevin. You have changed my life. You have given me so much happiness and hope. I never could have dreamed I could be this happy. I would love to marry you."

He stood and guided her up from her chair. They embraced, feeling as if they already were one. Kevin then placed an antique, diamond ring on her finger. As they drove home in the moonlight, the sparkle from her hand warmed her heart. Kevin had swept her off her feet.

– CHAPTER THIRTY-THREE –

After a brief engagement of five months, Maddie and Kevin were married in a small ceremony on Lisa's farm in front of family and close friends. She had decided to have a dress made for the occasion. Maddie didn't want a traditional white gown this time around. She wanted everything to be different. She was able to find an old picture of herself in the pale, yellow dress she had worn to her prom. She had never felt more beautiful than she did that night. She remembered clearly the look on Kevin's face when he saw her. Not that he would remember what she wore then, but she decided to fashion an updated version of the dress. She would explain the dress to him later. She knew that Kevin would appreciate the meaning behind it. Maddie's hair by then had grown out enough so that she no longer needed a wig. She found a beaded headband that would compliment her shorter style. Lisa stood as a witness, as did Kevin's daughter, Molly, and his son, Ryan. It was good to have all of her loved ones surrounding her. She had been accepted into Kevin's family with open arms and had formed a good relationship with his children.

After the wedding, they enjoyed a barbeque style reception. Bright and early the next day, they were off on the first real vacation in Maddie's life. Two weeks in the Hawaiian Islands was more than she could imagine.

Maddie adjusted her wide-brimmed hat as her husband of a few days splashed around in the ocean. He was having a ball, and Maddie enjoyed watching him. He was so full of life and had shown her more of the world than she ever dreamed she would see. She had been trapped in a small, country town, and now she was breathing in the warm, tropical air of a place far away from Westville. She could not have imagined how her life would have changed once

Kevin reentered it. He walked towards her, completely soaked, and pulled Maddie up from her beach chair. He led her out into the clear, blue water. Until this vacation, she had not been in the water since Matt had died. She had promised herself that she would never swim again. Kevin had worked her though it, and she now realized that she didn't have to hang on to the promises she had made then. Those promises were made to herself as a way of coping with the pain of losing Matt. He led her out to the deeper waters, encouraging her to trust him. He could touch the bottom but she was several inches shorter than he and could not. He held her close, and she allowed him to support her with his strong arms. She looked at him and felt such a deep love for him. Tears welled in her eyes as she looked at him.

"What's the matter honey?" he said in a soft laugh. "Don't cry." He held her close as the water lapped around them.

"I'm sorry. I'm just really happy, that's all." She held him tight.

"I know. Me, too." He stroked her short, cropped hair.

She pulled back to see his face. "I'm overwhelmed. I can't believe I'm here with you and have survived all that has happened. Excuse the metaphor, but it's like I have been treading water for so long. I've been close to drowning for so long, and now I can finally stand on solid ground. You are that solid ground for me, Kevin. I don't know what I would have done if you hadn't come back into my life. I would probably be dead by now." Kevin looked at her as if to say it was not true. "I know I would have given up a long time ago."

"Well, you didn't, and look at you now. You are Mrs. Brewster, husband of the great grocer," he laughed and she smiled. "Everything is going to be okay now, I promise. We have our whole lives ahead of us."

They had a magical time on their honeymoon. Kevin had arranged a helicopter tour of the islands, horseback riding, and many romantic dinners, during which they saw many beautiful sunsets. After the honeymoon, they returned to live in Kevin's home. Maddie was comfortable there with him and felt no need to change anything. She loved being able to look anywhere and see Kevin's touch on things. Most of her belongings consisted of what she had purchased new for her apartment. They held no sentimental value. All of her previous furnishings had been left at the farm. Over the course of their trip, she had many opportunities for reflection and made the decision to sign over the farm to the boys. Randall and Johnny had proven they could handle the responsibilities of it, and she was ready to sever her ties with the place. They deserved to call it their own. It brought the closure she needed to feel complete in her new life.

As a wedding gift, Kevin had built a studio for Maddie in the sunroom of the house. She was wonderfully surprised. With Kevin's encouragement, she had begun painting every day. She started with landscapes and stills, loving every minute she spent in the studio. She would paint for most of the day and stop in time to cook dinner for them. She looked forward to seeing him come home each night. It was not just the fact that they were newlyweds that made them want to be together. It was a mature appreciation for each moment they were blessed to have together.

A couple of months passed, and Maddie began to harbor a nagging feeling that she was meant to be doing something more than staying at home being self absorbed. Something important had been left undone. She couldn't put her finger on it for a while, until one day it dawned on her. The events of the past year had been put in place for her, to show her what she was meant to do with the gift that she had been given. It was no coincidence that she had become friends with Delores. Her mind started to run a mile a minute, and she had to stop herself before she got carried away. It was exciting, and Maddie could hardly wait to talk to Kevin about it. Listening intently, he gave her his whole-hearted support. She had been given many gifts, her survival being the most important, followed by Kevin, and her art. She wanted to incorporate all three and had come up with the perfect way to do it. She had received so much personal satisfaction when she painted Delores' portrait and had been touched by the family's reaction. She wanted to experience that again.

What unfolded was a ministry of sorts. Maddie gained permission from the hospital to offer her services as a volunteer to paint portraits of whomever requested one. Starting slowly, she got to know the nursing staff, and soon became a mainstay on the palliative care unit. It was a floor designated for patients who were too sick for aggressive treatment. They were the patients who wanted to die peacefully and comfortably. It was hard at first to see so many people suffering, but she learned that life is not forever and there is a beauty in recognizing death will come and being able to accept it with grace. Having been so close to death herself, she could relate in her own way to what they might be feeling. She was overwhelmed many a time at the extent to which that some had to suffer before they were taken. It was something she never would understand but found great satisfaction and purpose in providing even a small gesture of comfort to those who were passing on from this life. Over a period of two years, she painted over one hundred portraits, including one of Kevin's father before he passed. Kevin's job offered the financial means for her project but, as people began to take notice of what she was doing, donations started flowing in. They offered her a small office in the hospital, but Maddie preferred her own studio. It was there that she could recreate on canvas whatever memory the patient or family requested. It comforted Maddie to know that she could provide a beautiful focal point in an otherwise sterile environment. It was her goal to capture a moment of joy in their lives, something they could reflect on and possibly drift off to.

It was midmorning when Maddie reached the hospital. She had delivered her latest portrait and stopped by the nurse's station to find out what her next project would be. She was surprised to find that the nurses didn't have anyone in mind for her yet. The census was low, so they only had a few patients on the unit. They asked her to come back tomorrow, confident that they would have someone in mind. Maddie was not disappointed. After finishing each portrait, she felt emotionally spent. She tried not to get attached to her subjects but it was nearly impossible. She always made it a point to spend time with the family and the patient prior to painting. Maddie felt her heart was more into the portrait that way. She didn't want to paint as a job; she wanted to paint as a gift of herself.

Maddie turned her thoughts to how she would spend the remainder of the day. Kevin would be working until seven that day, and she decided she didn't want to go home just yet. She walked down to the hospital cafeteria and bought herself a muffin and some coffee. She sipped and munched as she walked to the car. An idea had popped in her head, and she decided to visit the boys on the farm. She hadn't been out in a few months and felt the need to check in on them.

As she pulled into her old driveway, she noticed her brother-in-law's truck parked near the barn. He was still actively involved in helping the boys. Maddie suspected that since her nephews had gone off to college, Doug had gotten lonely. Lisa told her that Doug spent a fair amount of time with the boys and had taught them a lot. As she entered the barn, she heard the sound of Doug laughing with Randall. The resemblance of Randall to Ray was still shocking to her. It was clearer than ever to her now as she looked at him. He was now twenty-one years old and had grown into a very handsome, young man. He was ready to finish his last year of college and then would join Johnny back on the farm.

When he heard Maddie laughing with the other men, Johnny came out of the office. She counted them all as family. Johnny walked up and greeted her with a big hug. They talked and looked around the place showing Maddie all that they had accomplished. Maddie was happy to see flowers planted out in front of the house. The old farmhouse had a fresh coat of paint, and she noticed they had added shutters to all the windows. As they neared the house, the front door opened and a petite woman with long, dark hair appeared. She was a very pretty girl and had dark brown eyes. For a moment, Maddie thought of herself at that age, living at the farm, young and carefree. Following her was Nicole, Johnny's wife of three years, proudly showing evidence of her first pregnancy. She was due to deliver a son any day. What she saw touched Maddie. The younger girl took her place beside Randy, and they interlocked hands. Randy introduced her as Danielle, his girlfriend. He said that after he was done with college, he was going to build a house on the land and then settle down with Danielle. The girl blushed when he spoke.

Maddie asked the boys if they would mind if she took a walk for a while. Drawn to her favorite path, she surprised herself by saying she missed the land and felt it calling to her. As she walked alone, she thought of the boys and of the lives they now led. They were building their families and establishing memories on her farm. Soon, Johnny would be a daddy, and another young child would roam these trails in search of some exciting new adventure. She hoped they would have many children, for she thought that the farm was a wonderful place to grow up. There was so much to explore and do. The landscape was breathtaking, and Maddie was glad that once again she could appreciate it.

As she neared the fence that marked her turn-around, she again surveyed the old Shultz place. It, too, had changed since she last traveled the path. The renters were gone and, from the looks of the reconstruction, whoever lived there now planned to stay. As she stood looking, a young man rounded the house carrying a bag of tools. When he saw Maddie, he waved hello and, to her surprise, started walking towards her. As he neared, Maddie struggled to recognize him. He immediately must have known who she was because he smiled warmly as he grew near.

"Mrs. Stevens, it's good to see you." Maddie didn't correct him because she was still trying to place the face that was greeting her. "I can tell by your face you have no idea who I am. It's Ben. Ben Shultz."

"Ben, I'm sorry. I haven't seen you in years. How are you?" she said, giving him a hug.

"It's been a long time, but it's good to be back."

"Did you buy the place?" Maddie asked, hoping he had. She never liked having strangers living in her old friend's house.

"Yes, we did. My wife and I decided to buy it from the family's estate, and now we are knee deep in renovations. It's quite a job."

"I am beyond thrilled that you are living here. I had hoped someone in the family would reclaim it. I have such fond memories of your grandmother here."

"Me, too. I remember coming out here as a little guy and I loved it. After Grammy died, no one wanted to come back here. It was never the same without her. They rented it for years, and recently decided they should just get rid of it. After much convincing, I talked my wife into moving the family out here. The kids love it."

"How about your wife?" Maddie asked.

"Let's just say it's growing on her. Once the main house is complete, I promised her an in-ground pool. I had to bribe her in some way," Ben smiled.

"Give her time. She'll grow to love it out here."

Maddie talked with Ben and filled him in on her new marriage and new life. She mentioned Johnny and his wife, and Ben said he would plan on stopping down to meet them. He would love for his wife to meet a friend in the area. Maddie said goodbye and started walking back towards the house. Time was all it took to restore life and love to this land. She had a peace about all she had learned from her visit to her old home. Whether you are part of it or not, life moves on. Whether good or bad, the events that mark a place only exist for those who witness them. The next ones to pass on the same path will see things in a completely different way from the ones who trod there before.

Upon returning home, Maddie felt inspired to paint. She mixed a colorful palette and sat down to contemplate what to do. She sat for a while thinking of the day, then started with a simple landscape. She became lost in her thoughts and allowed herself to paint freely. When she painted for herself, she became unaware of her surroundings and drifted off into a different place. It was a quiet, creative place from which she worked by pure instinct. She had painted for several hours, and the finished product warmed her heart, bringing back fond memories of herself as a young woman. A slightly plump woman in her mid-sixties sat on the ground near a garden. Mrs. Shultz had beautiful, white hair that framed her face in a soft bob. She wore a pale, blue dress and a calico-print apron. A young woman in a pink dress patterned with daisies sat beside her. Cradled in the young lady's arms was a sleeping infant swaddled in a blue and white, checked blanket. *Matt was a very happy baby, so sweet*, Maddie thought to herself as she looked at his image on the canvas. She reached out to touch him, stopping before she reached him. Maddie had painted rosy cheeks on his delicate face. She sighed deeply as she thought of him as an infant and tried to remember his scent. The old farmhouse stood tall and white, framed by a bright, blue sky and glowing sun. The trio sat under a tree on a handmade quilt. Maddie closed her eyes, inhaled deeply, and could almost smell the freshly cut, green grass.

Lost in her thoughts, Maddie did not hear the garage door open. Kevin called her name from the kitchen, his voice breaking through the daydream she was envisioning.

"I'm in here," she called to him.

"You're right where I expected you'd be. Working on a new project?" he asked, embracing her from behind. "Mm, you smell good," he commented as he gently kissed her neck.

"Thank you." Maddie turned and kissed him on the cheek. Kevin pulled up a chair beside her.

"That's pretty. Who are they?" Kevin inquired.

"That's me," she said pointing to the young woman holding the baby, "and that's Matt," she said, voice trailing.

"And the old woman?" Kevin asked.

"That was my friend, Mrs. Shultz. She lived up the road from us. I learned so much from her over the years. She was like a mother to me," Maddie said.

"What made you think of painting this today?"

"I got done early at the hospital and decided to drive out to the farm. I saw the boys. Doug was there, too."

"Oh yeah?" Kevin asked, prompting for more.

253

"He really likes those boys. I think he hangs out there more than we realize." Maddie smiled. "I took a walk and ended up running into Ben Shultz, Mrs. Shultz's grandson. He and his family recently bought her old place. He is doing a beautiful job restoring the house."

"We'll have to drive out there sometime. I'd like to see it," Kevin said, taking off his shoes and stretching his legs.

"We should. I came back home and felt like painting. I guess I was a bit nostalgic, and this is what came out of it," Maddie said, once again admiring the scene she had painted. "I always felt at peace when I was around her . . ."

"It's beautiful, Maddie. You should hang it up," Kevin said, proud of his wife's obvious talent.

"I think I will. Looking at it makes me happy," Maddie said, glancing at her watch. "Yikes, it's six-thirty. I really lost track of time. Are you starving? I was planning on making dinner."

"How about we just make some eggs?" Kevin suggested.

"Sounds good. I've got some of that raisin bread left from the bakery. We could have toast."

"It's decided then. I'm going to go change clothes, then I'll help," Kevin said.

Maddie rinsed her brushes, tidied her workspace, and hung up her smock. She joined Kevin in the kitchen.

"Good day today?" Maddie asked as she set the table.

"It wasn't bad for a Wednesday. I caught Mr. Jaffers eating an apple again."

"Again?" Maddie said laughing.

"Yes," he said feigning irritation. "I don't know what to do with him. I've tried to tell him that we charge by the pound, and an apple doesn't cost 25 cents anymore. He just doesn't get it," Kevin said and chuckled thinking of the old man.

"I think it's cute," Maddie said.

"I guess. He's what, ninety? I guess he deserves a free apple when he wants one."

"I think so, too," Maddie said, putting the bread in the toaster.

"It drives the produce manager crazy."

"Chuck has way too much free time if he's stressing about Mr. Jaffers. When does he come in, maybe once a week?"

"It depends on whether or not we have a good delivery of apples," Kevin smiled.

After the impromptu dinner, they decided to take a walk around town. It was a beautiful summer night, the sun setting in reds and purples. Lawnmowers buzzed the familiar hum of a summer melody. Giggles and shrieks came from barefoot children as they jumped and reached for the glowing bugs that speckled the sky. Maddie commented on the colorful, overflowing flowerboxes and hanging baskets that decorated the front porches they passed. The air was warm, the breeze refreshing.

"I was thinking, Kevin," Maddie said.

"You were thinking?" he teased.

"Yes, I was thinking . . . if I were to paint something for you, what would you want me to paint?"

"Hmm . . . you, maybe." He smiled at her.

"You have enough pictures of me. Tell me something I don't know. Somewhere you've been that has left an impression on you."

"Well, let me think a minute." Kevin took a moment to respond. He reached for Maddie's hand and held it as they walked. "What stands out the most from my childhood were the times I would go fishing with my dad. We usually would go to a local lake or pond and take out his old, blue, fishing boat for the day. When we vacationed as a family, it was usually around a body of water. Mom and Dad both loved the water."

"Sounds nice," Maddie commented.

"One trip I'll always remember is our trip up the east coast. We stopped at several beach towns and ended the trip in Bar Harbor, Maine. It is a quaint town located right next to the ocean. There are cute little shops and bed & breakfasts scattered around the town. The Acadia National Park on Mount Desert Island is just beautiful. The view from up there is breathtaking. The Atlantic that far up is so clear, the water so cool . . ." Kevin said, sighing as if he longed for the place.

"Sounds wonderful," Maddie said.

"On one particular day, Dad took me fishing off a lobster dock. We took some bait and fished, watching the lobster boats come and go. At the end of the dock was a square-shaped, simple, white building. Inside, a counter lined one side. A man with a white apron greeted us when we entered. 'You look like some hungry folks,' he said as he handled a large lobster. A big, glass tank held several fresh lobsters, swimming their last swim. Behind the man, steaming stockpots covered a stove. A typical order consisted of a fresh-boiled lobster, corn on the cob, and a heavy-handed scoop of coleslaw. They presented the feast in a white, cardboard box lined with wax paper. Inside, a cup overflowed with melted butter, making the bottom of the box greasy. Dad bought us each a box and a root beer. We took them outside and sat on an old picnic table. It was the best lunch I've ever had. We threw the scraps we didn't eat over to some anxiously waiting seagulls lingering on the dock."

"They're not stupid," Maddie said, laughing.

"No, they were probably the best fed seagulls on the ocean."

"That would be a fun scene to paint," Maddie said.

"I'll have to take you there so you can see it firsthand," Kevin said, meaning every word of it.

"I would love that," Maddie said

"We'll do it then."

They turned and decided to head back toward home, all the while chatting excitedly about planning another vacation. Maddie wanted to see the world through Kevin's eyes, to be where he'd been, to experience the places he loved. She already felt she loved them, just from what formed in her mind as he talked. Maddie stopped to tie her shoe. When she stood, she suddenly felt dizzy.

"You okay?" Kevin asked.

"Yeah, I just got up too fast."

"You need to rest for a minute? We went a little far tonight. Maybe I wore you out," Kevin said, the concern evident on his face.

"I'm okay," she said, trying to shake off the odd feeling she had. They continued walking but, again, Maddie had to stop. She felt like she was in a daze, her vision hazy. "Kevin, I feel really weird," Maddie admitted.

"Do you need to sit down?"

"I don't know. I feel so weird . . ." Maddie's body began shaking in uncontrolled waves. Kevin grabbed her quickly and lowered her to the ground. The quick, uncontrolled movements continued and intensified. Kevin called her name, but she was unable to answer him.

"Maddie, speak to me honey!" Kevin said urgently, holding her head so she wouldn't hurt herself. Finally, she began to calm down and slowly was able to speak.

"What happened?" she asked anxiously.

"I'm not sure, Maddie. I think you might have had a seizure."

"Oh, no," Maddie cried.

"It's okay, honey, you're okay," Kevin said, trying to reassure her. Maddie tried to sit up. "Are you sure you don't want to lie down for a minute? Maybe you shouldn't move."

"I think I'm alright. Can you help me sit up?" Maddie said. Kevin helped her and supported her weight against him. They sat for a few minutes, and then Maddie decided she wanted to try to stand. Once she was up, she felt she was strong enough to walk.

"Why don't you wait here and I'll run and get the car. I can ask if you can sit on their porch," he said, pointing to a brightly lit house not far from where they were standing. Maddie and Kevin were the only ones outside. The sun had gone down, and the kids were in their houses, most likely in the tub getting their bedtime baths.

"No, I'm okay. We are five minutes from home. I can make it. We'll just go slow," Maddie said.

"You're worrying me, Maddie." Kevin secured his arm around her waist and held her close to himself to steady her.

"I'll be fine," she said, taking a few steps forward with Kevin's help. Without warning, the convulsions began again. He held her tight. The second seizure was longer, and Kevin found himself close to tears when it was over. Maddie was groggy, and he had difficulty keeping her alert. Kevin fished his cell phone out of his pocket and dialed 911. He didn't move her for fear of yet another seizure. He rested his hand on her chest so he could feel her breathing.

The siren of the ambulance was enough to stir Maddie. She started to panic when she awoke to the commotion. Kevin stroked her hair and kissed her forehead. "I'm here honey, you'll be okay," he kept repeating, trying to reassure her. The paramedics strapped Maddie to the gurney and hoisted her up into the ambulance. They allowed Kevin to ride along, and he sat near Maddie's head.

"Kevin, I'm so sorry," Maddie cried.

"Don't be sorry, sweetie. You are going to be alright." He kissed her hand. "I'm not going to leave you."

"Kevin, promise me something," Maddie said, looking into his eyes.

"Anything, Maddie," Kevin said fighting back tears.

"Promise me you'll take me to Maine, to Bar Harbor," Maddie pleaded.

"I promise sweetheart, I will."

– Chapter Thirty-Four –

As the ambulance doors closed, Maddie saw the last sliver of sun escape beneath the horizon. Twilight beauty had been replaced with the unnatural glare of fluorescent lights buzzing above her. Trying not to appear frightened, Maddie smiled at the paramedics assisting her. Years had passed since her episode in the store, but here she was again traveling toward an uncertain fate.

"How are you feeling, Mrs. Brewster?" a young brunette asked, then smiled sympathetically exposing matching dimples in her cheeks. "My name is Mindy, and this fella here is Jason." Maddie glanced his way at the introduction. Jason looked to be all of twenty years old, wore a crew-cut haircut, and bit his lip while he worked.

"Hey, how's it going?" was his response as he pumped up the blood pressure cuff on her arm.

How's it going? Maddie thought to herself. "It's going pretty terrible," she said aloud, not apologizing for her frankness.

"I'm going to take a listen to your chest, Mrs. Brewster," Mindy said and leaned towards her. Maddie could smell the hint of rose perfume on Mindy's wrist.

"Call me Maddie, please."

"Okay, Maddie. If you can just relax and breathe normally, I'll be done in a minute." Maddie closed her eyes and tried to calm herself. She listened as Jason talked with the driver and heard him say they'd be at the emergency room in ten minutes. Maddie had lost all sense of direction as she felt the ambulance shift and turn at various intervals. The small windows offered only dark skies and sporadic streetlights that flashed quickly by. As they came to a final stop, Maddie watched the windows flicker from red to white, white to red. The noise of the paramedics gathering

261

equipment seemed muffled, and her fingers began to tingle as if falling asleep. Her vision narrowed and, once again, she was lost in the grip of another seizure.

*   *   *

A familiar scent aroused Maddie, and she jumped at the sight of Kevin's face so close to hers.

"Maddie, Maddie, calm down, it's okay, honey. It's just me. I'm here," Kevin said, trying to soothe her. He smoothed her hair away from her face and leaned in to gently kiss her forehead.

She looked at him, then at the room around her. Her vision was still hazy and she felt very groggy. "Am I at the hospital? Maddie asked.

"Yes, we are." He watched her brow furrow as she contemplated what had brought her there. "Do you remember anything about tonight? Our walk?" Kevin asked.

"Not really. Bits and pieces, maybe," Maddie said, still searching to understand what was happening. "Did I fall?"

"You did, a bit . . ." Kevin paused to compose himself. "You had a seizure, honey. Actually, you've had a few." A tear dropped from his eye, and he annoyingly wiped it away with his shirtsleeve.

"A seizure?" Maddie said, then contemplated the word. "Why would I have a seizure?" she said and looked to Kevin for an answer.

"We're waiting to find out. We'll know soon enough. Are you comfortable? Warm enough?" Kevin said as he tucked the sheet up under her chin.

"I'm fine." Maddie searched her mind for what she knew about seizures. Lisa had a seizure during labor with the twins. She remembered it had something to do with her blood pressure. "Is my blood pressure okay?" she asked Kevin.

"It's been fine. Everything they've checked so far has been normal," Kevin said with an optimistic tone. He looked at her quickly but was careful not to hold his gaze too long to hers. Maddie could sense his uneasiness and reached for his hand. He squeezed it and didn't let go.

*   *   *

Five hours had passed, and Maddie had endured lab draws, an IV, CAT scan, and a chest x-ray. Kevin had endured three cups of coffee, a solitary walk outside to compose himself, a distracting conversation with a guy in the waiting room about how the Reds were doing, and a splitting headache.

Little was said about the test results. "Nothing critical," a resident physician said as he described the plan to watch her overnight in the ICU. The anti-seizure medication she received seemed to be working, and Maddie was able to doze on and off in between tests and assessments. Finally, at two a.m., workers wheeled her to her room. They both agreed it was best not to contact Maddie's family until later in the morning. Maddie said goodnight to Kevin, who then went to rest in the ICU family lounge. He said he couldn't bear the thought of her being there alone. The nurses were kind enough to direct him to a chair that converted into a bed. He was the only occupant in the dimly lit room.

When the sun crested over the parking garage next to the hospital, the rays shone into the window and gently woke Kevin from his sleep. Looking at his watch, the time revealed that only three hours had passed since he had fallen asleep. Maddie's eyes were closed when he entered her room, and he carefully moved a chair close to her bed so he could watch her. Before long, he heard two women talking and they stopped at the desk right outside of Maddie's room. Only a curtain separated them from him. The light yellow scrubs and white tennis shoes gave away that they were nurses. He listened as they discussed Maddie's case.

"This is Maddie Brewster. She came to us from ER around two this morning. A squad brought her in last night with complaints of seizures. She has a history of endometrial cancer, status post chemotherapy, and radiation of around three to four years ago. Surgical history is hysterectomy with tumor removal. No other pertinent history. CAT scan last night showed a large mass in her brain. No definitive diagnosis yet. Sounds like brain mets to me . . ." the nightshift nurse said to the dayshift nurse taking over.

"Oh, that's too bad. She's so young," the dayshift nurse responded.

"I know. I hate to see it in the young ones. Her husband is here with her. Vital signs have been stable and she has no complaints of pain. The monitor looks good. No seizures since I've had her, and she's been resting quietly."

"Do they know?" the dayshift nurse asked.

"Not yet. We're waiting for the attending to make rounds to break the news."

"Alright," the dayshift nurse said with a sigh. "Ready to move on to room three?"

"Sure. That's Mr. Reinhold. Seventy-eight-year-old man, had a stroke yesterday—" the nightshift nurse's voice trailed off as they moved away from Maddie's room.

Silence, interrupted by the rhythmic beep of the machines, was all that was left. Kevin slowly let out the breath he had been holding and turned to look at Maddie. She was awake and had heard everything the nurses had said. She looked at Kevin and her lips began to quiver.

"It doesn't sound good, does it?" she managed to say, voice trembling.

"No sweetheart, it doesn't." Kevin stood from the chair and sat on the side of her bed. He leaned over and embraced Maddie and felt her wilt in his arms.

— CHAPTER THIRTY-FIVE —

"Inoperable . . . metastasis . . . poor prognosis . . . buy time with two different types of radiation . . . no hope for remission . . ." These were words and a few phrases Maddie would remember. She chose to focus on the tree she could see outside from the window as the doctor spoke to them. Maddie didn't really need to know the details of the tests or how her disease had so sneakily progressed. She didn't want to know what was medically available to her, didn't want to endure more treatments or last ditch efforts. She was dying once again and there was no use running from it anymore. When she heard those nurses talking a little too loudly that morning, she had made peace with what was happening. Maddie had prepared for this day. She knew she was living on borrowed time, and the happiness she had found with Kevin couldn't last forever. God had not forgotten that prayer she had uttered so long ago. He was being kind with the delay in his answer. Maddie looked at Kevin and saw that he was trying to be strong as he listened to the doctor. He asked all the right questions and tried to be optimistic in asking for the best possible options. He never took his hand away from hers, and she could feel him hold it a little tighter whenever the doctor said something negative. When they were alone again, he turned, eyes revealing such sadness and despair.

"You okay, honey?" Maddie said and drew him close to her. Kevin rested his head on her chest and they were silent. She caressed his hair, hoping to calm him. Maddie spoke softly in almost a whisper. "Kevin, I think it's time." Kevin didn't move.

"Time?" he said, voice hoarse with emotion. She could tell he was starting to cry.

"I think this time we won't be able to beat the cancer." She paused to collect her thoughts as she felt Kevin quietly tremble beneath her. "I think we need to prepare ourselves for . . ." Kevin lifted his head up in an attempt to delay what she needed to say.

"Do you even want to talk about what the doctor has said? Should we think about trying to give you some more time? Us more time?"

"I don't think it will make much of a difference. From what I gathered, we are talking maybe a few months . . ." Maddie stopped. Putting a time limit on her life was something she had told herself she didn't want to do.

"I'm not ready, Maddie. We haven't had enough time," Kevin said.

"I know," was all she could say.

"Can we talk about it later? Can we wait to make a decision?" Kevin looked at her, eyes pleading.

"It doesn't seem like we have that option. It's happening now, sweetie. What we have treaded lightly around these last few years has found us again. God is calling me home, Kevin." Maddie tried to sound strong for him. They'd had many heart-to-heart talks about what they would do if the cancer returned. It was easy to make decisions then. It seemed so clear. Now, with Kevin vulnerable and afraid, she wanted to change her mind to please him, but that would go against what she knew she wanted. To live her last days in peace, no treatments, just peace, is what appealed to her.

"Can we just go back to yesterday when I found you painting in your studio?" Kevin said. "It doesn't make sense. You looked so healthy, so beautiful. How, only a day later, can you be lying in a hospital bed with a brain tumor?" Kevin ran his fingers through his hair and lowered his head.

"It doesn't make sense, I know, honey. I wish I could go back, too. I wish I could go back and do a lot of things. I wish I could change the past so I wouldn't be hurting you now." Maddie felt the tears come. "I'm so sorry that I've let you get attached to me and now I'm going to leave you. If only Ray hadn't died . . ."

"Maddie don't talk like that. Please don't regret the time we've had together. I'm glad Ray died. It's twisted, I know, but had he not died, you'd probably have passed a long time ago. Listen to me." Kevin now was directly in her face, his hands clasping her cheeks so she had to look at him. "I would do it all over again if I knew I'd only have a year to love you, a half a year, it doesn't matter. Having the opportunity to be with you, to love you, and have you love me as strongly right back is worth any pain I'll endure in seeing you go." Kevin was on the brink of tears. "I don't want you to leave me, I can't stand the thought of it, and it makes me physically sick to think of you dying. One thing is certain—you will die as my wife and not his. You will be loved and cherished until you take your last breath. You were meant to be with me, and I will carry you to your resting place." Kevin stopped and wiped the tears from his eyes. He looked at Maddie and managed to smile weakly at her. "This is so hard," he said, voice cracking.

"I know," Maddie said and reached for him. They held each other in silence as the gravity of her condition settled in.

Later that evening, nurses took Maddie to have another medication port put in. This would enable her to receive medication if her condition worsened and she could no longer take something by mouth for the pain or nausea she was bound to endure. She had not wanted to do it at first, for it reminded her of her previous treatments and the misery that ensued from them. Her doctor was gracious with his time, and talked to her at length about what to expect in terms of symptoms and the progression of her disease. He outlined a treatment plan to keep her comfortable, and he would be available to tweak the plan as needed for the unpredictable course on which she was about to embark. He complimented Maddie and Kevin on their courage and, again, stressed his availability to them day or night.

The doctor discharged Maddie the next morning, and they hoped it would be the last time she would have to spend time in a hospital. When they arrived home, Lisa and her dad were waiting for them on the front porch. Tears were shed over coffee and donuts, and quiet acceptance soon followed. They had been through this before with Maddie's mother and commented on how it would be easier if they hadn't. Watching a loved one die of cancer is not something a person wants to experience twice.

"I'm not Mom," Maddie said, trying to comfort them. We'll just have to see wait and see how I do," she said and looked at Kevin, hoping for some reinforcement.

Kevin cleared his throat before he spoke. "Her doctor has been great. He's prepared us for just about anything. He also has us set up with hospice." At the mention of Hospice, Maddie's dad got up from his seat and walked over to look out the window. Maddie motioned for Lisa to get up to go to him, but she shook her head no. She whispered, "He needs to hear this."

Kevin took the cue and continued. "They should send over a nurse tomorrow, and she's going to get everything set up for us. I've got several prescriptions I want to get filled today, so we'll have medicine on hand if we need it. Lisa, could you stay with Maddie while I run to the pharmacy?"

"Sure, Kevin. Why don't you go now? I can stay as long as you need me."

"Right, good idea." Already on task, he went over and

retrieved his wallet and keys. "Anything special you want, Maddie? Soda? Tea?"

"I'm fine, honey. You go do what you need to do. I'll be okay." Kevin came over and lightly kissed her on the cheek before leaving. Maddie looked at her dad who was still gazing out the window. She got up, slowly walked over to him, and put a hand on his shoulder. He bowed his head and began to weep. She didn't move but waited until he turned toward her and they embraced. He held her tight, told her he loved her, and how he wished he could take her place. Maddie reassured him that everything was going to be okay. She was making peace with the idea of her death, and someday he would, too.

Jack said a quick goodbye to Lisa and told his girls he needed to leave before he completely fell apart. He planned to walk to Smitty's to see if Gina could take off work early. He said he'd be useless for the rest of the day.

Lisa stayed and, when Kevin returned, they had lunch together. Over soup and sandwiches, Maddie and Kevin disclosed their plan to spend some time traveling up the eastern coast. There were places Kevin had promised to show Maddie, and he wanted her to see them while she was feeling well enough to enjoy it.

"What will you do if Maddie gets sick or you need her doctor?" Lisa said in her motherly tone.

"We'll come home then. We talked well into the wee hours last night about it," he said and looked at Maddie who smiled at him. "We'll keep going until she wants to come home. When she's ready to . . ." Kevin couldn't say the words.

"Lisa, I don't want to lie around Westville and wait to get worse. I want to fill my last days with all I can." The three were silent, and Maddie's words hung in the air.

Lisa turned to Kevin. "Are you sure you can handle this on your own? Is it safe?" Lisa said. "I hate to be negative, but what if you are in a situation where you don't know what to do? What if you fall apart and can't help her?"

"We talked about that, too. We might see if we can hire a private duty nurse or a caregiver to come with us. I can cash out some investments to pay for it. We don't know if we'll need a nurse but thought it might be a good idea. We are going to ask the hospice nurse about it tomorrow to see if it's even a possibility."

Lisa was quiet for a moment. "What about if I go?" she said tentatively. "Can the nurses teach you and I what to do so we can both take care of her?" She looked at Kevin who seemed surprised at the offer.

"I hadn't thought of that." He looked at Maddie who shrugged her shoulders as a response. "I guess we could ask them about that, too," Kevin said.

"I was just thinking," Lisa said. "Wouldn't she be more comfortable with family than with a stranger? I'd love the opportunity to spend time with you, Maddie, and to help you, Kevin. I know I'm not a nurse, but I'd be willing to learn anything so that I can be there for you, Maddie."

"I'd hate to take you away from your family for that long," Maddie said.

"Doug can handle the boys for a few weeks while I'm gone. As long as there is food in the house, they're fine. I can have my mother-in-law come to stay with them. She'd love it."

"Do you really want to come?" Maddie said, trying to control her excitement.

"I do. I wouldn't miss it," she said and winked at Maddie.

"I guess it's decided then. I actually feel relieved knowing you'll be with us," Kevin said and went over and hugged Lisa. "You're a good sister."

"I know," Lisa said and laughed. She gave Maddie a

hug and a kiss goodbye. She was off to talk to Doug and prepare for what tomorrow would bring.

*   *   *

"Everything packed?" Maddie said as she rested on the couch. Lisa scurried around the house, crossing off the items on her list as she found them. Kevin took a seat on the couch beside her.

"I think we're almost ready. You sure you're up for this? We don't have to go if you don't think you can handle it. I won't be upset, I promise," Kevin said.

"I couldn't think of anything else I'd rather do," Maddie replied.

"Good. I am so excited to take you on this trip. There is so much for you to see." Kevin squeezed her hand and smiled.

He had rented a small RV for the trip and packed it with food, medicine, and a wide array of medical supplies to cover any imaginable circumstance they may come across during their journey. There was room for Maddie to lie down as they traveled, a kitchenette in case she was hungry, and a small living area if she wanted to sit up and watch TV. Lisa had stocked and organized an area that would serve as a mini-medical station. The hospice nurse helped her make note cards that corresponded with symptoms of Maddie's disease, highlighting the best remedies to try.

With Maddie settled in back, Lisa took the passenger seat to keep Kevin company as they embarked on their last journey together. The RV headed east out of Westville at nine a.m. They spent most of the day traveling across Ohio and into northern Pennsylvania. Their first destination was Presque Isle. They stayed in a B&B overnight and spent the next day exploring the beach and lighthouse the park had to offer. When Maddie woke around ten a.m. the next day, they had a late breakfast and set off on a short eighty-mile jaunt to Niagara Falls, a sight Maddie had seen in books but had never imagined could be so majestic and moving. She was so close, she could feel the mist on her face and felt as if God Himself was breathing His peace on her. A leisurely day exploring the world wonder left Maddie tired. They stayed over and had a quiet dinner at the hotel before turning in early.

A day of travel the next day brought them through the Jersey tunnel into the bright loud streets of New York City. Kevin had not thought through the challenge of driving such a big vehicle through the packed streets but managed to get them to their hotel safely. They were situated close to Rockefeller Center, and the view from their hotel room spanned all the way down to busy Times Square. The sea of people, merging like waves in opposite directions, was a sight to behold. They spent the next four days visiting the popular tourist sites of The Statue of Liberty, Chinatown, Little Italy, Grand Central Station, Central Park, and even a show on Broadway. They spent the most care and time at the art museums. With Maddie seated comfortably in a wheelchair, hours passed while she drank in all the beauty the buildings encased. She loved everything she experienced. She had never even imagined a city so full of life, excitement, and chaos.

Maddie slept soundly after their excursions in the city. They made their way to the Hamptons where Kevin had arranged a stay at the home of a friend. Maddie was able to see the magnificent vacation homes where the rich played and socialized during the summer months. To be able to stay in one, with a breathtaking view of the ocean, was something Maddie never imagined a small town farm girl would experience. With the graciousness of Kevin's friend, they extended their stay when Maddie's vision became blurry and her coordination and strength declined. A call to the doctor advised Lisa to increase Maddie's steroids. When they took effect, her vision returned to normal, and Maddie had renewed energy to continue with the trip.

They took a ferry to Mystic Connecticut and ate pizza inspired by the movie titled by the town. Maddie's appetite was ravenous from the medicine, amusing Lisa and Kevin as they watched her devour the food. They spent the day touring the Mystic seaport and Mystic Arts Center. From Mystic, they made their way to Cape Cod. Housed in a historic hotel on the ocean, they enjoyed a wonderful clambake style meal as they watched the sun set. After allowing Maddie to sleep until late in morning the next day, the trio set forth on a ferry to Martha's Vineyard where they enjoyed a light lunch and a sip of wine. A driving tour of the island was a non-taxing way for Maddie to see a place she had heard about but had no idea where it even was on the map.

Once on the mainland again, they settled Maddie into the RV. They gave her some pain medicine and something to settle her stomach. As the day had ended on their tour of the Vineyard, her head had begun pounding and nausea had set in. Kevin waited for the medicine to kick in before driving again, and Lisa held her sister's hand until she fell asleep. Kevin and Lisa contemplated heading for home and questioned whether they were pushing her too hard. Kevin decided they would press on, remembering his promise to get her to Bar Harbor. He and Lisa knew that Maddie would deteriorate during the trip, and they needed to stay strong and see her through whatever happened. They had promised Maddie they would stay on course until she said it was time to go home. She was fast asleep and they owed it to her to keep going.

Lisa rested alongside Maddie tending to her each time she woke. The headache persisted throughout the day leaving Maddie in a medicine-induced sleep for most of the trip to Maine. They stayed the night in Portland with Maddie and Kevin in the RV and Lisa in a hotel. Kevin wanted Lisa to rest because he felt he might need her more than ever in the days to come.

Maddie awoke the next morning free of pain and nausea. Kevin helped her outside, and they walked to the beach, enjoying the cool water that swept across their feet as the tide came in. The sky glowed in pink, peach, and light yellow. They stood to watch the bright crest of the sun from below the horizon. The rays kissed the water making it glisten and shimmer. Maddie hoped she could capture its beauty on canvas if given the opportunity. She leaned back onto Kevin's chest and rested in his embrace as they watched the sun rise until it no longer touched the water. He carried her back to the hotel where they had breakfast with Lisa. Once settled into the bed of the RV, Lisa took vigil over her for the last leg of the trip.

Hours passed as Maddie slept. Kevin pulled into Bar Harbor towards late afternoon. They drove through the picturesque streets of the quaint town until they pulled into the driveway of a large home perched along the shore. Lisa woke Maddie and helped her freshen up. They entered the white gate flanked by enormous blue hydrangea bushes. The walkway to the house was lined in daisies that matched the yellow paint of the house and the bright, white gingerbread trim. Kevin guided Maddie up the steps onto a gleaming hardwood porch that spanned the entire front and left side of the house. Hanging baskets overflowing with impatiens of red and white decorated the space between the posts of the porch. White, wicker furniture housed overstuffed blue and white, striped cushions. An old, dry sink held a pitcher of freshly squeezed lemonade. Beside it was a milk-glass cake stand that displayed homemade sugar cookies and gingersnaps. Maddie told Lisa she felt like she was walking straight into a *Better Homes and Garden* magazine picture. She chose to sit on the porch before going in any further and found the cushions were as comfortable as the sight of them promised. As she nibbled on a cookie, a cool breeze touched her skin. As she looked up, a ceiling fan slowly turned and Maddie noticed the ceiling was made of wood that was every bit as beautiful as the floor.

Kevin had gone to check them in and shortly returned with an elderly couple. They introduced themselves as the proprietors of the lovely home, Mr. and Mrs. Bowman. The home had been in their family for more than a century, and they had opened it to the public as a bed and breakfast twenty-five years ago. The seven-bedroom house, each with ocean views, was one of Bar Harbor's finest accommodations, and Kevin had stayed there several times over the years.

Inside proved to be just as beautiful as the outside of the home. The color scheme continued with pale blues, white, and yellow. Wood floors continued from room to room, and up the stairs, enticing one to climb all the way to the third floor. Big picture windows abounded encasing gorgeous views from every angle. The kitchen was located in the back of the house. A large farm table that could seat twelve sat proudly before a wall of windows. Maddie was taken aback at the view she saw from them. When she approached the windows, she could see that the kitchen became the second level from the back of the house. The view of the ocean was the reason why. When she looked down, she could see where the side porch opened to a deck that spanned the back of the house. The wood deck ended seamlessly at the pristinely manicured lawn. The green grass had a gradual slope that ended as a stone-lined barrier where it met the ocean. Maddie paused to watch as the waves came teetering close to its edge. Lisa came up beside her.

"Can you imagine living like this?" Lisa said, equally as stunned as Maddie. "This place is amazing."

"It sure is," Maddie said. "Can you help me down there so I can get a closer look?"

"Sure, honey." Lisa turned to Kevin, who was conversing with the owners, and asked if he could help Maddie go outside. They exited a door off the kitchen and descended the stairs that led them to the deck. Kevin bore a lot of her weight as Maddie's strength was weakening considerably and her gait was very unsteady. She appeared stroke-like with her right leg lagging a bit behind her other movements. Slowly, she made it onto the lawn. She paused to take off her shoes enjoying the cool grass on her feet as she walked. Wood Adirondack lounge chairs perched toward the rocks offered a relaxing view of the water. Lisa walked up to the house and returned shortly with a blanket and several pillows. She arranged them to Maddie's comfort, then watched her sister close her eyes, soon to be lulled to sleep by the lapping of the waves.

When Maddie woke, she found Kevin quietly reading in the chair beside hers. Lisa, he told her, was exploring the shops of the town and would find dinner on her own. The air had grown chilly as evening approached them. The warm August days of Maine led to refreshingly cool nights as the sun took its leave. Kevin and Maddie began talking about the novel he was reading and the sights they had taken in on their trip. They settled on remembering their favorite times together; stories that evoked laughs as well as tears. As they reminisced, Mrs. Bowman brought out hot coffee, steaming crocks of soup, and warm bread. When the first stars began to twinkle, Kevin carried Maddie into the house. At her request, he made gentle, sweet love to her, perhaps for the last time.

He watched her drift off to sleep and admired how beautiful she was despite being so sick. Unable to sleep, he took a hot shower and, once dressed comfortably, decided to go downstairs to read. He found Lisa reading in the dimly lit living room. He took a seat in an overstuffed chair beside hers.

"Is Maddie asleep?" Lisa asked as she put her book down in her lap.

"Yes, she's exhausted," Kevin said. "I can't seem to relax and go to sleep."

"I can sympathize with you," Lisa said and stretched into a new position. "She seems to be a lot weaker today, don't you think?"

"She is. I'm not sure how long we should stay," Kevin said, revealing what had been worrying him.

"Has she said anything to you about wanting to go home yet?" Lisa inquired.

"No. We had a really nice talk tonight. We stayed down by the water for a few hours and not once did she mention that she wanted to leave."

"Then she's not ready yet. She'll let us know," Lisa said and gave Kevin's arm a quick squeeze.

"This is the hardest thing I've ever had to do."

"I know. You just have to keep going. When our Mom was sick, Maddie and I were so young. I remember not wanting to see her and wishing I were somewhere else. You know, she would ask for us girls, and I would try to find something else to do, anything to get me out of it. If it weren't for my dad's persistence, I probably would have never gone into her room. I know I was young, but I was old enough to know that it was wrong not to spend time with her. Now I look back and cherish those moments that I had with her. I didn't appreciate them then, but I do now. When I see Maddie suffer, part of me wants to run away. It would be easier to go home to my family, to run away so I don't have to feel so much pain," Lisa said and took Kevin's hand. "It's going to get worse, much worse, but I tell you one thing . . . you will never regret a minute of this trip. You will look back and see that you have shown her the world in these last two weeks. Thank you, Kevin. Your gift to her is also a gift to me. I have been blessed to spend this time with you and Maddie."

"I'm glad, Lisa. You've been such a strong support for me. I know I couldn't have done it without you." Kevin leaned over and gave Lisa a hug. "I guess we should get some sleep."

"Sounds good," Lisa said, then made her way upstairs to her room. Kevin quietly entered the room he shared with Maddie. He slipped under the covers, gently kissed her on the lips and listened to her breathe until, finally, he was able to rest as well.

– Chapter Thirty-Six –

Their first full day in Maine also would be their last. As if something had slipped into the air of the night and cast a spell over Maddie, she woke with no use of her legs. When her tears finally subsided, she was determined to see the beauty of this place that Kevin had promised. He helped her dress and carried her downstairs to meet Lisa. She, too, needed time to cry over this latest loss. They retrieved the wheelchair and put it to good use as they walked the streets full of trendy shops. They went to the docks, where they watched the lobster boats come in to unload their bounty. Maddie watched Kevin and Lisa enjoy a fresh lunch at the Fisherman's Landing dockside restaurant. Her stomach would not permit more that a few bites of bread, but the enjoyment of watching them eat was satisfying enough.

They rented a car and drove through Acadia National Park to the top of Cadillac Mountain. Touted as the highest point on the eastern seaboard, the view was spectacular. Kevin told them that the rays of the rising sun strike the mountaintop before reaching anywhere else in the United States. When they descended the mountain, he drove them to Sand Beach, which is comprised of thousands of tiny seashells. He made sure Maddie dipped her feet in the cool, clear water. Before heading back to the B&B, they stopped for tea and popovers at Jordan Pond. Like a master storyteller, Kevin told them the story of Mount Desert Island and the early settlers to the area. He spoke of the rich fishing waters that led to a successful shipbuilding industry. The beauty and charm of the land drew artists and philosophers to the area. It didn't take long for the wealthy to find this jewel, and he said the park and Island now was in jeopardy of being developed into a playground for the rich. In the early 1900s, an effort was made to preserve the land, and it had been protected ever since. Maddie's heart melted at the enthusiasm in Kevin's voice as he talked, and she was caught up with emotion for the man she loved.

Maddie looked out the window of the car as they wound along the scenic road back to the B&B. She wanted to take in all that she could of the beautiful landscape. Quiet and contemplative, she was lost in her thoughts. Maddie hadn't told Kevin or Lisa that her headache had started to return and that her arms felt very weak. Her body was telling her things she was unable to dismiss as a fleeting setback. Unfortunately, she felt that it was time to head for home. She could stay in Maine and would be happy to die there amongst the rocky shores, but that would be unfair to her dad. He was waiting for her, and they needed to be able to say goodbye to each other. The longer Maddie waited, the more at risk she was to miss the opportunity to spend some time with him.

As they pulled in the driveway of the Bowman estate, Maddie asked if they could again sit out in the chairs by the water. Kevin carried her and set her down gently. She asked if Lisa would come and sit with her for awhile. Kevin left her and soon Lisa came to join her. Maddie reached for her hand.

"Hey sis," Maddie said and motioned for Lisa to sit down.

"Hey," Lisa said and relaxed back into the chair. "What a day, huh?"

"It was. This place has a magic all its own. I feel a calm and peace here," Maddie said.

"I'm so glad I came," Lisa said. "Do you know I probably never would have thought to come up here on my own? It wasn't even on my radar as a potential vacation spot. I'd love to take Doug and the kids here. The boys would love that park, such a great place to hike, and I bet you could camp somewhere around here."

"You should do it. If there's one thing I've learned from Kevin it is to just go. If you want to see it, dream of seeing it, you have to just go. That's what living is all about."

"That husband of yours is something else. He's just great, Maddie. I'm so glad you guys found each other."

"Me, too," Maddie said and then looked at her sister. "Lisa, can you promise me you will keep in touch with Kevin when I go? You are the one who can comfort him when I'm gone. I feel that you have formed a good friendship on this trip, and I want that to continue. I want him to still feel connected to our family in some small way."

"Of course I will, Maddie," Lisa said then looked out to the ocean. She wiped a tear from her cheek.

"It's going to be okay," Maddie said. "I love you, Lisa."

"I love you, too," Lisa said softly.

They sat in silence together, and when Maddie felt she could handle it, she told her sister that it was time to head for home, time to start the process of saying goodbye.

They stayed overnight and woke early to get a good start on the trip home. As the RV pulled out of Bar Harbor, they paused to see the sun rise over Cadillac Mountain as if to bid them farewell.

Initially, Kevin had planned several stops on the way home that Maddie would enjoy seeing. That all changed when he looked into Maddie's eyes and, without her saying a word, sensed that her time was coming to an end. They had managed her symptoms quite well, but he was concerned now that she would make a turn for the worse before he could get her home. He and Lisa took turns driving and stopped only when necessary to refuel and eat a little something. Maddie succumbed to the pain of the headache again and needed to be heavily medicated to rest comfortably. Unlike before, there was an urgency now, and the miles could not pass quickly enough for them.

Kevin was relieved to finally pull into the drive of their home. It was two a.m., and the neighborhood was quiet and still. Maddie and Lisa were fast asleep, and he decided not to wake them. Instead of going inside, he slept on the small makeshift couch. It wouldn't be long before Maddie would stir, and then he could take her inside.

As Maddie slept into late morning, Kevin was able to contact the hospice nurses again and also made a call to let the doctor know they were again home. He arranged to have a hospital bed delivered and concentrated on making room in her studio for it. Clearing away her art supplies was difficult, for he knew that she would never paint again. He noticed the picture on the easel and remembered it was the one she had painted the night she got sick. He looked at it and was taken aback by a realization he had not thought of before. Maddie's last painting would be the one that comforted her. He felt a chill run through him and took a moment to study the picture. Maddie had captured a moment in her life that had brought her joy—just like she had tried to capture something memorable for the many dying patients for whom she had painted at the hospital. God must have whispered in her ear to paint one for herself.

Kevin made a place for the painting next to the window so that the soft light would reflect off the image to make it glow. After reconnecting with her family, Lisa retuned to help Kevin set up the room. Maddie settled well into the room and was alert enough to see her painting. She admired it and also was touched by the timing of it all. Her periods of sleep grew more frequent and longer in duration but, when she woke, it was as if a gift of clarity had been granted, and she was able to spend time with her dad. She said farewell to friends and family who stopped to see her, spent time with Lisa laughing, and had quiet, precious moments with Kevin. It wasn't long before she began to speak of things that didn't make sense, often forgetting where she was or what was happening to her. She remained responsive to her close loved ones but soon was too tired to lift her eyelids to see them when they spoke. She'd softly whisper, "I love you" whenever she heard Kevin's voice, and her breathing seemed to calm whenever he was near.

It was just after the sun rose, a week since being home, when Maddie took her last breath. Kevin was there alone with her and held her hand as he watched her go. She had swept into his life as a beautiful soul, a priceless masterpiece, and now it was time to let her go.

CPSIA information can be obtained
at www.ICGtesting.com
Printed in the USA
BVHW042137181122
652333BV00015B/48